I don't want Elizabeth to be my wife, Nick mused to himself.

It may have taken him a long time, but he'd finally accepted his wife's death. But, God help him, there were so many memories, so many similarities. The way Elizabeth stirred her coffee. Her mannerisms and patterns of speech.

And then Nick thought back to the night he and Elizabeth had made love. Two bodies perfectly in sync, moving as one. So totally in tune that, when he whispered his wife's name without thinking, Elizabeth had responded without question, wrapping her arms around him, pulling him closer.

Nick slammed his fist down hard. If he didn't get some answers—and soon—he was going to lose it big-time. He had to know once and for all: Was he in love with two women—or one?

Dear Reader,

Once again, you've come to the right place if you're looking for that seductive mix of romance and excitement that is quintessentially Intimate Moments. Start the month with *The Lady in Red*—by reader favorite Linda Turner. Your heart will be in your throat as rival homicide reporters Blake Nickels and Sabrina Jones see their relationship change from professional to personal— with a killer on their trail all the while. And don't miss the conclusion of the HOLIDAY HONEYMOONS miniseries, Merline Lovelace's *The 14th...and Forever.* You'll wish for a holiday—and a HOLIDAY HONEYMOON—every month of the year.

The rest of the month is fabulous, too, with new books from Rebecca Daniels: *Mind Over Marriage;* Marilyn Tracy: *Almost Perfect,* the launch book in her ALMOST, TEXAS miniseries; and Allie Harrison: *Crime of the Heart.* And welcome new author Charlotte Walker, as she debuts with *Yesterday's Bride.* Every one of these books is full of passion, and sometimes peril—don't miss a single one.

And be sure to come back next month, when the romance and excitement continue, right here in Silhouette Intimate Moments.

Enjoy!

Leslie J. Wainger
Leslie J. Wainger
Senior Editor and Editorial Coordinator

Please address questions and book requests to:
Silhouette Reader Service
U.S.: 3010 Walden Ave., P.O. Box 1325, Buffalo, NY 14269
Canadian: P.O. Box 609, Fort Erie, Ont. L2A 5X3

YESTERDAY'S BRIDE

CHARLOTTE WALKER

Silhouette

INTIMATE™ MOMENTS®

Published by Silhouette Books

America's Publisher of Contemporary Romance

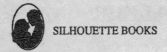 SILHOUETTE BOOKS

ISBN 0-373-07768-8

YESTERDAY'S BRIDE

Printed in U.S.A.

CHARLOTTE WALKER

has been a free-lance, nonfiction writer for several years, working for the Midwest public relations firm she and her husband co-own. Some of her most memorable assignments include an interview with a Russian trade delegation that toured the United States on a technological exchange mission and a "contract killer" feature story. Most recently, she created a commemorative writing project, distributed worldwide, which recognized Garth Brooks as the fastest-selling recording artist in history.

Despite working in the nonfiction field, she has always been an avid reader and was never able to shake her true love of fiction. Yearning to challenge her creativity and unleash her imagination, she switched to writing what she's always loved to read—romance.

Charlotte lives in Illinois with her husband, a fourteen-year veteran detective who serves as her "personal expert" on police-related research, and her teenage son, who is a "daily reminder" of the ever-changing, constantly developing human psyche.

This book is in loving memory of my father, Red, whose quiet love is with me every day of my life...
My mother, Jalette, who made me believe that I could do anything...
My husband, Jerry, who supported and encouraged me down this unforgettable path...
And my son, Dusty, who restores my faith and inspires me daily.

Prologue

He methodically thumbed through the newspaper, scanning every page, until he found the headline he'd been searching for. Grinding out his cigarette, he focused his full attention on the article.

LOCAL DOCTOR AND SONOIL DRIVER DIE IN FIERY CRASH

CHICAGO (AP)—Dr. Danielle Davis, age 31, and John Stevens, 47, died yesterday in a fiery collision on the lower south side.

According to a witness at the scene, the vehicle driven by Dr. Davis failed to stop for a red light and collided with the Sonoil gas tanker at the intersection of Halsted and Roosevelt.

Police sources stated the collision ruptured the tanker, causing an explosion which consumed the Davis vehicle and severely burned Stevens who was driving the tanker. Stevens died later at Michael Reese hospital, resulting from the injuries.

Captain Ronald Sutherland of the Chicago Fire Department stated, "By the time we arrived, the car, identified as the Davis vehicle was completely engulfed in flames. We were lucky to contain the blaze and keep several of the surrounding buildings from igniting."

Nick Davis, husband of the victim and a detective for the Chicago Police Department, told authorities that his wife had been visiting her sister in Springfield, Illinois, and was returning home at the time of the accident.

This brings Chicago's Fourth of July fatalities up to five for the three-day weekend.

He wadded up the paper and tossed it on the floor, then sat back and lit another Marlboro. Smoke curled through his teeth as he swore, "Dammit, Lizzie, how could you have panicked and run that light?"

Chapter 1

Almost 15 months later, 6:15 p.m.

Purple shades of evening veiled the dimly lit alley. Except for a few faint street sounds and the distant barking of a dog, all was quiet.

Crouched nearby, the woman could smell the full Dumpsters that lined both sides of the narrow street. Her haggard face gave no evidence of its former beauty. High cheek bones and a straight, perfectly formed nose were the only clues to her youth. A mane of brown hair, matted and tangled like unbraided rope, capped her head. Once beautiful hazel eyes, now neither sharp nor clear, guarded her shopping cart full of treasures…everything she owned.

The day had been so confusing, but she remembered digging through a trash can. After carefully making sure no one was looking, her trembling hands had pulled out a tattered teddy bear. Overwhelmed with emotion, she'd lovingly wrapped it in a faded blue rag. Her shaking hands had told her this toy was important...it represented some connection...held a clue to her past. But what?

Darkness threatened to envelop her as she cradled the bear in her arms, wanting to cry, though she didn't know why. Sitting there, crumpled and dirty, she tried desperately to remember. She closed her eyes and concentrated, only to see the handsome, smiling face of the man whose piercing blue gaze haunted all her dreams. Strangely comforted by his image, she was finally able to relax.

As evening settled around her, her mind cleared and she saw someone...a child. She stood to get a better look. A small boy bounced a basketball down the sidewalk. She could hear his playful laugh, see his precious face. As he looked up, she heard herself laugh, too. Tears filled her vacant stare, then spilled, streaking her hollow cheeks.

Suddenly, the sound of screeching brakes ripped through her like a bolt of lightning. Her mouth went dry, perspiration beaded her forehead. The boy! She had to warn the boy! Dropping the stuffed animal, she ran frantically out of the alley. He was just ahead of her. The roar of the automobile's engine filled her head. Dashing in front of the car, she screamed, "Look out!"

She spoke only once before losing consciousness— barely a whisper. *"This* child will live."

An hour later, the wail of the ambulance as it sped from the scene of the accident and raced to Michael Reese Hospital turned Nick Davis's blood to ice water. Another tragedy. Just one more torment to plague his already sleepless nights.

The victim's taken care of, Detective, that incessant voice in his head nagged. *Now get cracking and do your job.*

He turned to his lieutenant. "What have we got?"

"Here." Handing over a badly scuffed, brown purse, Lieutenant Kevin O'Malley studied Nick's unreadable stare. "It's got one of those paper identification cards cheap wallets have." At Nick's nod, he added, "Looks like she filled in her name and address."

Nick methodically examined the bag, wanting desperately to turn back the hands of time, yet knowing from experience that it was impossible. "How do we know it belonged to the victim?"

O'Malley cleared his throat. "It was under your car, Nick." He pointed across the street. "And that witness standing by the Dumpster confirmed it was the victim's."

Nick motioned, then waited as the reluctant man, followed by his small dog, came forward. "What's your name?"

"Buster."

Nick clapped down a hand on the street person's shoulder.

A low growl came from the pup.

"How do you know this handbag belongs to the woman who was hit?"

"I know, 'cuz it's the only purse Elizabeth ever had." His voice cracking, the old man wiped his eyes with his dirty sleeve before continuing, "I've seen her carry it a thousand times."

The dog whined.

Nick unzipped the bag and recovered a billfold which was empty except for the identification card. No money. No photos. Nothing. "Elizabeth Gleason."

Buster nodded.

"Looks like you're right, pal," Nick told him. "Has she been around long?"

"About a year, maybe more. We all sort of look after

her. Make sure she's got a place to stay and something to eat.''

''Why's that?'' Nick coaxed.

''Most of the time poor Elizabeth walks around in a kind of daze.'' Buster shook his head. ''Is she going to be all right?''

Nick's gut clenched. ''They'll do everything they can.'' *Trouble is, sometimes their best just isn't good enough.*

''What in the hell is taking so long?'' Nick Davis slammed his fist on the counter that separated him from the wide-eyed nurse he'd cornered. ''I want some answers, and I want them now!''

Another bout with this man's volatile temper startled, but still failed to intimidate, the understanding RN. ''They're doing every thing they can, Detective Davis.''

Nick's large hand snaked out and grabbed the pristine sleeve of her uniform. ''Look, Katherine,'' he continued through gritted teeth, ''she's been in that operating room for hours—''

''And they'll let you know as soon as possible,'' the nurse assured him, all the while working to pull free from his viselike grip.

As Nick watched her sidestep the desk and head down the hall, he muttered under his breath, ''Robo-Nurse.'' But then, what did he expect after interrogating her like some punk he'd dragged in off of the street?

Davis subconsciously patted the pocket of his shirt. God, what he'd give for a cigarette right about now. He wondered how he had made it over a year without one. Not that he'd had a choice. Dani had refused to take no.... Nick's fingers instinctively sought the ring he wore around his neck.

Like the ancient Egyptian legend, this phoenix had also

risen from the ashes. After putting out the car fire on that hot July afternoon—one year, two months and twenty-one days ago—all that remained of his wife, and his life, had been her wedding band. Clenching his jaw, Nick traced the delicate engraving with his fingertip. He didn't have to read the words. *Love Forever, Nick* was inscribed in his heart, as well.

Sometimes just touching it helped....

Nick checked his watch—11:45 p.m. Perspiration trickled down his back.

And sometimes it didn't....

For the past four hours Nick had done nothing but relive today's accident over and over again in his mind. It had happened so damned fast. One moment the street had been clear. The next, a boy had darted into Nick's path. He remembered slamming on his brakes. Then, a woman had shoved the child out of danger.

Nick closed his eyes, still hearing the squeal of his tires. The woman's scream. The sickening thud.

He dropped into a nearby chair and braced both forearms on his knees. He'd seen enough fatalities to know it didn't look good for the woman he'd hit. Her face had been covered with blood and one leg had been badly broken.

After the ambulance had taken her to the hospital, Davis had checked the alley and had come up empty-handed, except for her shopping cart. Now, he glanced down at the tile floor and nudged a brown purse with the toe of his shoe. There, in one dirty little pile at his feet, lay the rest of the street woman's worldly possessions. One tattered red sweater, a stuffed bear wrapped in a rag, and a billfold made of cheap plastic.

Nick had already phoned headquarters and reported that the identification card he'd found inside the billfold was in the name of Elizabeth Gleason. He clasped his hands together and drew a ragged breath. If she didn't survive, at least he would know who to bury.

God, not another funeral.

Fifteen years on the force had taught him to trust his instincts. But not this time. This time he was too burned out to make a life-or-death call. Now, all he could do was wait. And waiting was one of the very few things Nick Davis was not good at.

Every bone in her body ached. Each time she drew a breath, her head throbbed as if it would split in two. Not daring to move, she lay perfectly still while consciousness, steeped in darkness and shadows, played an elusive game of hide-and-seek with her...and the stranger that had stood by her bed.

Unwilling to open her eyes, she heard two women enter the room. Their voices were soft, soothing. Gentle words that made her want to smile, if only it didn't hurt so badly.

"Good morning," one woman said quietly. "Let's see how you're doing today."

A warm hand carefully lifted her arm so competent fingers could settle momentarily at her wrist.

A steady beat.

"What's her prognosis?" the other woman asked.

"It's still touch and go."

A steady beat.

"Her leg was pretty badly fractured, but her head injuries are what have the doctors worried. The way it looks now, even if everything goes well, she'll still have a long road ahead of her."

A steady beat.

"Reconstructive surgery?"

"Eventually. That's what I heard."

A steady beat.

"Can you believe Detective Davis? I thought we'd have to call security to throw him out even long enough to take her vitals."

Her pulse quickened.

"Poor guy," the woman sympathized. "He's been through hell this past year."

"I'll say. That man's been a walking time bomb ever since Danielle died. When was it?"

"A year ago last summer. Fourth of July weekend, I think."

Her pulse pounded.

Her hand was released and carefully placed by her side.

"You know, this accident could push Nick right over the edge."

"You think so?"

"Sure. The way I figure it, this will either snap him out of it or just snap him—period."

Her heart hammered hard against her ribs.

"You might be right about that. Even *he* can only take so much."

Muffled sounds followed the clinking of a metal chart against the end of her bed.

"How's she doing?"

"Pulse is a little erratic this morning but, under the circumstances, she's hanging in there."

"Great. Now, maybe Davis will go home and get some rest."

"I wouldn't count on it. He hasn't left this room since they brought her in two days ago."

The door swooshed open, then clicked shut.

She was alone.

How many days had Nick spent pacing the damned hospital room, hoping for some sign of life from the woman, wondering if she was ever going to regain consciousness? *Four,* he answered himself.

He carefully studied the woman one more time. Surely all the tubes and machines she was connected to would pull her through this. Her head was bandaged mummy-style except for her eyes, nose, and mouth. A large cast encased one leg that hung suspended from a pulley-type contraption above her bed.

Nick turned away and stared out the window, into the darkness, wanting to smash his fist through the glass. He ignored the hunger gnawing at his belly and refused to give in to the bone weary fatigue that threatened to drain every drop of his strength. He guarded her like a sentinel. *This time* he was prepared to face death...and defy it.

The next afternoon, there he stood again. How often, the woman wondered, had she struggled past the haze of drugs only to find his ominous silhouette standing there?

Watching. With brooding eyes.

Waiting. Edgy and angry.

Silent. Always silent.

This time, she fought through the pain and managed to speak in a voice that was little more than a whisper. "Where am I?"

When he turned, her breath caught. Those magnificent eyes. *He* was the man from her dreams.

"You're in the hospital." He headed toward the door. "I'll get a nurse."

So he *was* real, not just a dream. Suddenly, afraid of losing him, she tried to reach out, but her arm was anchored by an IV. Ignoring the pain in her jaw, she rasped, "Don't go."

He faltered. "I'll be right back," he promised, hating to lie. She fought back the tears when he shut the door behind him. God, she had so many questions. She had to clear her head. But, how could she think straight, when all that was on her mind was the tall man with the dark hair and mesmerizing blue eyes?

A cold sweat glazed Nick's palms as he stood outside the woman's door. Damn. He didn't want to talk to her. Didn't want to know her. Refused to care. All he wanted was for her to do him one big favor and live. On his way toward the nurses' station, he caught sight of a familiar face. "Katherine, hurry. She's awake."

One Year Later

"What do you mean, start at the beginning?" Elizabeth Gleason stood and placed her hands on the desk that separated her from the doctor. The soft, classical music she usually found so soothing during her sessions, seemed to drone on incessantly today. "For God's sake, Dr. Franklin, you're my psychiatrist. You, better than anyone else, should know that I have no beginning."

"What I understand," Mary Franklin began patiently, "is that until now, you wanted no part of delving into your past." She looked Elizabeth in the eye. "A year is a long time to wait. Not to mention the fact that you were so adamant about not wanting to know. I have to wonder what changed your mind?"

"I didn't just lose my memory," Elizabeth insisted, raising her voice. She paced, stopping directly in front of the doctor's beautifully polished mahogany desk again. "Don't you get it? I didn't just lose my memory," she repeated. "I lost *me.*"

"And so it's been," Dr. Franklin answered calmly. She paused. "All right, Elizabeth. Just answer one question. After all this time, why now?"

Elizabeth walked over and stared out the window at the trees that were already beginning to change color. As hard as it was for her to believe, autumn had come around again. Over the past twelve months, she'd battled her way through surgeries and physical therapy—not to mention the recent flashbacks—and not one of those struggles compared to...the dream.

How could she explain this sudden, overwhelming need to know? She turned back and confronted the sophisticated woman who had taught her so much. "I honestly don't know."

"Well," the psychiatrist said, smiling, "we've come a long way on a whole lot less, haven't we?"

Elizabeth nodded. "I guess we have."

"I'll see what I can find out," Dr. Franklin promised. "In the meantime, I want you to continue concentrating on living one day at a time."

"Thanks." This time, it was Elizabeth who smiled. "There's something I'd like to ask you about the time I spent in the hospital."

"What is it?"

"Was there a man in my room?" She held her breath and waited for an answer.

Unsure of the direction this question was aimed, Mary told her, "I know there were doctors and nurses, both male and female."

"No." Elizabeth shook her head. "One man. Tall and dark. I remember his dark ponytail and angry blue eyes."

Dr. Franklin leaned back in her chair. "Why is this important now?"

"I've started having this dream."

"About him?"

Elizabeth nodded and clasped her hands together. "I need to know if he's real or a figment of my imagination."

Dr. Franklin rolled a pencil between her palms. "And, you feel if he wasn't in your room, there has to be another explanation?"

"Maybe."

She laid the pencil down and leaned forward. "If he isn't a part of the present, do you think he may have some connection to your past?" Dr. Franklin scribbled on a note-pad as she spoke, then looked directly at Elizabeth. "Is this what changed your mind about wanting to find out about your life before the accident?"

Elizabeth nodded. "I thought, if I could put him into perspective, I could break this weird connection with him. And maybe get some sleep at night," she added with a smile, trying to lessen the urgency behind her words.

"Dreaming about a man isn't at all unusual but, under the circumstances, I can appreciate your concern. Let me check into this for you. He may have been a paramedic or even a police officer."

Elizabeth let out a sigh of relief. "I'd appreciate it."

"Consider it done," her friend promised. "By the way, how's the soup kitchen coming?"

"It'll open on Monday. Just three more days." Elizabeth beamed. "It's been a lot of hard work, but I needed to do it. Running the place will be my way of repaying all the homeless people who kept me alive when I was on the streets."

"You still don't remember anything about that part of your life, do you?"

Elizabeth shrugged. "Only what I've been told. That I was living out of a shopping cart at the time of my acci-dent. And, according to the ID I carried, my name is Eliz-abeth Gleason."

"Well, dear, up until now you refused any other information."

"I know," Elizabeth admitted. "But how am I going to run a kitchen for street people and encourage them to get their lives back on track, if I haven't taken that step myself?"

Mary nodded. "Good point."

With a deep breath, Elizabeth continued, "Maybe with your help, I can finally put my past to rest." She paused at the arch of her friend's brow, then added, "After all, how many times have you told me that I have a brand-new life ahead of me?"

"More than a few," Dr. Franklin conceded.

"Well, before I step into the future, I have to find out why I wake up sobbing in the middle of the night. Someone out there has to know. They just have to."

"Dammit, why didn't I lock that door?" Nick Davis glared up from behind the stacks of *bureaucratic bull* covering the top of his desk. The faint knock that had interrupted his concentration was just about the last straw. It wasn't until she walked into his office that recognition softened his irritated features and lightened his mood. He'd always appreciated a classy woman, regardless of her age, and pushing sixty hadn't stopped this one from being a knockout.

Over the years, he'd worked with Mary Franklin on numerous cases and her cool head never failed to impress him. "Doc." He flashed her a sincere grin. "What brings you down here?"

"Got a minute? I'd like to talk." She waited patiently while Nick shoved aside his paperwork and rose to clean off a nearby chair.

"For you, I'll make the time." And he would. Nearly a year ago, he'd asked Mary to take time from her busy private practice, as well as her occasional police work, to help Elizabeth Gleason. She'd agreed and had willingly kept him apprised of the woman's progress as well. He'd been certain if anyone could help the bag lady get her life in order after the accident, Mary would be the one to do it.

Flattered by his genuine warmth, Dr. Franklin stepped over a stack of brightly colored folders in the middle of the scuffed linoleum and sat down. She knew for the past two years Detective Davis had rarely offered more than— well, at best, an extremely hard time to anyone. But, she also knew why.

He hitched one hip on the side of his desk and folded both arms comfortably across his chest. "What's up?" The shrill ring of his phone momentarily interrupted their conversation. "Take a number," he barked before slamming down the receiver and turning back to her.

"Is your fuse always that short?" she asked.

"No, Doc, sometimes it's a whole lot shorter," he answered truthfully. "I know you didn't come here to psychoanalyze me, so what can I do for you?"

Respecting his right to act like a jerk occasionally, she asked, "What can you tell me about Elizabeth Gleason's past?"

Short and to the point. That's what he loved about the doctor. "I have all the details in her file," he acknowledged, crossing the room to shut his door. For some reason, the noise from the booking room seemed to grate on his nerves more than usual today. "Why do you want to know?"

"Elizabeth came to see me today and she has decided she'd like to know."

Nick snapped his fingers. "Just like that?"

Mary shook her head. "Probably not. But, that's the way it seems to her."

"This is good, right?" He rounded his desk to dig through a battered metal cabinet.

"I hope so," she confessed. "Elizabeth has come such a long way. Physically she's had a tough time recuperating, but that hasn't been nearly as difficult to deal with as the loss of her identity."

Nick may have had to suffer the guilt connected with driving the car that hit Elizabeth, but at least he was spared most of the financial worry. Because the accident happened while he was on duty, the city had been liable for her medical expenses. In the months to follow, Nick had even located a renowned plastic surgeon who, with Elizabeth's consent, had used several innovative reconstructive procedures to repair the damage to her face.

Already riddled with blame, the one thing Davis thanked God for was that he hadn't been responsible for her memory loss, too. Their investigation had determined she'd been living on the streets without any recollection of her past for over a year before he hit her. Unfortunately, that relieved the city of any liability for her psychiatrist's bill, so Nick was paying that himself. He pulled a manila folder from the file drawer and handed it to Mary. "Maybe this will help."

"Thanks." She patted the folder. "Elizabeth needs to make some kind of peace with herself. Besides, her new job will be enough of a challenge. I don't want anything else adding any pressure."

"New job?" Nick frowned as he sat down behind his desk. "I thought you said she liked working at the boutique."

"She did," Mary assured him. "But Elizabeth has some pretty strong feelings when it comes to paying back debts—"

"She doesn't know, does she?" Nick interrupted.

"That you've taken care of all my fees? No, Nick. I promised you she'd never hear that from me. But, she's been having dreams and from the description she gave me, I'd say they're about you. Won't you reconsider and just meet with her once? She doesn't have to know about the financial side of our arrangement."

He looked her square in the eye. "We had a deal."

"Yes, we did," she nodded. "And I won't go back on my word."

Thank God. The last thing in the world he needed was this Gleason woman feeling obligated to him. Or, worse yet, fixating on him. He shifted in his seat. "So, what's this new job of hers?"

"She's reopening a soup kitchen for the homeless down on Maxwell Street."

"What?" Nick's voice boomed. He jumped up so fast he tipped over his chair. "Dammit, Mary, I worked undercover for months getting that place shut down. Do you know how dangerous that neighborhood is? Especially now. Don't you read the newspaper?"

She simply nodded and let him rant.

He pointed to the folders scattered across his floor. "See those files? Those are exactly why you have to stop her." He waved wildly in the general direction of the window. "Someone out there is murdering street people. I'm working twenty hours a day to stop this bastard, and you hand deliver a self-proven, class-A victim right into his lap. How in the hell could you go along with this?"

Her cool stare caused him to self-consciously grab his chair off the floor and shove it behind his desk.

"Elizabeth Gleason is not a child who can be told what to do. She has very definite ideas on how she wants to live the rest of her life." Mary raised a well-manicured hand to silence him. "You don't know her like I do. She was extremely defenseless when I first met her, and she's still vulnerable in some ways. But don't kid yourself. There's an unbelievable amount of strength and determination in that woman."

"She can't do this, Doc," Nick said without blinking, palms planted firmly on both hips.

Mary shrugged. "She already has."

"How?" He raised his hands incredulously. "How in the hell did she pull it off?"

"Simple. She made inquiries and did her homework. You know how in vogue having a *social conscience* is nowadays. This town is full of politically correct, wealthy backers looking for a cause." She shrugged. "And as they say—the rest is history."

Frustration radiating from him, Nick shoved both hands into his pants pockets. "That place was a magnet for every scumbag on the south side before, and you and I both know history has a way of repeating itself." He turned his back on her. "Is Elizabeth Gleason prepared to handle that?"

"She sees this as her opportunity to repay the people on the street for taking her in. After all, they kept her alive."

Nick spun around. "As opposed to me—who tried to kill her?" The barely discernable flinch that crossed Mary's perfect features had him instantly closing the gap between them. "Sorry, Doc." He took her hand apologetically. "Even after more than a year, I guess I'm still a little off the wall when it comes to the accident."

"I know you are," she sympathized. "But, don't you see? Being hit by your car was the trauma that snapped her back to reality. In the end, you may have actually given Elizabeth her life back."

Nick started to protest, but his respect for Dr. Franklin

made him at least file her remark away for future reference.

Taking advantage of his uncharacteristic silence she added, "Besides, reopening the soup kitchen isn't your decision."

He gave her fingers a slight squeeze. "Mary, aside from this lunatic we're after, that place was nothing more than a flophouse for dopers and drug dealers. Gang members hung around there like flies on sh—" He stopped abruptly, trying to clean up his simile. "Like flies at a picnic."

She smiled at his sweet consideration. "Maybe so, but I discussed the neighborhood's background with her and she's still committed."

"You mean she *should be* committed," Nick corrected.

"No, she *should be* able to move forward and live her own life," Mary emphasized. "You can't run it for her, Nick. No one can."

Ticked off that Dr. Franklin was actually making sense, Nick held up both hands in surrender. "Okay, okay. Don't tell me. This is why you get paid the big bucks, right?"

"Something like that." Mary smiled as she rose. "Thanks for the file. I'll see that you get it back."

"No hurry." He walked her to the door.

She looked up at him and secured his chin with one peach-colored nail. "You're not going to do something foolish, are you?"

Careful, Nick old boy, she's not buying your innocent act.

"Scout's honor, Doc," he answered truthfully. *There's not a damned thing foolish about it.*

Chapter 2

Cigarette smoke curled over the top of the newspaper as he read the headlines.

ELIZABETH GLEASON TO OPEN SOUP KITCHEN

CHICAGO (AP)—Amnesia victim, Elizabeth Gleason, who wandered the streets nearly a year ago, being cared for by local homeless people, recently found a way to repay their kindness. Ms. Gleason will be reopening the Maxwell Street soup kitchen on Monday. Meals will be served every evening at 5:00 p.m.

According to local doctors, amnesia is often a temporary condition, and many victims can be expected to regain their memory. Maybe Ms. Gleason will remember her past and, like the soup kitchen, have a chance to begin again.

He took a long draw off his Marlboro, then touched its smoldering tip to the edge of the paper. As flames curled through the article, he warned through gritted teeth, "You should have stayed dead."

"You look like hell on wheels, Davis."

Nick slammed a dilapidated Cubs' cap on his head and glared at the lieutenant. "Stuff it, O'Malley." Despite their banter, Kevin O'Malley was one of the few men on the force Nick would trust with his life. The burly man staring him down had spent the last fifteen years passing on everything he knew about being a good cop—a damned good cop—to Nick Davis. And never once during that time had O'Malley cut him any slack. Regardless, or maybe because of that, Kevin was the one cop Nick would want to see if his back was against the wall.

"Top o' the day to you, too, nose wipe." The thirty-year veteran sidestepped his way into Davis's office and eyeballed the detective's ragged garb. "Goin' slummin'?"

Without looking up, Nick grabbed the filthy sleeves of his long underwear top and pushed them up to his elbows. "You know exactly where I'm going." Leveling his gaze, he challenged the red-haired Irishman, "Is there a problem, Lieutenant?"

O'Malley just shook his head. "That soup kitchen is legit now, and you know it."

Davis adjusted the leg of his jeans to better conceal the ankle holster he'd just strapped on. "That place is trouble and *you* know it."

"Maybe. Maybe not. Time will tell." O'Malley clapped a fatherly hand on Nick's shoulder. "Until then, play nice for a change, will ya?"

Nick fought the grin tugging the corners of his mouth.

"I told you, I'm just going to check the place out." At the other man's snort, Nick continued, "Mother, may I?"

O'Malley grunted as he headed toward the door. "Just don't stir it, Davis," he barked over one shoulder. "One complaint and you're outta there. You got that?" He stepped over the stack of folders lying on the floor. "And clean up this dump."

Nick did smile then. How many times had O'Malley ranted and raved, only to throw his own badge on the table to defend Nick's highly unorthodox methods to Chicago's most polished brass? The slam of the door that followed only widened Davis's grin.

Elizabeth had been serving dinners for only a little over half an hour and her left leg was beginning to ache. The dining room was equipped to serve one complete meal a day to fifty people and it had to be close to capacity by now.

She worked quickly, and had stopped momentarily to refill one of the stainless steel servers...when *he* walked in.

Elizabeth could *feel* his presence. She turned toward the door and spotted the tall, muscular man leaning against the frame as if he owned the place. Not exactly the build nor the demeanor of a street person, she thought.

Many of the destitute people she'd met were humble. Some of them were angry. But, the one common bond they all shared was their pride. This man's attitude, however, had nothing to do with pride.

He stood, half in shadow, half in fading sunlight, just far enough away that she couldn't make out his face. She rubbed her eye, then winced, wondering again why she had let Dr. Franklin talk her into contacts. *Why not go for a different look and change the color of your eyes? Invent a whole new you,* the doctor had challenged. Elizabeth forced her attention away from the man, only to sense he had taken his place at the end of the line.

As familiar faces shuffled past, Elizabeth grabbed metal tongs and picked through the heaping pan of fried chicken. She saw Thelma coming through and pulled out a drumstick.

"I just can't get over how beautiful you look, Elizabeth," Thelma declared. "If you hadn't come back around and told us who you were, we'd never have recognized you."

"You guys are about all I can remember, but a little more comes back all the time," Elizabeth replied. As Thelma turned to walk away, Elizabeth's brows knitted together. She didn't care for Thelma's color one bit. "Don't forget to button up that sweater before you leave," she added quickly. "It's getting cooler outside after dark these days."

Buster, who, Elizabeth remembered, had a particular taste for green beans, followed Thelma through the line. Elizabeth even added a couple of gizzards to his plate for his amazing little dog, Whizzer.

"I don't give a damn what Thelma says, being hit by that car was the best thing that ever happened to you, Elizabeth." He gave her a lopsided grinned. "I ought to know, I was there that night. If it wasn't for me, they might not have found your purse."

"And I've still got it, thanks to you, Buster." She smiled as he walked away.

Funny, she mused, it hadn't taken her long to remember their preferences. If her retention was this sharp, maybe Dr. Franklin was right. Maybe she had a good chance of recovering from the amnesia, after all.

At one time or another, in the faint pen-and-ink sketches

she called her memory, many of these people had reached out to her. Some had offered shelter. Almost all had shared their food. One had saved her life.

"Cat got your tongue tonight, little darlin'?" the old gentleman asked in a voice as rough as sandpaper.

Elizabeth patted his shaky hand. She never failed to get a lump in her throat when he called her that. "Not where you're concerned, Joe."

Joe had told Elizabeth he'd found her fifteen months before the accident, lying facedown behind some bushes. He'd scrounged around and found her some clothes to replace the bloody ones she'd been wearing and had tended to her injuries with all the care and finesse of a loving mother. She owed this man her life.

With a wink, she added an extra spoonful of mashed potatoes and leaned forward to whisper, "I miss you." His embarrassed grin warmed her heart but the raspy cough that followed him to a nearby table sounded a little too much like bronchitis to suit her. She made a mental note to contact the nurse at the clinic first thing in the morning.

"Welcome." Elizabeth smiled, reaching out to fill the next plate. "I don't believe I know you. My name's Elizabeth."

"Name's LeRoy Stratton." The man nodded. "You've probably seen me around."

She shook her head. "No, I don't think so."

He faced her. "Maybe you just forgot."

Elizabeth took a closer look. The man was over six feet tall, medium build—but muscular—sandy-colored hair and blue eyes. "Sorry." She shook her head. "If I've seen you, I don't remember."

"Nothin' to be sorry about, Elizabeth." He glanced at his plate. "Looks mighty good. Thanks."

"You're welcome." When LeRoy walked off to find a

seat at a nearby table, she noticed the man's slight limp and instinctively took a step back. Her grin faded.

Suddenly the overwhelming sensation she'd experienced earlier washed over her again—only stronger. Without looking, she knew the stranger from the doorway had stepped in front of her.

Why am I afraid to make eye contact? More to the point—why am I afraid not to? she wondered. The solemn promise she'd made to herself at the end of her first session with Dr. Franklin—to always face her fears—forced her to look up. *That can't be him!*

That can't be her! One look at Elizabeth Gleason and Nick Davis's itinerary for the evening went straight to hell. He'd planned to slip unnoticed into the shelter and check it out. That was, until he laid eyes on her.

At a glance, something about this woman seemed vaguely familiar, but Nick shook it off, thinking he'd probably passed her a hundred times on the street. Then he took another look—a closer look. Forget it. There was no way the woman in front of him could be Elizabeth Gleason. Surgery or no surgery, she didn't look much more than thirty years old. Elizabeth was his age, thirty-seven.

His eyes slid down her curvy little body and back up to the interesting angles of her face. Where the hell had all that silky, copper-colored hair come from? Or the full, moist lips that, until now, had greeted everyone with a friendly smile and a kind word. He felt as if he'd just been sucker punched.

Couldn't be the fact that you nearly made road pizza out of such a beautiful creature, could it, pal?

Nick told the nasty voice in his head to kiss off. He'd already paid his dues over this woman. Unfortunately, his conscience wasn't about to let him off that easily. His fingers itched to grab her by the arm and drag her somewhere private to warn her of the dangers in this neighborhood.

But what had Mary Franklin so tactfully pointed out? None of his business, she'd told him. What Mary was forgetting was that, as a police officer, Elizabeth's safety *was* his business. Unfortunately, working undercover prevented him from making that particular point to Elizabeth just now.

Nick watched the woman's thin gauze shirt gently rise and fall with each breath. His heart thudded hard against his ribs. He wiped the back of his hand across the thick stubble on his cheek and shook his head.

This time the good doctor was wrong. But, it was more than that. Nick couldn't put his finger on the reason yet, but aside from his sworn duty to protect and defend, Elizabeth Gleason was very definitely his business. And, as always, he had every intention of taking care of business.

Elizabeth's hand shook as she offered the plate of food to the stranger whose same penetrating blue gaze had haunted her sleepless nights for as long as she could remember.

But how could he have been in your dreams before the accident? The ones you had when you were still on the street?

Elizabeth dismissed the idea of having known this man during her time on the streets as grasping at straws. After all, she was struggling to piece her life together and a familiar face would be a good place to start.

She struggled to maintain eye contact in a desperate attempt to ignore the thick dark hair that hung to his shoulders—his broad, hard-as-a-rock shoulders. Or, the shadow of his beard that outlined his full, sensuous lips. Her eyes were drawn to his mouth.

Remember the kiss in your dream?

When she nearly dropped the plate, he steadied her hand, his strong fingers closing over her wrist for support. Flesh against flesh. Their eyes locked.

Unable to find her voice, Elizabeth whispered, "Sorry."

The confusion Nick saw reflected in her eyes ripped a hole in his chest that no police badge could ever cover. Gritting his teeth, he took the dish from her trembling hand. "No problem," was all he said before he turned and headed for the nearest table.

Nick sat down and concentrated on getting a feel for the people around him. He immediately zeroed in on one guy seated to the rear of the room, who hadn't taken his eyes off Elizabeth since Nick spotted him. Even seated, he appeared to be tall, in his early forties, with blond hair and a hard-as-nails look on his face. Already finished with his meal, the man sat quietly, talking to no one, smoking a cigarette and watching Elizabeth's every move.

Nick tried to read the stranger's expression. Maybe the guy was just fascinated by such a beautiful woman. Davis took another look at Elizabeth and decided that was a very definite possibility. Not that the why mattered. He'd keep an eye on her admirer, just in case.

Elizabeth finished serving the last few people in line plus a couple of stragglers who wandered in. When everyone was finally seated, the room hummed with muffled conversations and clanking silverware. Several street people who had volunteered to help out in exchange for their meals had already started cleaning up in the kitchen.

But tonight, instead of joining them, Elizabeth busied herself in the dining room. Time after time, her gaze was drawn to the tall, dark-haired man who had rattled her composure by simply walking through the door.

He sat, facing her, and talked quietly with the people seated around him.

Had the man in the hospital room been real, or just a dream? Is this the same man? Is he a total stranger? Or, is all of this just a desperate attempt to find a clue to my past?

Confused and frustrated, Elizabeth cuffed her sleeves and headed for the kitchen. Washing dishes was always therapeutic, so she decided to let her help go early tonight. Maybe scrubbing a few pots and pans would take her mind off everything...*and everyone?*

Nick found Elizabeth alone, her back to him, elbow deep in soap suds. Her flowing skirt swayed back and forth to the rhythm of a Beatles song that blared from a nearby radio. Soundlessly, he walked up behind her and tapped her on the shoulder. The next thing he knew, she brought up her forearm in self-defense and caught him under the chin with the back of her soapy knuckles.

Elizabeth had been totally lost in thought, wondering if she'd been in love the first time she'd heard "If I Fell," or if she'd ever been in love at all, when a touch from behind triggered a flashback that slammed her back in time.

A hand on her shoulder.

The blinding sun.

The tall silhouette of a man.

An explosion of pain.

A black void.

After it was over, Elizabeth just stood there—stunned. Before this, she'd never experienced any such flashes while she'd been awake. All the others had come to her in her dreams. Finally, she thought, a breakthrough. Not that it hadn't scared the holy bejesus out of her. Because it had. A shudder coursed through her veins as fear and exhilaration wound themselves around one another like two warring snakes.

Her heart was still pounding. In fact, her hand was throbbing, too....

That's when Elizabeth realized what she'd done. Wide-eyed and embarrassed, all she could do was look up into the face of the stranger and stare.

Nick's chin stung like hell, but that wasn't what bothered him. As soon as his pride backed off long enough for his cop instincts to kick in, he realized he hadn't simply startled Elizabeth. She had overreacted to the point of hand-to-hand combat because she'd been terrified. In the meantime, there they stood like Laurel and Hardy, soapsuds nearly covering the look of shock on both their faces.

Nick watched her struggle to stifle the urge to giggle. The more she tried to hide her amusement, the more intense it became, until she gave up and dissolved into uncontrollable laughter. Caught up in the mood, he had to admit she looked damned cute with bubbles in her hair. He figured they both probably looked ridiculous...until she touched him.

Elizabeth caught her breath and gradually regained her composure. "I'm so sorry," she finally managed to gasp, reaching out to scrape the soapsuds off his stubbly cheeks in a gesture so natural, it passed unnoticed...by her.

Her hand was soft and smooth against his rough cheek. Her voice was throaty and appealing. Nick felt the tension ease out of his body, and for the first time in over two years, he did more than offer a polite smile. He gave in to the warm, inviting laughter that was desperate to escape his lips.

Wiping the frothy suds off her nose with his fingertip, he fought the flood of emotions raging within him. However brief the window, relief had sneaked right past him. And it felt great. Until the guilt set in. But his wife, Dani, was dead, he had to remind himself. And he wasn't.

And this sure feels good, doesn't it, Nick old boy?

It did. He'd be a liar if he denied that. Nick clenched his jaw. A little over a year ago he'd nearly had to scrape Elizabeth Gleason off the front tire of his car. This uncharacteristic chink in his armor was probably just some kind of delayed reaction to finally meeting her, face-to-face.

Satisfied with his pseudoshrink explanation, he ignored the attraction, or reaction, or whatever the hell was going on between them. He'd never met a woman yet he couldn't handle—except maybe Dani. Rubbing his throbbing chin, he grinned in spite of himself.

"With a backhand like that, you must be hell on a tennis court."

Elizabeth started to say something, but stopped. Like so many times before, she realized she didn't have a clue how to answer. Maybe she'd played tennis. Maybe she hadn't. Once again, she was forced to hedge.

"Well, I don't know if *hell* is exactly the right word." And she didn't. But what she did know was that this man looked remarkably like the one she'd seen, or thought she'd seen, in her hospital room. Now was the time to find out once and for all. "So, what's on your mind, Mr.—"

"Davis. Nick Davis." He figured he might as well use his real name. After all, he didn't plan to stay undercover more than a couple of days on this. It shouldn't take long to convince her reopening the kitchen was a mistake.

She extended her hand. "Nice to meet you."

Nick gave her fingers a quick squeeze, trying hard to minimize body contact.

"I guess you already know who I am," Elizabeth probed, still fascinated with his all too familiar face.

"No, I don't." Nick's gaze narrowed at her hopeful expression. "Should I?"

"I could swear we met last fall."

Does room 317 at Michael Reese Hospital ring a bell? his conscience ragged.

Nick knew she had regained consciousness while he'd been at her bedside, but Dr. Franklin had assured him Elizabeth's recollections during that period of time were almost nonexistent.

"Sorry." He shook his head. "I'd remember a face as pretty as yours." He nearly choked on the truth.

"My mistake, I guess," she conceded.

"No problem." Nick heard the doubt in her voice and immediately glanced around the huge, commercial-size kitchen to try to change the subject. Two stoves and ovens, two refrigerators, and what appeared to be a walk-in upright freezer all appeared spotless. "You did a good job on this place. Quite an improvement."

"You've been here before?"

Nick slid his hand into the pocket of his jeans and relaxed. "Yeah, I was here the day the cops shut it down." At the arch of her brow, he couldn't help but wonder how a woman with her apparent savvy could end up wandering the streets.

He looked around the room again. Anyone who could pull together a project like this had to have a lot on the ball. A lot more, it seemed to him, than the Elizabeth Gleason he'd read about in her file.

Right now, Nick needed time. He hadn't realized the renovations to the shelter would be this extensive. Somebody had sunk some big bucks into this joint, and it was going to take a damn sight more than one undercover cop not wanting it reopened to pull the plug this time.

Elizabeth leaned against the counter and crossed both arms over her chest. She studied the tall, well-built man, searching his face, wondering why something about him still nagged at her. He was too sure of himself. There was an underlying confidence that just didn't jibe with his outward appearance.

For some reason she couldn't explain, being alone with men his size always frightened her. Who was she kidding? They scared her half to death. But Nick didn't. Rather than feeling intimidated and threatened, she actually felt comfortable with him. "What can I do for you, Mr. Davis?"

He leveled his gaze. "I thought you might need some help. You know, maybe do some work around here in return for my meal."

"You want a job?"

"Yeah." Nick angled his head in the direction of the sink. "If you could use the help, I'll wash dishes for a few days."

"Dry," Elizabeth stated, meeting his cool blue stare.

He hooked both thumbs in the back pockets of his jeans. "Excuse me?"

"I said you can dry." She grabbed a dish towel and tossed it his way.

Nick snagged the cloth in midair. He looked at Elizabeth and rolled his shoulders restlessly. He'd never done dishes with any woman but his wife. Until tonight.

She smiled up at him. "I always wash."

"You're the boss." Nick shook off her sultry voice and fought the knot forming in the pit of his stomach. Dani had always insisted on washing, too, and he'd teased her unmercifully about it. Not that he'd given a damn about the dishes. He'd just liked to rile her up. Lord knows, no one could have held a candle to her when she was being feisty. He swallowed hard.

In his head, Nick knew if he stopped burying himself in his job and decided to live again, he'd be compelled to face countless reminders of Dani. In his heart, he had chosen not to.

Unfortunately, shutting down this soup kitchen might just force his hand. This could be the fork in the road where the real world and his cop shop would meet head-on. And, for once, this might be the very confrontation Nick Davis couldn't do a damned thing about.

He distanced himself, watching Elizabeth as they worked. Her hair wasn't as red as he'd first thought, but more of a chestnut. Just a shade richer than Dani's? Nick turned away and exorcised the thought. He wouldn't compare them. Not now. Not ever.

Slowly, deliberately, Nick's attention drifted back to Elizabeth. Her green eyes were nearly as impressive as her beautiful smile. When his gaze locked on the fading scar along her jawline, his stomach rolled. Since her only ID had been the small card that comes in cheap billfolds, he had no idea what Elizabeth had looked like before, but she was truly beautiful now.

At the time of the accident, he had refused the gory medical details, but he knew there had been some fairly extensive damage to her face. The huskiness in her voice was a result of minimal damage to her vocal cords. And she seemed to favor her left leg a bit. But, considering the shape she had been in, he knew she was lucky.

With Nick collecting the dirty dishes from the dining area, Elizabeth could hardly keep up. He was fast and efficient. Certainly not the work habits of a man who would find it difficult to get a job.

Elizabeth would love to know Nick's story, but she respected the privacy of the street people too much to ask. Hard times didn't give anyone the right to pry. Then again, she mused, maybe he would open up on his own.

When he set another stack of plates on the counter beside her, she stole a glance at the clear-cut line of his profile. She had to admit he was classically handsome, with compelling blue eyes and firm, sensual lips. There was an inherent strength in his face, a confident set to his shoulders. Hardly the posture of a man who would confide in a perfect stranger. As they worked, Elizabeth caught his melancholy stare and offered him a smile. The faint grin he returned held an unmistakable touch of sadness.

It was times like this when Elizabeth wished she had some type of life experience to draw on—something personal to share. Intellectually, she could listen and offer compassion and understanding, but nothing of herself. And that bothered her.

Nick saw the flicker of sorrow in Elizabeth's eyes. How did she cope with having a cumulative past that could be measured in a matter of months? God knows, during the last two years, he'd done everything he could to forget his. He'd worked until he was exhausted. Gotten rip-roaring drunk. And, when all else had failed, he'd even prayed.

Before tonight, Nick would have sold his soul to wipe the slate clean. But, after talking to Elizabeth, he'd seen her occasionally falter, unsure of how to answer. He knew she must constantly wonder…if she did—or ever had—or even could do or know something? Looking at her again, he realized there was definitely one thing a whole lot worse than memories…not having *any*.

After putting the last dish away, Nick snapped Elizabeth with the damp towel. Only this time, rather than sneak up on her, he made sure she saw it coming. "Looks like we're finished."

"You will be, if you smack me with that again," she threatened with a grin.

Nick waved the white cloth like a flag. "I'll surrender my weapon, if you give up yours," he bargained.

"Mine?" She yanked the dish towel from his hand and tossed it into a large wicker laundry basket.

He grabbed her hand and held it up. "Exhibit A," he teased. "Your right hook."

His touch was warm and firm. She felt the raw strength that surged just beneath the surface. "That was an upper-cut," she announced, unsure exactly how she knew the difference.

Nick released her fist. "Touché." As far as he knew, she and Dr. Franklin hadn't taken in any boxing matches during the past few months. So, he was encouraged to find she'd begun to recall fragments of past information. That was a good sign. He hoped the doctor's confidence hadn't been misplaced. She believed the flashbacks would increase and, in time, Elizabeth would fully regain her memory.

Despite the fact that nothing about this man seemed to make sense, Elizabeth had learned to trust the only part of herself she could rely on—her intuition.

Exhibit A? Touché? Not your usual street jargon. But then, there isn't anything ordinary about Nick Davis, is there?

As crazy as it seemed, her instincts not only said he was okay, but her feelings went beyond that. She was strangely drawn to him.

"By the way, if you don't have a place to stay, we have several rooms upstairs." It still never ceased to amaze her how many of the homeless had refused the charity, as they called it, of a clean bed.

Nick sensed the sincerity of her offer. The honesty. "Thanks, but I'll be fine." Too bad he couldn't give her the same kind of truthfulness in return. But, he learned a long time ago, undercover was just another word for deceit.

Tonight Nick had seen the side of Elizabeth that was filled with the drive and commitment Mary Franklin had warned him about. He had witnessed firsthand how hard Elizabeth had worked to whip the soup kitchen back into shape. Her care and concern were genuine, and he had no doubt she understood the needs of the homeless and had their best interests at heart.

But Nick knew the streets. The gangs. The dopers. Living in this neighborhood was dangerous, and Elizabeth was right in the line of fire. He only hoped she wouldn't hate him too much when the kitchen was closed down, and this was all over.

"You're sure about having somewhere to stay?" she repeated, wondering why the thought of his leaving bothered her. She reasoned that simply having company was nice for a change. Someone besides Dr. Franklin to talk to. Maybe she missed that kind of closeness.

Since Elizabeth's release from the hospital, she'd spent so much time recuperating and then refurbishing the shelter that she hadn't had time to make many friends. Okay, no friends, except the street people that moved in and out of her life. Not that she was lonely. Because she wasn't. She was too busy. Too involved.

"Positive." He turned to go.

"How about a cup of coffee for the road?" she offered, still hoping he'd stay just a little longer. "I'll make a quick pot if you'd like."

The trace of vulnerability in her voice wrapped tenuous fingers around Nick's heart and gave it a gentle squeeze. "Sure."

Within minutes, they sat across the table from one another, the steaming pot between them. The moment he picked up his mug, Elizabeth pinpointed exactly what had been bothering her since Nick walked in. His clothes were dirty. His shoes were filthy. His cap was even grungy. But not his hands. They were immaculately clean with neatly trimmed nails.

She remembered the shame of waking up in the hospital and seeing her grimy hands and broken, dirt-caked fingernails. Just the thought of walking around like that still upset her. The idea of being incapable of caring for herself was unnerving, not to mention inconceivable. According to Joe, she'd been badly hurt when he found her. Surely that was the explanation. If only she could remember.

Nick had watched her grow quiet. "Is everything okay?" he asked, knowing, if nothing else, she had to be tired. Hell, he was beat.

"Sorry. Guess I spaced out for a minute," she confided, pleased that his eyes weren't probing, but merely concerned.

"Anything you want to talk about?" *Like she's really going to spill her guts to someone who looks like he just crawled out of a compost pile.*

"Oh, I don't know," she hedged. "Let's talk about you."

Nick took a long swallow from his mug. If nothing else, he had to give her credit for trying to turn the tables on him.

"Not much to tell."

"Everybody has a story." Elizabeth decided she would only ask once, but wouldn't press him. Methodically folding her napkin, she glanced up and met his unreadable expression.

"That's a fact," he nodded. "Mine's just not very interesting. How about yours?"

Elizabeth shook her head. "Mine either." She took a deep breath. "This," she looked around, "is my life. The soup kitchen and I are going through a similar metamorphosis. We're starting over together. And this time, we're in it for the long haul. End of story." And that was the truth.

Nick's gut tightened. Why in the hell did he feel as if he'd just dropped a litter of puppies down a well? Couldn't be because his reason for coming to the kitchen was to close down the only thing this woman had in the world, could it? "That offer for a job still stand?"

Elizabeth smiled. "Absolutely." Having him around might be fun. "And, since you're working here," she offered nonchalantly, "I can throw in a load of your laundry during the evening, if you'd like."

"No thanks," Nick declined, feeling like the lowest form of reptile on Earth. Just in case, he stretched his legs to make sure they hadn't evolved off while he'd been talking. Grateful he wouldn't have to slither away, he stood.

Elizabeth teased, "Don't tell me my reputation with a washing machine has preceded me?"

Knowing she hadn't wanted to embarrass him, Nick appreciated her considerate attempt to keep his pride intact, so he played along. "Why? Is there a story behind that, too?"

"I swear that I had nothing to do with everyone's underwear turning pink." She crossed her heart. "They're all lying."

Nick smiled. "Sounds like you were framed."

"I knew you'd understand." She grinned, glad he hadn't taken offense at her offer. Or, if he had, at least he'd gracefully let her off the hook.

Feeling awkward for the first time in one helluva long time, Nick cleared his throat. "Well, I'd better go."

Disappointment, unfamiliar and unwelcome, settled over Elizabeth like a shroud. "You can leave through the dining room."

On his way out, Nick stopped and ground out an oath. "You need a dead bolt on this door."

Confused by the edge to his voice, Elizabeth assured him, "That lock works."

Why don't you just pull out your badge and give her a direct order, hot dog? "That's what you think." Before stepping outside, he ordered, "Lock it."

Elizabeth flipped the latch and hadn't taken more than two steps when she heard the door click open. She whirled around and found Nick standing behind her, looking grim—not at all smug.

She had to close her mouth to ask, "How did you do that?"

Without a word, he handed her the metal pick he'd used.

Elizabeth didn't mind backing down when she was wrong. "I'll buy a dead bolt first thing in the morning."

"Smart lady." Nick winked. "I'll install it."

"I'd really appreciate that." She looked around thoughtfully. "I'm responsible for all this, you know, and when I think of what might have happened..." Eyes wide with gratitude, she gave his arm a pat. "Thanks."

Still think she'll be grateful when you close down her kitchen? Her brand-new beginning. Her reason for living. "No problem." God, why did she have to look so vulnerable? Unwilling to meet her gaze, Nick took the tool from her hand and turned away. "Good night."

"See you tomorrow, Nick. Don't forget, you've got a job to do." She felt wonderful.

He felt like hell. "Yes, Elizabeth, I do."

Chapter 3

Nick had just finished installing the new dead bolt lock on the front door when he heard Elizabeth and the older man named Joe come in the back entrance. Intrigued by the nature of their conversation, he stood out of sight in the dining room and listened.

"Please don't argue with me, Joe." Elizabeth had gotten nothing but flack from him all morning. He'd balked at seeing a doctor, but that was mild compared to the fuss he'd put up over getting his prescription filled. Now that they were back at the soup kitchen, she simply popped the penicillin tablet into his mouth the moment he opened it to protest. Mission accomplished. She shoved a glass of water into his hand and ordered. "Swallow."

Satisfied by his gulp, she ignored the pout that followed and kept right on pitching. "The nurse said your bronchitis was caught in time, but medicine alone isn't enough. You have to take care of yourself to get well."

The old man wrinkled his nose and huffed, "She's just pushin' pills."

"She's trying to help you." Elizabeth patted his threadbare sleeve. "And so am I," she added quietly.

As Joe's expression softened, she continued, "Tell you what, if you sleep here, we can roast marshmallows just like we used to."

"How we gonna do that?" he muttered.

Elizabeth draped her arm over his rounded shoulders and surveyed the kitchen. "The burner on the stove?"

"Not the same as a *real* fire under the stars," Joe grumbled.

The slight quirk at the corner of his mouth was all the encouragement she needed. "Maybe not, but what if I turn off the lights and light some candles? How does that sound?"

"Okay. All right." Joe handed her the empty glass. "But I'm just doin' this for you, little darlin'."

"The why's not important, sweetie," she crooned, giving him a wink. But it was to her. She'd made a lot of promises to herself during the past year, and one of the most important ones had been to take care of Joe. Whether the old softie liked it or not.

Nick shook his head and grinned. Poor guy never had a chance. And, as Elizabeth barreled through the door to the dining room, he figured his odds were just about as bad.

She screamed and jumped back. "God, Nick, you scared me half to death."

He dropped his hammer, just missing his thumb, and swore. "You're dangerous, you know that, lady?"

She pointed an accusing finger. "How did you get in here, anyway?"

Her snapping eyes and flushed cheeks reminded him of

how combative she'd been when he startled her in the kitchen last night. Elizabeth hadn't merely reacted, she'd been primed for self-defense. The question was still—why?

For someone who didn't remember her past, she seemed wound pretty tight. If he could settle her down a little, maybe she'd open up and tell him. "I kicked in the door," he said sarcastically, twirling the old lock on the tip of his finger. "How else?"

Remembering how he'd picked the lock in a matter of seconds the night before, a sheepish look crossed her face. "Right," she nodded. His impertinent grin did nothing but aggravate her further. "What's so funny?"

"I was just thinking," Nick began, angling his head in the direction of the kitchen. "Maybe you should've read poor Joe his rights before browbeating him into submission."

"What for?" Her gaze met his. "It worked, didn't it?"

His eyes narrowed. "So the end justifies the means?" As a cop, he'd found that to be true on more than one occasion. But then, he'd discovered a whole lot on the job that was better left alone. Like the gang-bangers. The neighborhood. This shelter.

"That depends," she considered. "When it comes to protecting someone I care about, I'll do whatever I have to."

That makes two of us, pretty lady. He wondered how hard Elizabeth would fight him, once she knew he'd come to close the shelter. God, he hoped she'd be reasonable. So, why did the phrase *fat chance* keep coming to mind? Not that it mattered. Either way, he'd do what he had to do—as always, without regrets. He pushed away thoughts of *the inevitable* for the time being. "Even a camp fire?"

"If that's what it takes to get that sweet old man to sleep

between clean sheets, let the marshmallow virgins run for their lives. There's going to be a sacrifice tonight."

Nick's rich laughter echoed through the empty dining room. "Now that's quite a visual."

Elizabeth couldn't explain the kick she got from making Nick laugh, but the rush that coursed through her veins spoke for itself. "It is, isn't it?" Though she had no idea where it came from or why it had started, this lighter side to her personality both pleased and surprised her. As happy as these occasional glimpses of the *real* Elizabeth Gleason made her, they also gave birth to a million more unanswered questions about the woman she had once been.

Intelligent and understanding, she would guess. Honest and trustworthy, she was sure. But, so much more than that…she would hope.

Her smile faded as old familiar feelings of doubt settled around her. Damn, she swore under her breath, it always came down to this. How could that kind of woman—the one she'd begun remembering—end up wandering the streets? It just didn't make sense. She wondered if it ever would.

Nick watched the emotions wash across her face one after the other, and his gut tightened. Innocent and defenseless—that was one dangerous combination in a woman. He frowned. What was it like to go through life not knowing why some things pushed your buttons and some didn't? Must be a heavy load for a lost soul to carry. "Don't look so sad." The quiet, soothing words were out of his mouth before he could stop them.

"Sad?" Elizabeth echoed her own desperation.

Barely able to handle his own vulnerability, Nick knew he couldn't take on Elizabeth's, too, so he masked his concern with humor. "You know, feeling guilty about those marshmallow virgins," he teased. "Forget it. This day and age you'll be lucky to find one in the whole bag."

"Especially if they're males," she shot back.

Grateful to see her spirits lift, Nick felt a little of his own load lighten. He grinned. "Lady, you've got that right."

Elizabeth's eyes met his, and for just a moment she sensed a connection with this handsome stranger. Not at all like sharing a joke, or even a secret. It was more like a comforting jolt of familiarity. But without the why…or the who. Hidden deep in the shadows of her mind, the why remained more elusive than smoke. The who, more evasive than her memories. And, the reality of both was far too much for Elizabeth to handle right now.

"So, let me get this straight." She walked around him—slowly. "You—broke in—to install a new lock?"

Nick picked up the hammer. "That's about the size of it."

Elizabeth noticed that today his jeans and T-shirt were every bit as clean as hers. Apparently her offer to launder them hadn't offended him too much. Or maybe just enough? She shifted her attention and flipped the dead bolt. "Nice job."

"You're welcome."

"You're getting paid on Friday. How's that for thanks?"

Nick pinned her with his gaze. "I asked if you needed any help. I never asked for money."

His attitude didn't make one bit of sense to Elizabeth. After all, the man was destitute.… Or was he? She stepped into his path. "What are you *really* doing here?"

He picked up the box of tools. "You mean besides breaking and entering?"

"No. I mean you just don't add up," Elizabeth answered honestly.

He took a step toward her, admiring the fact that she didn't blink. "You mean *measure* up," he corrected.

"No, I don't." Elizabeth's words were sincere. "Look, if you're in some kind of trouble, I'll do whatever I can to help."

God, Dani would have loved this woman. A fellow do-gooder. Another Ivory Tower sociologist. Why couldn't they ever understand the difference between real life and theory?

Nick shook his head. "I'm not in trouble, and I don't need your help. I'll work for meals. That's what I'm *really* doing here."

Like hell! "Fine." Nick Davis's story still didn't wash. Granted, he didn't seem dangerous—in the true sense. But no man—she glanced at his long dark hair and soft sensuous mouth—who looked like he did was harmless, either. She smiled up at him and extended her hand. "A deal's a deal."

He smiled right back. "Then you'll let me help?" If he was going to keep her safe, he had to have some excuse for sticking around.

"Absolutely." She nodded, more determined than ever to find out why Nick Davis was doing odd jobs at a homeless shelter in exchange for food.

Shortly after lunch, Elizabeth closed the manilla folder and met Dr. Franklin's steady gaze. "It's like reading someone's biography," she admitted. "But not mine."

"And you expected…"

"I don't know. Something."

"You don't know what you'd hoped to find?" the doctor prodded.

Elizabeth sucked in her breath and enunciated each word carefully. "I wanted to remember my life." The edge to her voice was unmistakable. "Realistically—" she shifted in her seat "—I thought at least something would ring a bell."

"But nothing did?"

"No." Elizabeth watched Dr. Franklin jot down notes as she continued, "I read the words and they were just that—words."

"For now."

Elizabeth shrugged. "I guess."

"But...?"

"But shouldn't they mean *something* to me?"

"Not necessarily. Give it time." Dr. Franklin laid down her pen and smiled. "Just plant the seeds and let them grow."

Elizabeth tapped the folder with her fingernail. "How long?"

"As long as it takes."

Elizabeth sat a moment, considering the doctor's comment, then shook her head. "No. That's not good enough."

"For now, it has to be."

"No." Elizabeth raised her voice. "It doesn't. This report—" she seemed to spit out the words as she flipped open the folder "—says I had a husband named... Stewart." She looked incredulously at Mary Franklin. "A husband—"

"Who died in a fire at your home, Elizabeth. That trauma may be exactly what put you on the streets."

Elizabeth shook her head again.

"It would be an awfully big piece of the puzzle," Dr. Franklin pointed out. "Maybe you should think about it."

"This says," she said, then paused to find the description, "he had blond hair and brown eyes, was five foot ten and weighed 195 pounds."

"And...?"

"How can I make you understand?" Elizabeth ran both hands through her hair in exasperation. "There is only *one* man." She leveled her voice as well as her gaze. "This—" she gouged the paper with her fingernail "—is not him."

"Your mind has a way of protecting—"

"Protecting me from what?" She gestured around her. "My own life?"

"Sometimes."

"Well, not this time."

"And you propose to do what?"

"I don't know. Something." Impatient, she stood. "I'd like to go to—" she opened the folder and found the line labeled Address "—1122 North Wisconsin Avenue."

"Now?"

"Yes." Elizabeth straightened her shoulders. "Right now."

Dr. Franklin glanced at her schedule. She had some free time. "Would you like me to go with you?"

Elizabeth took a deep breath. "I think I need to do this alone."

"Suit yourself, Elizabeth. Call me later, if you'd like to talk."

"I will." She pulled the report from the folder. "May I have a copy of this?"

"That one's yours."

Elizabeth glanced at the paper. "No," she said, then looked at the doctor. "I don't believe it is."

By two-thirty Elizabeth was turning onto Wisconsin Avenue. She studied the row of small ranch-style houses, praying something would jog her memory:

At 1116 North Wisconsin Avenue, a blue house with a cyclone fence around the yard. *Nothing.*

At 1118—a tan house with a screened-in front porch and an attached garage. *Nothing.*

At 1120—a small white house with black shutters and no garage. *Nothing.*

She slowed to a stop—1122 North Wisconsin Avenue. Only a blackened shell remained. She pulled up in front of the overgrown lawn and parked.

Nothing.

Her only thought as she looked at what was left of the house was that someone should remove the shards of glass from the windows so none of the neighborhood kids would get hurt. She looked around...that is, if there were any children on this street. *God, shouldn't I know that?*

Frustrated and confused, Elizabeth's anxiety turned to anger. She didn't give a damn how deeply buried her memories were—if she and her husband had lived here, she would remember. Crossing both arms over the steering wheel, she rested her forehead against them. "Think, dammit, think."

Nick received the call from Dr. Franklin around two o'clock. She'd called, as always, after Elizabeth's session, but this time with talk of a possible breakthrough. Just what they'd been hoping for. Unfortunately, the enthusiasm in the doctor's voice failed to excite him. Quite the opposite. For some strange reason, her encouraging words disturbed him.

If he drove like a bat out of hell, he could arrive at the Wisconsin Avenue address enough ahead of Elizabeth to park one street over and run back on foot.

Positioned in a nearby garage less than twenty minutes later, he slapped a cobweb away so he could see through the window closest to the street. Still unable to put into words why he was there, Nick just knew for some reason he had to be.

"Sorry, Doc," he whispered as he watched Elizabeth's car inch down the street, "I've got a feeling you called this one all wrong."

Sweat trickled down Nick's back as Elizabeth pulled up in front of the charred skeleton of a house. Even from his vantage point he could see her blank expression crumble into despair.

At that moment, he realized exactly why he was standing in a filthy garage on the south side of Chicago in the middle of the afternoon. O'Malley could send a rookie to pick up his car because Elizabeth was going to need him. That was exactly what had drawn him there. Just how, he wasn't sure.

Nick had suffered enough pain in the past two years to understand the anger and frustration Elizabeth would feel when she realized she didn't belong here. And she didn't. Somehow, he was sure of that, too. He knew from experience, that when control gave way to circumstance, resentment was about all that was left. That, and maybe a good friend—if you were lucky. He wanted to be that friend. That was the least he could do, considering what they'd both been through.

Nick knew he could pick up the pieces of his life and go forward—without Dani. But without her, his life was just a memory. His days consisted of little more than going through the motions.

Elizabeth could start over without looking back, but she would never know exactly who she was or where she had been.

Right now, Nick wasn't sure which was worse. But if the expression on Elizabeth's face was any indication—he left the garage and ran toward the car—she was in a hell of a lot more pain than he was.

Elizabeth sat up and took a deep breath. There had to be something around here familiar enough to spark an inkling of recognition. But there wasn't. When she realized there never would be, tears stung her eyes and spilled down both cheeks. This was the house of a stranger.

Elizabeth never saw him coming, but the instant Nick appeared at the passenger door, relief—not surprise—washed over her. She flipped the lock, and he slid in beside her.

"Come here," he whispered, as though he'd done it a thousand times before. Why did taking her in his arms feel so right? When she began to cry again, he pulled her closer and braced himself for the guilt. But this time was different. This time it didn't come.

Without question, Elizabeth melted against him. Why did Nick holding her feel so much like going home? She turned to him for comfort as though it were the most natural thing in the world. Settling into his strong embrace, she inhaled his scent. *So familiar?* The beat of his heart against hers severed her last thread of control. She sobbed uncontrollably and clung to Nick Davis, suddenly certain that he was the man who had haunted all her dreams.

Elizabeth was the first to pull away, secure in knowing Nick would hold her as long as she needed. She patted his damp shirt and tried to muster a smile.

"Sorry about the mess."

"Forget it."   *Fat chance. How does it feel to know you crossed the line and let your assignment become personal?* Without regret, Nick turned off the voice in his head and wiped away Elizabeth's last tear. "Want to talk about it?"

She straightened in her seat. Nick hadn't surprised her

by showing up, but had she actually expected him to be there? she asked herself.

That was impossible.

How could she find consolation from a man she'd known not even a full day, and not one shred of comfort from the place she'd called home for fifteen years?

That shouldn't be.

Why did this neighborhood seem more foreign to her than a total stranger?

It just didn't make sense.

When Elizabeth turned to Nick for answers, his blue eyes were filled with life and pain and undeniable warmth. She took a ragged breath. "Yes, I think I would like to talk about it. But not here." Swiping both cheeks dry, she started the ignition.

"Sure." At the moment, one syllable was about all Nick trusted himself to say. Any more than that and he would do a lot more than cross the line. He'd spill his guts.

Ten minutes later, they sat in a diner separated by a scarred tabletop and an awkward silence.

Elizabeth thoughtfully stirred her coffee.

Patience never came easy to him—not even on a good day—but the clank of her spoon was beginning to irritate the hell out of Nick. When he glared at her cup, it dawned on him—no cream or sugar. How many times had he asked Dani why she stirred black coffee? His jaw clenched.

Nick stared into Elizabeth's face, searched every nuance. *What in God's name did he expect to see?* She appeared to be lost in thought, debating exactly how much to tell him.

"Two years ago this past summer, Joe said he found me lying behind some bushes and that I'd been badly hurt."

"Why didn't he find a way to get you to a hospital—or at least call 911?"

"Joe doesn't have much use for hospitals," she explained. "I don't know the whole story, but from what I can piece together, his daughter died about four years ago. Whatever the circumstances, Joe has never quite handled the loss, much less the doctor's failure to save her."

Nick knew exactly what she meant. Cops saw families torn apart by death all the time. Losing a loved one was bad enough, but turning on one another was about as ugly as it got. Some families pointed fingers and dished out blame by the truckload. Others, like Joe, chose a different route. "He gave up?"

"Yeah," Elizabeth nodded. "Somehow, he managed to take care of me, but even after I recovered physically, I still couldn't remember a thing. Not who I was or where I lived. I wouldn't even have known my name if my ID hadn't been in my purse.

"With his help, I lived on the streets until about a year ago when I was hit by a car. I don't remember the accident, per se, but I woke up in the hospital. To make a long story short, after several surgeries and a year of counseling, I've managed to make it this far."

"And you still don't remember anything about your past?"

"No." She shook her head. "In the beginning, I didn't want to pursue my prior life."

"Why not?" Nick watched the question hit home.

"I'm not exactly sure why I was so adamant." And she truly wasn't. "Maybe I hadn't recovered enough to handle it."

He gave her time to think before asking, "What changed your mind?"

She looked out the window, then glanced up nervously. "I started having this dream again."

Nick took a drink. "A nightmare?"

"Not really. In fact, I'm not sure if it's a dream—or a memory resurfacing."

As Nick watched her stir her black coffee again, he shifted restlessly in his seat. "A memory?"

"Yeah. I have flashbacks," she clarified. "Like the other night, in the kitchen."

"When you nearly decked me?" He absently rubbed the spot beneath his chin that was still sore as hell.

She reached out to touch his hand, then pulled back and grabbed her cup instead. "Exactly. That was the first one I'd had while I was awake."

Nick leaned forward, bracing his forearms on the table. "What was it like?"

"Scary." She gripped the coffee cup tighter. "But it was so clear. I remembered feeling a tap on my left shoulder and turning my head to look out a window. A man was standing there, but the sun was in my eyes. It was so bright I couldn't see his face, but his silhouette was tall and muscular.…"

Nick urged her on. "Did he hurt you?"

The cup almost slipped out of her grasp. Elizabeth's voice was barely a whisper. "Yes." *My God, he had!*

Nick caught the cup and set it down. From the way her eyes had widened, he figured she'd never connected the man and the pain before. He held her trembling hands in his and cursed the bastard under his breath. "Are the flashbacks always frightening?"

"Not at all." She hoped to hell her instincts were right, because she'd decided to jump in with both feet and confide in Nick. "When I have the recurring dream," she began carefully, "it's like looking at a photograph. The foreground is crystal clear, but the background's hazy."

"What's in the picture?"

Elizabeth held her breath, barely exhaling before she

answered. "You. You're all I see." She looked out the window and waited for him to say something—anything.

Nick never changed his expression, despite the fact that Elizabeth had avoided his eyes just like Dani used to do when she was unsure what his reaction would be. "How do you explain that?"

"How do *I* explain it?" Elizabeth pulled her hands away and faced him. "How do *you* explain it?"

Jesus, Nick could hear O'Malley now. *"Standard police procedure, Davis. Never get involved while you're undercover. It's sloppy, not to mention dangerous. And it's hard as hell to protect someone when you're dead."*

In fifteen years on the force, Nick had never thought about breaking that rule—until today. The smartest thing he could do right now would be to walk away from Elizabeth. The dumbest thing he could do would be take another look at her quivering lower lip. The best thing he could do right now was try not to get in any deeper.

"You probably just remember me from the street," he told her, stretching the truth to the max.

"Maybe you're right, but I swear these dreams go back to the summer *before* last—that's over two years." Overwhelmed by conflicting emotions, Elizabeth halfheartedly shrugged. "Of course, the information I was given also said I was raised by my grandmother, and at age eighteen I married a factory worker named Stewart Gleason." Frustrated, she looked at Nick. Why did she feel that he, of all people, should know better than that?

Nick already knew all about Elizabeth's marriage—hell, he'd written up the report himself. So why did the very thought of old Stewart still rub him raw? "I suppose you don't believe that either?"

"Don't you think it's a little odd that I can't remember a fifteen-year marriage?"

God, she looked confused and alone. If only Nick didn't feel so damn connected to this woman. But he did. And worse than that, he sensed there was a helluva lot more where that came from. "Take it easy," he soothed, tracing her pale cheek with his finger. "That's why they call it amnesia."

Even now, his touch seemed familiar—which only baffled Elizabeth more. "Then why do I remember you?" she asked softly, taking his hand in hers.

"Maybe I'm the first person to come along since your memory started returning, and somehow the pieces of then and now simply get mixed together." He watched her clouded expression clear just a little.

"Maybe," she repeated, determined to ask the question that would lay most of her fears to rest. "But, there's one thing I need to know."

Nick looked at Elizabeth sitting across from him, wide-eyed and just a shade pale. He sensed she was going to ask something of him that he wasn't prepared to give—but would anyway. She'd been through enough, and he'd be damned if he'd deny her again. "Shoot."

In one deep breath she asked, "Were you in my hospital room after my accident last year?"

The raw need in her voice left him no choice. There was no way in hell Nick would lie to her now. "Yes."

Relief washed over her like a soft, spring rain. "So, I'm not crazy after all."

"No," he assured her, willing to reveal just enough of his story to ease her mind. And, even before the words were out of his mouth, he knew she would never blame him. "I'm the one who hit you."

"You?" Elizabeth hesitated a moment. "I never wanted to know the details, but they said a city employee hit me, and that's why all my expenses were covered—even my psychiatrist.''

Nick nodded, ignoring the perspiration trickling between his shoulder blades.

Elizabeth's shock faded into quiet words of sympathy. ''How awful.'' Had the accident torn Nick's life apart? ''I can only imagine what you must have gone through.''

Her selflessness touched him. ''You were the one fighting for your life.''

''Exactly.'' She smiled. ''And you gave it back to me.''

This time, he was the one who averted his eyes and looked out the window. ''You don't have to say that.''

''I'm serious, Nick. Think about it. Before you hit me, I was living on the streets in a daze. Unfocused, unsure and unreachable. The trauma of being hit by the car snapped me out of it.'' She threaded her fingers through his, coaxing his gaze back in her direction. ''You have nothing to feel guilty about.''

''I wouldn't go that far.'' He gave her hand a gentle squeeze. ''Quit—before you start thanking me.'' He grinned, secure in the unexplainable knowledge that the woman who returned his smile was no stranger. ''Besides, I'm the one who's grateful to you.''

''Me?'' She sat up a little straighter in her chair. ''Why?''

''You saved me from running over a boy that day. I hit you when you pushed him aside.''

Elizabeth pulled her hands from his and covered her ears.

The child's laughter.

The squeal of tires.

The sound of her feet against the pavement.

The feel of the boy's nylon jacket beneath her hands as she shoved him.

The excruciating pain.

Nick steadied her shoulders the moment her eyes focused. "Another flashback?"

She slid both palms down her cheeks and nodded. "The boy."

Tears stung her eyes. "I saved him."

"And me," Nick added softly. "He would have died and I couldn't have lived with that." *And he knew that was true.*

The ache in his voice was nearly Elizabeth's undoing. "No. I'm sure you couldn't." And, somehow, she knew exactly what he meant. "No child can ever be replaced."

It was such a simple phrase. Isn't that what Dani had told him after her miscarriage, when he'd tried like hell to assure her they could have other children? Or was his mind working overtime, digging for similarities? Was he wishing Dani's mannerisms off onto some poor woman who didn't even really know her own name? Sickened by his own selfishness, Nick threw down a couple of dollars for the coffee. "Ready?"

"Sure." Elizabeth realized immediately that she'd struck a nerve, but sensed his abrupt mood change wasn't aimed directly at her. So she met his thunderous expression and respected the intensity of his reaction by not asking questions—at least not right then.

Their conversation had already taken her a giant step closer to finding out why Nick Davis was keeping secrets and working for meals on Chicago's south side.

Chapter 4

"What do you mean, play hooky tonight? I've already been gone half the afternoon." Elizabeth craned her neck to see past a garbage truck as she changed lanes.

A horn blared. "Just what I said." Nick adjusted the side mirror so *he* could see, too. Evidently old habits, like old control freaks, die hard.

"That shelter is my responsibility. I simply can't—"

"What are your days off?" He hung on as she leap-frogged through traffic.

"Well…I—"

"Exactly," he interrupted again. "You think you have to be there twenty-four hours a day, seven days a week. But you don't. You've got a rotating staff of volunteers that helps run that place."

"I know," Elizabeth sighed.

"While we're on the subject, how *did* you pull off re-opening the soup kitchen—in such style?"

"I have to give a lot of credit to the investigative reporter that kept tabs on me after my accident."

Nick admired her lovely profile and could just about imagine what kind of tabs this guy kept. "He took that much interest in your story?"

"She," Elizabeth corrected.

Nick unclenched his teeth.

"I guess she expected me to be some illiterate social misfit, and when I wasn't, it piqued her curiosity."

"Apparently hers and a lot of other people's," Nick observed.

"The follow-up article she wrote last spring generated enough interest to kick off the entire project."

"So that's how you got your backers?"

"Well, that and with the help of my psychiatrist. Dr. Franklin said her friends were always looking for a legitimate tax write-off."

So the good doctor had crossed the line for Elizabeth, too. Oddly comforted by that fact, he continued, "Sounds like urban funding at its best."

"Don't knock it. The shelter's backers not only arranged the finances, but they contacted every service organization around. Thank God almost all the groups' charters require community service from their members."

"Funny how money can set the wheels into motion, isn't it?" Nick cringed as she cut off a cab. "All one fat cat has to do is holler 'Jump' and every wanna-be hanging on his coattail asks 'How high?'"

"Call it what you will, but in less than a week those people initiated enough donations to renovate the entire shelter."

Nick grunted.

"I'm serious." Elizabeth faced him as she stopped for the traffic light. "You can't believe how many people showed up to clean and repair that place from top to bottom. Stores even donated building supplies and paint—"

"That's dandy." This time, Nick cut her off. "But you still need a life outside that place."

Frustrated, Elizabeth shrugged. "I know, but I love what I'm doing."

"That goes without saying," he assured her. "Your dedication's obvious, but you still need some time off."

She frowned. Did she really want to stifle the spark of excitement his suggestion had ignited? "Take the night off, huh?"

"Recruit an extra volunteer for this evening. It's as simple as one phone call." When Elizabeth didn't jump down his throat, Nick sensed a crack in her resolve. He touched her arm to hold her attention. "After what you went through today, you deserve it."

Elizabeth started to protest, then changed her mind. She hadn't been the only one who'd been affected by her emotional turmoil this afternoon. She'd seen old hurts reflected in Nick's eyes, and the regret she'd heard in his voice had been unmistakable.

"Just say thanks, Gracie," he joked, trying to lighten her mood. Funny, he hadn't thought of the old classics since... Somehow, nothing seemed the same without Dani to share it.

"No," Elizabeth shrieked and slammed on the brakes. "It was—"

The memory hit her full force.

"—say good-night, Gracie!"

When she turned to him, eyes wide with excitement, Nick braced his palms against the dash. "Okay. Okay." He grabbed the wheel.

"I remember," she cried. "George Burns and Gracie Allen."

"Yeah, right. They were great. But about your driving—" Nick's eyes darted as the car swerved from lane to lane. "Have you ever had a flashback while you were behind the wheel?"

She slapped his hands away. "You mean before this one?" The oath that passed his lips was enough to make her blush. "No, it's never happened," she swore, holding up three fingers. "Girl Scout's honor." She stared at her hand—which was still in midair—and screamed again.

The car zigzagged. "Dammit, Elizabeth, pull over," Nick ordered.

The car came to a screeching halt in a nearby parking lot. Wide-eyed, Elizabeth turned to him. "I was a Girl Scout." The words came out in barely a whisper.

He opened his arms and pulled her close. "And probably a damned good one. But if you're going to have some kind of chain-reaction recall, I think you should at least live to experience it, don't you?"

She nodded and snuggled closer, comforted by his strong arms wrapped around her. Confiding good news right now to Nick seemed just as familiar as when she'd shared the bad news earlier. For now, Elizabeth pushed the how and why of it aside. "My memory's really going to come back." She sighed.

He pulled her closer. "I know it is." Hallelujah. Maybe if that damned soup kitchen wasn't the focal point of her entire life, he'd be able to shut it down without losing Elizabeth's... Losing what? Her trust? Respect?

Think again, pal. You've done nothing but lie to her since the day you met her. And, it looks like your time is running out. Better make a decision, Detective. Just how important is Elizabeth to you?

Important enough, Nick reasoned. Maybe she won't hate

me for doing my job. Then again, maybe she will. Either way, it was a risk. But one he had to take.

"I'm really going to regain all of it." She shuddered, suddenly frightened at what remembering might mean. Her past was bound to change her. It had to. Soon she would have memories of another life. A childhood filled with dreams. Family ties. Love?

He squeezed her tighter. "Uh-huh."

Elizabeth couldn't believe it. There she sat in a grocery store parking lot—in broad daylight—in the arms of a stranger, teetering dangerously on the brink of a new beginning. One healthy push was all that stood between her past and her future. And leaning back, she stared hopefully into the pale blue eyes of the only man who could shove her through that looking glass.

But the question that really haunted her was whether or not he would follow her to the other side? Shaken by the possibility that he might not, she forced herself to concentrate on the present. He was with her now.

"What do you say, Davis? Let's throw caution to the wind and take the night off."

"You've got it," he agreed, more than pleased to see her smile. "But this time—I'll drive."

Nick Davis was not a patient man. O'Malley had always accused him of being a pit bull when he had something on his mind, and today was no exception. Especially after the emotional afternoon he'd spent with Elizabeth.

This evening, however, it was driving to the beach in Elizabeth's compact car, her seated next to him, that had him questioning the wisdom of this little night out. The hot pink logo, All Mine, emblazoned across the front of her T-shirt was making his palms sweat.

The dregs of rush hour traffic were hell, especially on

a less than tolerant cop. Nick glanced anxiously at the clock on his dashboard and pressed the accelerator closer to the floor. Nearly five-thirty. Thank God, they were almost there.

Within minutes, he was able to park near the lakefront. He helped Elizabeth from the car, then closed the door and positioned her against it—more to get his hands on her than anything else. "Stay put." Her eyes widened at his order, but before she could protest, he added softly, "Tonight, I'm going to serve you."

Elizabeth smiled at the thought. Respecting Nick's wishes, she stood back and watched him lift the huge wicker basket from the trunk. It didn't take him long to find a spot nearby to spread the blanket. As soon as he was finished, she moved to sit beside him. Nick stopped what he was doing and looked—no—stared at her. In that split second, she swore something in his eyes pleaded silently *Go ahead and ask me. I want you to.* She blinked once and the sensation was gone, time was back on track.

As though the words had been spoken, Elizabeth wondered if what Nick wanted her to ask was what she needed to know.... Who he was. Why he'd walked into her life. What he wanted. Regardless, she planned to have the answers soon.

"Nice touch," she told him. Silverware from the kitchen, not plastic knives and forks. Cloth napkins he'd gotten God only knew where. The steamy blues of Eric Clapton's "Layla" drifting provocatively from the cassette player he'd borrowed from her. As Clapton's silky voice begged to have his weary mind eased, Elizabeth yearned for the same relief. "This is really—"

"Ambience," Nick offered, completing her thought.

Ambience? From a man who claimed to live on the

streets? Maybe. But every time Nick's ambiguity generated another doubt, Elizabeth's need for the truth grew.

"That, too," she nodded, trying unsuccessfully not to give in to his sexy grin. "But I was going to say how lovely everything looks."

He rewarded her easy laugh with one perfect rose. "Flattery," he began in a low husky tone, "will get you everywhere."

Elizabeth stroked the delicate red petals. "Where did you get this?"

Nick winked. "I mugged one of those flower sellers down at the bus station."

Elizabeth was speechless.

"Look, if you don't want to accept stolen property, I can respect that." Nick reached for the stem, only to have his hand slapped away.

Stolen property? Some day, she planned to piece together all of Nick's inconsistencies and innuendos. Because, this man was not who he pretended to be. She watched his long, dark hair blow in the breeze. His facade should have frightened her, or at the very least made her wary. But it didn't.

All she could do now was watch him and wait. Given time, the truth always had a way of surfacing. She wasn't sure why she believed that, she just did. "Very funny, Davis, but it's been so long since I've had flowers—" *Had it been?* "I guess."

Sincerity softened his tone. "Then I can't think of a better reason, can you?"

Nick's grin nearly pulled the plug on Elizabeth's life support system which, after the music, the flower, and possibly reading Nick's mind, was shaky, at best.

Without another word, he popped the cork on a chilled bottle of chardonnay and poured.

Charmed by the effect of Nick's self-proclaimed atmosphere, Elizabeth sniffed the fragrant rose and toasted, "To botanists." She clinked glasses with Nick.

"And bald, flower-peddling guys who hang around bus stations and pester the tourists," he rambled, trying to take his mind off how breathtaking she looked in the golden glow of the sunset. Who was he kidding? His feelings for her went far beyond anything he was ready to admit.

Whether he wanted her to or not, this beautiful woman stirred something familiar deep inside him. He struggled to pinpoint why just being near her turned him inside out. Was it the tilt of her head? The arch of her back? Or something tucked away in his mind's eye—just far enough out of reach to make him want to drive his fist through a wall in frustration every time they were together?

Elizabeth leaned back and sipped the wine. "Ummm."

Her throaty sigh caused his gut to tighten. "Good?"

"Uh-huh." She closed her eyes and tipped her face toward the fading rays of the sun, dreading to ask how he'd come up with the money for all this. "Nick, I was just wondering—"

"California," he said, answering her question.

She opened one eye and squinted at him. "What?"

He pointed to the label on the bottle. "Domestic."

"Right." Elizabeth gave up and closed both eyes again. She might not know a lot about Nick Davis, but she knew better than to try to pump him for information.

Edgy and restless, Nick stood. He didn't like feeling this way. Didn't understand it. "Sit here and relax while I gather some firewood for later. Once the sun goes down, it'll cool off in a hurry."

Elizabeth watched him walk away. Tall and muscular. Dark hair hanging to his shoulders. She sighed. Whoever he was, Nick Davis was quite a man.

And apparently she wasn't the only one who thought so. She sat up straighter and craned her neck to watch a blond jogger with a Spandex body and a cheerleader's smile offer Nick a more than hopeful glance.

Elizabeth held her breath.

Nick grinned back...

Elizabeth waited.

...and kept on walking.

Elizabeth exhaled.

Okay, so he'd become important to her. Much more important than she was willing to admit. But, why *this* man? It didn't make any sense. She knew virtually nothing about him, except he was passing himself off as a street person. And for some reason that defied explanation, she trusted him anyway. As he walked back toward her, Elizabeth contemplated what forces between heaven and earth had brought Nick into her life.

She watched him unceremoniously dump the armload of wood next to the blanket, then squat to rearrange the twigs and branches into one neatly woven pyramid. "Are you always this precise?"

O'Malley's comment about the clutter on Nick's floor rang in his ears. "Let's just say I've always had my own way of doing things."

Elizabeth sensed a story behind his smirk but ignored the temptation to ask. "It must be nice to know yourself like that."

Nick considered her words. He had learned to depend on his life experience as a reference point. So without that, what did Elizabeth base hers on? How did she feel when she reacted to a situation without knowing why? Was there some place deep down inside she could turn to for comfort? "Guess that makes me pretty lucky in your eyes, doesn't it?"

"Yeah." She pulled up her legs and hugged them close.

The match he struck flared as he tossed it on the wood. "You know, at the rate you're going," he said easing himself down beside her, "it won't be long before your memory returns."

Elizabeth watched the flames jump from branch to branch until they engulfed the entire wooden triangle. *Maybe that's the way it will be for me. Some day, these little sparks I'm remembering will connect with one another and ignite my entire past.* "I just get impatient."

Nick brushed a stray curl from her cheek. "That's understandable." He would never forget the paralyzing frustration of sitting by Elizabeth's hospital bed after the accident, knowing he was helpless. He had fought the fear and won. But the anger that had bubbled just below the surface hadn't been such an easy battle. "Waiting must be hell."

Elizabeth couldn't remember ever having a friend, but if Nick's quiet understanding was what that was like, she was grateful to have one now. "Some days are worse than others," she admitted.

"Like today?" he asked softly, regretting the sadness in her eyes.

"Oh, yeah," she sighed.

They sat in silence, each absorbing the comfort of the moment. The beauty of the sunset. The shimmery surface of the lake that appeared to burst into flames as the sun sank into the west. The rich orange glow that crept along the horizon as the late afternoon shadows gave way to evening.

Finally surrounded by the soothing darkness, Nick relaxed. "You realize," he began, putting his arm around her, "that this day's not over yet." He felt her snuggle against him and understood immediately that the closeness she sought was not sexual.

Sensuality would have definitely been easier for Nick to handle—because he'd thought about it...a lot. He knew exactly the angle he'd have tilted her head. Expressly the way he'd have cupped her face in his hands. Precisely the path he'd have nuzzled down the soft column of her throat, before tracing her lips with the tip of his tongue. He couldn't explain why, but he'd spent the afternoon wondering what might happen between them tonight. He'd expected just about anything...except maybe this.

But, the trusting way she laid her head on his shoulder asked for something much more complicated. Emotional intimacy, not seduction. So he pulled her close and, at least for now, was content to watch the crackling fire with her by his side.

What was it about sharing a sunset that united two people's souls? Elizabeth wasn't sure, but, sitting here beside Nick, she felt as though she'd known him forever. And that made her smile.

Today had been the first time she could remember someone else actually sharing a part of her life. And it felt wonderful. Without thinking, Elizabeth lifted her head from Nick's shoulder....

Nick never saw it coming. But, when Elizabeth's mouth covered his, the connection between them rocked him so hard all he could do was dig his fingers deep into the warm sand and hold on for dear life.

He never moved a muscle. Didn't have to. The moment her lips touched his, Elizabeth felt as if she'd been struck by lightning. Without saying as much as a word, Nick Davis had invited her into the future.

Some cops had it. Others didn't. Even after yesterday, having his mind blown halfway to hell and back by one solitary kiss, Nick's internal radar could still sense trouble a mile away. And tonight was the night. The knot tightening all day in his gut had spoken—loud and clear. So, he waited.

Less than an hour later, his cop instincts kicked into overdrive. Right again. He spotted the Blood's colors the moment they walked in. *Bingo, O'Malley. I told you'd they'd show up. You owe me a six-pack.* Before they could move, he was in their face.

"Beat it, Chico." Nick's quiet words were edged with promise. Luckily, Elizabeth had gone into the kitchen and couldn't hear him.

"Hey, Davis," the punk sneered. "What are you doin' in *our* neighborhood? Somebody's cat stuck up in a tree?" He high-fived one of the other gang members and the rest snickered.

"I said, take a hike." Nick balled his fists when he saw the kid's jaw clench.

Chico jerked his head toward Elizabeth as she pushed through the kitchen door. "Check it out, guys. Looks like Davis already got the kitten down." He ogled her again. "Safe and extremely sound."

The instant Nick grabbed Chico, the hoots and whistles died down.

"Nick!"

He faced Elizabeth's outrage. "I was just telling the boys here that we're closed for the night," he said, tightening his hold on the gang leader.

She pried his hands away from the kid's throat. "Help yourselves to dinner." She shot Nick a look that would have flattened a bull elephant at twenty yards. "There's plenty left."

"Change of plans," Nick assured her, through gritted teeth. "They're not staying, after all. Are you, boys?"

Chico rolled his shoulders and arrogantly smoothed the front of his leather jacket. "Thanks, kitten, but not tonight," he leered, before leveling a meaningful glare at Nick. "We'll come back some time when we're *really* hungry." As he turned on his heels, one snap of his fingers had the others following him out the door.

"The kitchen," Elizabeth growled. "Now."

Nick dodged the swinging door only to find her ready and waiting on the other side. But not nearly as ready as he was. Before she had a chance to open her mouth, he boomed, "Are you nuts?"

"Me?" Elizabeth slapped both hands on her hips to keep from taking a swing at him. "How dare you turn them away?"

"That wasn't just anyone." He was furious. "The Bloods are one of the roughest gangs on the south side."

"They came in here to eat." Elizabeth stomped her foot. "And, as long as that's all they do, they're welcome."

Nick's sarcastic laugh was more like a snarl. "And how do you propose to stop them, if they decide to do *otherwise?*"

"What makes you so sure they will?" she argued.

"What makes you so sure they won't?" Frustrated, he ran a hand through his hair. "Look, the gangs are part of the reason this place was closed down the first time. They not only came in and took over, but a lot of them used this building as a front for dealing dope—among other things."

Elizabeth shook her head. "I'm not turning them away. I'll handle—"

"You won't handle squat," he shouted. The instant flush of her cheeks caused him to lower his voice. "Listen to me, Elizabeth, these aren't just defiant, misunderstood teenagers."

She huffed and looked away.

Why in God's name, after all these years, did this still surprise him about women? He'd never been able to talk Dani out of doing volunteer work on the south side, either. He'd ranted about the dangers of the neighborhood. And she'd preached about a greater danger—losing faith in mankind. He shook his head in agitation. "You actually hope there's some good left in those punks, don't you?"

"Yep."

Nick cupped her chin, forcing her face back to his. "Most of them have a rap sheet a mile long."

Elizabeth's eyes narrowed.

Adrenaline still pumping, he traced her jawline with his thumb. He'd give her a little time, but if there was one more incident, he'd blow his cover to protect her. "Have it your way. But, if this doesn't work out, you'll reconsider. Deal?" He offered his hand.

"Deal." Elizabeth's hand slipped into his like a glove, but she didn't buy a single word of his compromise. She knew he'd never give up this easily. But then, neither would she. Smiling up at him, she suggested, "Now let's get back to work."

By the time the last dish was dried and put away, Nick had had plenty of time to think about the Bloods. He knew exactly what Chico's threat about being *really hungry* had implied, and that the warning had gone right over Elizabeth's head.

It never ceased to amaze him that some people could truly believe in humanity as a whole. To them, anything less was inconceivable. Dani had been like that. And so was Elizabeth. Unfortunately for Nick, this wasn't some imagined similarity. "You know," he began, "maybe I'll take you up on your offer to stay here."

Elizabeth checked her watch. Exactly two hours and twenty-three minutes. That's how long it had been since Nick's run-in with the gang. Actually, she was surprised it had taken him this long. "I don't need your protection."

No, what you need is a good, hard shaking and a whole different spin on reality. He gave her a patient grin. "Of course not."

"We may have a different philosophy on life, but I know a line of bull when I hear one." When Nick bent over to tie his shoelace, Elizabeth noticed a wide silver necklace around his neck. Even though she'd never touched it, she knew the feel of the chain, the imprint of each link as it slid through her fingertips. The vivid image disturbed her like the billowing of a curtain on a moonlit night, hinting at memories too dark to see.

"Let me get this straight." The edge to Nick's voice was unmistakable. "Chico and his playmates just came in here for a nice hot meal, but I'm the one feeding you a crock of—"

"I think," she interrupted, stopping momentarily to steady her voice, "that until they prove otherwise, I have no choice."

"Well, I do." He had intended to cut Elizabeth a little slack, but he'd be nuts to back off and wait for something else to happen. And it *would* happen.

"Like what?"

Nick huffed, "Like shut down the kitchen."

"You can't do that."

Nick sighed. "I can and I will." He started pulling the silver chain from beneath his T-shirt...

Elizabeth's blood ran cold. The necklace, in all its icy clarity, surfaced link by link in her mind's eye. Her lips mouthed the word *undercover.*

...and showed her his badge. "I'm a police officer."

"You lied to me," she shouted.

Nick shook his head. "You never asked."

"I never pried."

"Exactly my point. You're too damn trusting, Elizabeth. Too nice for this part of town. These people—"

Elizabeth's spine stiffened. "These people took care of me when no one else would." She pointed an accusing finger. "Certainly not *the system*. You call *these people* dangerous? Gun-waving, egocentric, hot dogs like you are far more dangerous to society than *these people* will ever be. They saved me, and now it's my turn to give something back to them."

Nick stood his ground. "But not your life."

She swallowed hard and squared her shoulders. "Don't be ridiculous."

"Think about it, Elizabeth." He leaned toward her, intent on making her understand. "You've already cheated death twice."

"And, I suppose you thought you could just flash that badge and I'd melt into a puddle at your feet." She shook her head, refusing to give in. "Forget it, Nick. The kitchen stays open."

"We'll see." He slammed both hands in his pockets to keep from throttling her. "For now, you'd better pray you're right."

The warning in his voice made Elizabeth uncomfortable, but she still didn't back down.

Nick headed for the door. "I'll see you in the morning." *I'll just stake out the place from that vacant building across the street.* His gut still tightened at the thought of leaving. "Lock up," he ordered in a last-ditch effort to protect her.

Elizabeth followed him into the dining room.

One moment they'd been standing there, the next an

explosion had them diving for cover. Nick pushed Elizabeth to the floor, using his body to shield her from flying glass.

"What the hell?" he growled.

Tires squealed down the street.

"Damn," he swore, jumping to his feet. With no positive ID on the car, he'd never be able to confirm what he knew had just gone down. Not that he needed to.

Nick had pushed the Bloods tonight and they'd been stupid enough to push back. *Huge mistake, boys.*

Helping Elizabeth to her feet, he brushed the glass from her hair, then wrapped his arms around her trembling shoulders. "Are you all right?" He felt her nod.

"Are you?" she whispered.

"Never better." He moved her aside and crunched through the broken glass, that covered the floor, to inspect the damage. Typical drive-by shooting. The Bloods had left their mark. "We might be in one piece, but this window sure as hell isn't."

Without a word, Elizabeth headed for the kitchen and the broom closet. It wasn't until she emerged from the kitchen that she noticed the blood trickling down Nick's cheek. "You're hurt." She dropped the dustpan and two brooms. "I'll be right back."

By the time she returned with the first aid kit, he'd made a quick call to the precinct. A squad car was on the way.

Nick bucked under her ministrations. "It's nothing."

"Shut up and sit still, or I'll suture your mouth shut." Elizabeth held Nick in the chair with her knee while she swabbed his cut with peroxide. "Good thing this cut wasn't any deeper or I would've had to call an anesthetist just to get it cleaned up."

She applied a dab of first aid cream. "And you know how nasty those guys get when they're on call."

Nick stared at her.

Elizabeth stood, confused. "I would guess," she added lamely, wondering why she'd made that type of comment in the first place. "All done."

She picked up the broom and, without another word, started to sweep the debris from the dining room floor, then stopped. For some reason, Nick's silence aroused old fears and uncertainties. As Elizabeth watched him pace, she continued to search for some plausible explanation for her comments about sutures and anesthetists. But there was none. So much for solutions, she thought wearily.

Nick unlocked the front door when he saw O'Malley pull up. "It's about time," he snorted. "Were you pedaling that thing, or what?"

O'Malley checked his watch. "Five minutes and thirty-seven seconds isn't exactly slow motion, Davis." Stepping over the broken glass the lieutenant shook his head. "I didn't think you'd been down here long enough to pi—" O'Malley stopped midsentence the moment he spotted Elizabeth. "Excuse me, ma'am." Not taking his eyes off her, he continued, "I meant, who did you tick off this time?"

Nick stepped between Elizabeth and the officer. "The Bloods. If you can stop hassling me long enough to stay with me a minute, I was trying to tell you I *ticked off* the Bloods."

O'Malley snorted.

Turning, Nick said, "Elizabeth, this is Lieutenant Kevin O'Malley. Lieutenant, this is Elizabeth Gleason."

The police officer stared. "Not the same lady from the accident last year?"

Nick nodded. "O'Malley arrived first on the scene after—" Nick violently rejected the year-old, crystal clear memory "—I hit you. He did an outstanding job that night."

"There are so many people I've never gotten to thank,"

she offered quietly. "I'm glad you're no longer one of them. Thank you, Lieutenant O'Malley."

"My pleasure, ma'am." The lieutenant took another long look and sighed. "It's a miracle, isn't it, Davis?"

"Yeah, it sure is," Nick agreed. "Now let's get the damned paperwork out of the way, so we can get this place cleaned up."

The lieutenant meticulously jotted down the details as Nick dictated them. Before leaving, he helped Nick sweep up all the glass and locate a large sheet of plywood left over from the renovation.

When they were alone again, Elizabeth, who had remained uncharacteristically quiet during the whole procedure, spoke. "Okay, Davis, if you want me to admit it, I will. You were right about the gang. There, I said it."

As Nick double-checked the nails on the makeshift cover over what was left of the window, he wondered why it had taken an act of terrorism to convince her. He took an extra pound at the last nail and locked the front door without so much as turning around.

"You heard me." Elizabeth's voice was no more than a whisper.

"Yes, I did," he admitted solemnly. When he finally faced her, Nick swore an oath that would've made O'Malley blush. Elizabeth had a death grip on the broom she'd picked up and her face had turned pale, almost ashen. *Dammit, Davis, she nearly got her head blown off tonight.*

Oh, yeah. Nick definitely planned to take care of this whole mess, but first, he crossed the room and pried the wooden handle out of her hand. "Come here," he whispered, taking her into his arms. "Trust me, Elizabeth, everything is going to be all right."

Chapter 5

Elizabeth leaned into Nick's strength. Even in the midst of bullets and shattered glass, his soft words and strong arms managed to calm her. One touch from him and her heart had stopped pounding. One word, and her breath had steadied to an even rhythm. Elizabeth clung to him, secure in knowing that this moment in time had been inevitable. Call it destiny or fate, but some unearthly power had bound her to Nick Davis—of that she was certain.

During her months on the street, when all else was lost, her only memory had been of the handsome stranger with the piercing blue eyes. Whoever Nick Davis had been, he belonged to her now.

Nick felt her tremble in his embrace, and his anger over her earlier stubbornness melted like ice cream on a hot August night. Pulling her closer, he murmured soothing words and promises he had every intention of keeping.

He couldn't explain how, he didn't have a clue why and he didn't care. But like the intricate pieces of some grand cosmic puzzle, their souls had traveled through time and space to come together.

He gently lifted her into his arms. "Where's your room?" he asked, inhaling the soft fragrance of her hair as she rested her cheek against his chest.

The heartbreaking questions that had plagued the last year of Elizabeth's life vanished, suddenly unimportant. Somewhere deep inside, she knew all the yearning and wondering would end tonight. That agonizing wait to cross some inevitable threshold would be satisfied, because Nick Davis was the elusive unknown she'd been searching for—the only answer she would ever need.

As Elizabeth's trembling stopped, she wrapped her arms around Nick's neck, and pointed to a stairway at the far end of the dining room. "First door to the right," she said sighing.

Grateful for the light from a small lamp on the nightstand, Nick kicked the bedroom door all the way open. He felt the mattress give beneath the weight of his knee as he carefully placed Elizabeth in the middle of the bed. Straightening, he offered her a halfhearted smile. "Rest."

Elizabeth shook her head. "Don't go."

"Close your eyes and try to relax. I'll be downstairs." Damn, she was too pale to suit him.

Never taking her eyes from his, Elizabeth reached out and took his hand. "Don't leave me."

"Give me five minutes to make you some tea." At her frown, he added, "I'll be right back. I promise."

Elizabeth nodded, biting her lip to keep from calling him back. As he turned and walked away, she couldn't help but wonder what price Nick would pay for confessing he was a cop. Common sense told her he'd committed a mortal departmental sin by blowing his cover—even to protect her. Realizing the dangerous position he'd put himself in, she only hoped that was all it would cost him.

In the kitchen, waiting for the water to boil, Nick braced both hands against the sink as he stared out the kitchen window into the darkness. He'd crossed a critical boundary he'd never before considered stepping over. Chalk it up to gut instinct, or something as simple as a judgment call, but he'd do it again in a heartbeat. He'd risk his badge—hell, his life—to protect Elizabeth. And maybe, just maybe, that's exactly what he'd done tonight.

Pouring the tea, Nick hurried back upstairs and found Elizabeth propped against the pillows. Still a little too pale to suit him, the smile she offered helped soothe his troubled mind.

"Drink some of this."

Accepting the warm mug, she took a sip and smiled. "Chamomile?"

Nick nodded as he sat on the edge of the bed. "Thought it might help you sleep." He smoothed her tousled hair and patiently waited until she'd finished every drop.

"This was awfully sweet of you." She set the empty cup on the nightstand and pressed his palm against her cheek.

Such a pretty face, he thought. So smooth and soft beneath his fingers. "I'm just sorry you had to go through this."

"I don't know what I would have done if it hadn't been for you." She brushed a kiss across his knuckles.

He hooked a stray curl behind her ear with his free hand, wondering if she could look any more beautiful than she did tonight. "You mean, aside from me throwing you down on the dining room floor?" he gently teased.

"Oh, I don't know." She arched one brow. "I kind of liked that part."

"Maybe without the bullets and flying glass." Nick laughed as he grabbed the quilt off the end of the bed and covered Elizabeth. "Try to get some rest."

Feeling safe and relaxed, she took his hand. "Lie down with me. At least until I fall asleep."

Without a second thought, Nick kicked off his boots and lowered himself beside her. He held her close and felt her settle comfortably against him. A feeling of *going home* washed over him like a warm ocean breeze. Deny it or not, holding Elizabeth felt right. And *right* was something Nick Davis hadn't felt in a long time. He closed his eyes and, just for the moment, refused to let time and reality stand in his way.

Elizabeth surrendered to his embrace. His strong arms wrapped around her, and the warmth of his body seeped into her very being. When his eyes finally closed, she traced the furrows between his brows and the lines that bracketed his mouth. When they disappeared beneath her featherlike touch, something familiar stirred deep inside her.

For the first time since she could remember, Elizabeth felt very much alive. She wasn't the least bit tired, and sleep was definitely the last thing on her mind. Shifting, she gathered her courage and pressed a tender kiss on Nick's lips.

Nick felt Elizabeth's soft mouth against his. When he opened his eyes and searched her face, the quiet certainty he saw dissolved his apprehension. Worry gave way to need, and concern surrendered to desire.

In the golden glow of the lamplight, he traced the hollows of her already flushed cheeks with his fingertip. When her eyes fluttered shut, something hauntingly familiar stirred deep inside, reminding Nick that Elizabeth now belonged to him. Maybe she always had.

He pulled her close and kissed her, gently at first, his lips covering hers in an almost reverent gesture as if sealing some holy vow. He felt her mouth soften against his, and that one symbol of sweet surrender told him everything he needed to know. *His world* had finally been made right again.

For the first time in what seemed like an eternity Nick had found peace. He filled his lungs with Elizabeth's fragrant scent. Comfort and warmth washed over him like a refreshing sea breeze. Like a starving man, his mouth devoured hers, savoring the very essence of what was now and would always be Elizabeth. He pulled away and looked at her—desperate to memorize every detail—only to discover the ugly black-and-white void he'd been living in had returned to one of vivid color and beauty. He felt complete.

Elizabeth sighed. Nick's gentleness had awakened a secret place in her heart. A place of long ago. He'd unearthed all her womanly feelings, the ones her mind had buried from the past, and coaxed them back to the present. To him.

Overwhelmed by emotion she tried to speak—to tell him—but, unable to put her feelings into words, she pressed her trembling fingertips to his lips.

The clear, unwavering look in Nick's eyes told Elizabeth he understood that tonight destiny had chosen their path. Two bodies. Two souls. Entwined for eternity…as it had been, so it would be. She smiled.

He reached for the neckline of her silk peasant top, then hesitated.

Elizabeth's eyes never left his face as she took his hand and pressed it to her breast.

His last shred of control snapped like a dry twig underfoot. Expertly flicking each button free, he exposed a silky ivory-colored chemise that made his mouth water. He met her gaze and the fire in her eyes was everything he'd hoped for and, yes, if he was honest, dreamed it would be. He watched her sit up and discard her blouse, then reach for him. Her fingers made a nimble path down the front of his shirt, quickly tossing it alongside hers on the floor.

Elizabeth's hands roamed over Nick's well-muscled chest and shoulders. In one smooth stroke, she ran her palms down the length of his arms, stopping only once along his rock hard biceps before clasping his hands in hers.

Fingers still linked, Nick pushed Elizabeth back down on the bed and pinned both arms above her head. A smile tugged the corners of his mouth.

Advantage, Davis.

But the proud tilt of her chin and the mischief in her eyes warned him the woman beneath him could give as well as she got. He'd seen that look before and liked it, but it was the other expression, the one now challenging him, that stirred his soul. He felt Elizabeth wiggle beneath him, then heard her shoes hit the floor. His grin faded.

Disadvantage, Davis.

Elizabeth watched Nick's playful expression dissolve into a subtle, smoldering gaze that grew in intensity with every breath he took. This time, his lips came down firm and passionate on hers. She tried to pull him close, but he deliberately held his weight above her, denying her body the pleasure of molding to his, only allowing their lips to touch.

But what a mouth. Elizabeth responded to Nick's soft, sensuous kisses as he coaxed and teased, nipped and licked. His attacks were swift—an assault on her senses. His retreats were skillful enough to make her beg for more.

Driven by desire, Elizabeth pulled up both knees, then wrapped her legs around Nick's waist.

Nick thought the feel of her warm ankles against his skin was his undoing until he noticed the silky skirt that had slid up her bare thighs and fanned around them on the bed. "My God, Elizabeth, are you trying to kill me?" he rasped.

"Not yet." Her voice was hoarse with need.

The promise of her words fueled the fire in Nick's blood. He cupped the fullness of her breasts. Mesmerized by their weight in his palms, Nick gently squeezed and kneaded them until the fascinating rhythm was almost more than he could bear. He stroked them, gently pulling each one, and heard himself moan with pleasure when each tip hardened like an exotic pebble between his thumb and finger.

Elizabeth writhed beneath him, sighing and gasping at his skillful touch. She clutched his sweat-slicked shoulders—desperate to pull him closer.

"Patience, sweet Dani," he whispered in a ragged breath.

Elizabeth looked into his flushed face and saw a desire that could only be matched by her own. "But I've already waited so long," she heard herself say.

"I know," he rasped.

And somehow she knew that he did.

Nick yanked her skirt down around her ankles and pulled the silky chemise over her head. He unhooked her bra and slung it toward the ever growing pile of clothing on the floor. Elizabeth worked feverishly at unsnapping and tugging down Nick's zipper, freeing him to shimmy out of his jeans and underwear. He then turned his attention to slipping Elizabeth out of the lacy triangle that stood between him and heaven on earth.

Nick spotted the scars from the accident and Elizabeth tried without success to cover one leg with the other. "Don't," he whispered. "You are so beautiful." His voice was husky and sincere.

When he bent to plant a row of kisses the length of each fading reminder, Elizabeth's heart nearly broke. A lifetime of need welled up inside her, refusing to remain a prisoner, demanding to be set free. She offered her leg freely, without reservation, then pulled herself up and arched against him, dropping her head back into his waiting hand. Her hands worked to guide him as she released every fantasy and desire that had been suppressed for so long. Unable to wait another minute, Elizabeth challenged Nick's every move, making him take her.

In a sensuous tangle of arms and legs, Nick gave Elizabeth everything she asked for and more. So much more. He massaged and stroked her body until it hummed from his touch. His lips teased and his tongue tantalized until she cried out. Every gasp was silenced with a kiss, each moan heightened by another thrust until they stood together on the brink of ecstasy. Then, like a tidal wave, they were engulfed by a crest of passion so strong it relentlessly pulled them under time and time again before releasing them spent and exhausted into one another's arms.

At long last—they were one.

Nick awoke before dawn with Elizabeth snuggled against him, her head resting peacefully on his shoulder. He could feel the steady beat of her heart against his ribs, hear the easy rhythm of her breathing. Careful not to disturb her, he eased out of bed and slipped into a nearby chair.

His intense feelings for this woman were not unlike the

gut instincts that had saved his butt time and time again on the job. They started deep down in a spot he knew too well.

Years on the force had taught him to trust that voice in his head. The one that whispered, *Pat down this mutt one more time, Davis,* only to find a well-concealed knife that would have probably been used to slit his throat.

He'd learned real fast to respect that hard-to-describe, sixth sense that kept him from getting his head blown off by screaming, *Turn right, not left,* when he'd searched a deserted warehouse, only to find exactly what he'd been looking for.

And since Nick trusted his instincts, he was positive he understood that he was making love with Elizabeth, not Dani, tonight. Even though their lovemaking had been as familiar as a melody they'd danced to a thousand times before.

Elbows planted on both knees, head braced between his hands, he couldn't for the life of him figure out why he'd called her Dani. Much less why she hadn't noticed. The reason for his slip of the tongue remained just out of reach, as elusive as the gossamer, silvery mist that mysteriously disappears just before daybreak.

And afterward, when he awoke full of hope for the future, it was as though Elizabeth had slept this way with him—her soft curls nestled against his neck, her slim arm resting familiarly across his chest—every night of his life. No, he wasn't confusing Elizabeth and Dani.

As daybreak filtered through the sheer eyelet curtains, Nick noticed the small, tattered teddy bear from her shopping cart now seated on Elizabeth's dresser. He slipped back into bed, knowing, without question, he would lay down his life to protect this woman.

* * *

Less than twenty-four hours after the shooting at the shelter had occurred, Nick headed to the precinct. The Bloods had been rounded up and hauled in for questioning. O'Malley and a couple of the others were handling the rest of the gang, but Nick insisted Chico be cut from the pack.

Nick elbowed his way through the crowded booking room. "Chico, my man." He snagged the gang leader by the arm and slapped him on the back hard enough to knock the chip off his shoulder. "After you," he insisted, pushing the punk across the hallway into an interrogation room, and slamming the door shut behind him.

"Sit down." Visions of Elizabeth lying on the floor surrounded by broken glass played in Nick's head as he shoved Chico down on one of the two folding metal chairs situated in the middle of the floor.

Nick liked the room's stark surroundings. Its obvious lack of barriers served a purpose. Institutional gray walls with no windows weren't designed to instill hope. And that's just the way he wanted it. Keeping a suspect off balance gave Nick leverage and, right now, that's exactly what he needed.

He stared Chico down. An hour could seem like a helluva long time in a place like this, if you were smart enough to shut up and let the guy sweat.

"You can't hold me here, cop man, and you know it," Chico snarled, breaking the silence.

Nick got in his face. "Let me tell you what I know." He enjoyed the flicker of fear reflected in Chico's eyes. "There's only one way out of here, pal, and that's through me." He stepped back and folded both arms across his chest, then smiled. "You ain't going nowhere."

"What did I do?"

Nick glared at him. "Does shooting out the soup kitchen's window last night ring a bell?"

"I don't know nothin' about that."

"Yeah, right." Nick sneered. "It was just a coincidence."

Chico shrugged. "I want to talk to my lawyer."

"Lawyer? So now you want to play by the rules? You still don't get it, do you?" Davis shouted. "We're not playing by the book any more, scumbag. The minute you shot that window out, we started playing by *my* rules." Like a streak of lightning, Nick kicked the chair out from under Chico.

Leather jacket bunched in both his fists, Nick yanked the gang leader to his feet. "Come on, Chico, I'm dying for a piece of you," he begged through gritted teeth. "Just give me a reason."

"What do you want, man?" Chico's words were cautious.

"From this moment on, if *anyone* as much as spits on the sidewalk within a ten-block radius of that kitchen, *you* will answer to me." Nick hauled Chico up a notch higher—until he was on his toes. "That better be the safest neighborhood in town, my man," he growled. He let go of Chico with such force the gang leader's body landed against the far wall. "Because if it's not, you're mine."

A noise. Elizabeth sat straight up and reached for Nick only to find the other side of the bed empty. She checked the clock on the dresser. Where on earth could he be at 5:00 a.m.? The run-in with the Bloods two nights before had made her cautious, so she crept downstairs.

A light. Elizabeth eased the kitchen door open a crack. The sight of Nick at the table and the aroma of freshly brewed coffee should have at least laid her fears to rest. But for some reason they didn't.

For the past two nights she and Nick had made love.

The most erotic, most intimate love she could ever imagine two people sharing. Nick's tenderness had caught her off guard, like some precious secret he'd saved just for her. His fiery passion had swept her off her feet, and kept her there—willingly, wantonly.

Was it always so easy and natural? Did everyone come together as they had, in such perfect unity? No awkwardness. No nervousness. Just an undeniable commitment of their bodies, their souls.

Elizabeth walked into the kitchen. "Have you been down here all night?" she asked, stopping to massage the tightness from his broad shoulders.

"Nope," he answered without glancing up. Nick hadn't slept a wink. Around 2:00 a.m. he'd phoned O'Malley to check in only to be summoned to the scene of a crime less than two blocks from where he'd left Elizabeth sleeping. Another street person—female, Caucasian, midforties, looked sixty. Not a pretty sight. But one, like so many others, that he would take to his grave.

This morning, Nick had to live with the fact that the sick son of a bitch who did it was still out there. And if that wasn't enough to push him over the edge, throw in the fact that the same bastard could stroll right through the front door this evening and have Elizabeth serve him dinner.

The bitterness in Nick's voice stopped Elizabeth and she took a good look at his face. Drawn lines bracketed his tense mouth. Rage veiled his bloodshot eyes. Something had turned him into a very angry man.

Elizabeth sat down beside him and asked quietly, "What's wrong?" When he didn't answer, she decided to make small talk until he was ready to open up. "If I hadn't seen the dining room window still boarded up, I'd swear I dreamed the whole ugly mess the other night."

"You realize the cops don't have enough manpower to guarantee it won't happen again." He noticed that she never flinched at the impact of his words. *Damn stubborn woman.*

"I understand." Elizabeth watched his jaw clench as she spoke. Whatever was wrong, he seemed to get more irritated by the minute.

He slammed down his empty coffee cup and stared at her. "I don't think you do."

The tension that hummed just below the surface of his flatly spoken statement warned her, once again, something was very wrong.

Without a word, Nick got up and refilled his mug. He contemplated gripping the hot coffee pot with his bare hands to keep from shaking the living daylights out of Elizabeth.

Instead, he sat back down and decided to make one last pitch. "The Stalker hit again." The moment the words were out, he could smell her fear. That was good, but would it be enough?

Elizabeth's blood ran cold. She'd followed the newspaper and television coverage of this grisly case for some time now. "Did you know the victim?" Maybe that would explain his anger.

Nick shook his head. "A bag lady, ID'd as Annie."

The name wasn't familiar to Elizabeth, but that didn't mean anything on the street. Most of the people she'd met simply went by the nicknames they'd pick up. "How bad was it?" The granite hard look in Nick's eyes answered her question before the word *murder* escaped his lips.

Elizabeth gripped her cup tighter. "It's getting worse, isn't it?"

"Oh, yeah." He took her hand for emphasis before continuing. "And more frequent."

She racked her brain for the details, but couldn't—or didn't want to—remember. "How many days since the last attack?"

"Ten."

"That must mean something, don't you think?" She searched his grim expression for hope, but found none.

"Whoever's doing this is getting braver."

"Oh, great." Elizabeth's heart thudded dully against her ribs. "Where did this happen?"

"A couple of streets over." He paused intentionally. "An alley behind one of those warehouses."

She stood and moved to the window above the sink. Her struggle to make a new life had been so difficult. A weaker person might have given up or at the very least given in. But not Elizabeth. She'd battled death and won, and despite all odds, she had overcome what others had called hopeless physical and emotional traumas.

Elizabeth watched dawn approach. As the first golden threads of daylight spread through the nighttime sky, she was reminded of the rays of hope that had begun to shine through the darkness that had once been her life. She braced both hands on the countertop and managed a smile. "So, what's your point, Davis?"

Nick studied the determined tilt of her chin and knew he was in for a fight. And, just like always, he jumped in with both feet anyway. "I think you know the answer to that."

Mindful of their new relationship, Elizabeth turned around slowly, tempering her response, and hoped he would follow suit and leave it at that. "I appreciate your concern, but I won't willingly close these doors."

He was standing now and faced her, toe-to-toe. God, for two cents he'd just slap a lock on the front door of this joint right now. "Then I'll have to do it officially."

"Yes, you will." Elizabeth stood her ground. Obviously the delicate state of their personal life ranked second, next to being right, on Nick's priority list. "Right now, the people in this neighborhood are scared and this kitchen is exactly what they need."

Damn, he had to wrap up this case in a hurry. O'Malley had been dogging him for a collar. The Bloods had already left their mark, and a cold-blooded murderer still walked the streets. And, if all that wasn't bad enough, smack dab in the middle of all of this, there stood Elizabeth. The hot-blooded, hardheaded, pain in the butt was so far under his skin, Nick had a rough time finding the exact spot where she stopped and he began. When he looked at her, he saw his future. "And, I need you." His words were sincere.

Totally defused by Nick's unexpected turnabout, Elizabeth just stood for a moment and looked at him. She knew they'd never agree on the kitchen, but Nick would never give up this easily. Not in her lifetime.

But, all the signs were there. The frown lines had softened around his mouth and between his brows. A hint of mischief glinted in his penetrating blue eyes. His lips curved just enough to make her wonder...or hope? Elizabeth planted both hands on her hips. "Davis, did anyone ever tell you that you fight dirty?"

He smiled before dragging her to him. "It's been said."

The strength of Nick's well-muscled arms and the wide expanse of his shoulders made Elizabeth feel safe and protected. "The answer is still no," she insisted in a voice that wasn't nearly as steady as she would've liked. She wrapped her arms around his neck and whispered in his ear, "But about what you said," she hesitated. "I feel the same way about you."

For Nick, hearing the words hadn't been necessary, but once Elizabeth spoke them something shifted deep inside him. Slowly at first, he felt his defenses lower—a sensation as welcome as summer sunshine, as exciting as a shooting star. And, he liked it. He grinned and tightened his hold on Elizabeth. "Until this situation is resolved, no more going out by yourself," he ordered in a low, yet firm tone.

Elizabeth sighed. "Look, Nick—"

"Day or night," he insisted.

"But—"

"No more staying in alone, either."

Nick's icy stare caused Elizabeth to swallow her sassy comeback. "You're not kidding, are you?"

"No, I'm not." He toyed with an auburn tendril of her hair as he spoke. "When I can't be here I want a volunteer with you."

"Don't worry," she assured him, as much as herself. "I'll be careful."

Nick released Elizabeth, placing both hands on her shoulders. "You have to be." He stepped back, needing but not wanting some distance. "I won't lose you, too."

Elizabeth started to ask him who else he'd lost, but before she could find the right words he had turned and walked away. The next sound she heard—Nick leaving for work on his motorcycle—triggered a vivid memory. Standing alone, her bare feet planted firmly on the cool linoleum, she suddenly remembered another kitchen.

Closing her eyes, she saw a warm, sunny room decorated with copper pots and woven baskets. The scent of potpourri was as fresh in her mind as if it were simmering on the stove beside her. A tall crystal vase overflowing with lilacs sat on a beautiful window seat. This was *her* home. Exhilarated, she tried desperately to hold on to the tenuous memory. But, as quickly as it had come, it was gone, leaving only a glimmer of hope behind.

Elizabeth hugged herself and sat down, at least grateful

for another glimpse of what had once been her life. There would be more, she assured herself. And when the picture was complete, she'd know exactly where Nick Davis fit in the puzzle, because he, too, was a part of this. Someday soon, she'd unlock the right door in the recesses of her mind and find him standing there in the shadows...waiting for her.

Chapter 6

It was barely daybreak, and Elizabeth had already had quite a morning. News of gruesome murder. Visions of another kitchen—one she truly believed had been hers. She shook her head and yawned. Craving a little of *the ordinary,* she promised herself one more cup of coffee, then she'd get going.

The back doorknob rattled.

Oh, God. I'm alone....

Her heart leapt to her throat.

And the murderer is still out there....

Holding her breath, she slipped out of her chair and silently eased the phone off the hook. As fast as her trembling finger could move, she punched 611—

611???

Elizabeth cursed silently as she fumbled to redial 911. Forcing herself to look down the hall, she spotted a familiar face looking through the back glass.

One step short of a coronary, she cradled the receiver.

Hurrying to open the door, she offered a shaky laugh. "Geez, Joe, you scared me half to death."

Joe shrugged.

"Hey, I thought you promised to spend at least one night here." At his blank stare, she asked, "Why didn't you show up?"

"Sorry, little darlin'. I've been busy."

Letting him pass, she locked the door before following him back to the kitchen. "What are you doing out at the crack of dawn?" She listened carefully to see if his bronchitis sounded better.

"Couldn't get back to sleep."

Satisfied his voice wasn't as raspy and his cough had eased up, Elizabeth made her way to the counter. She pointed to a chair and poured him a cup of coffee. "Then can I interest you in a little caffeine for your insomnia?"

He sat down and took a drink, then smiled. "My Peggy always made me coffee." His grin faded.

"I'm sure she did." Knowing how difficult it was for Joe to discuss his daughter, Elizabeth sat down beside him and gave his shoulder a comforting pat. "Have you been feeling better?"

"I'm fine," he assured her. "And before you ask, I've been taking my pills every day."

Elizabeth grinned. "You know me too well."

"Guess I do." He shrugged.

Trying to take his mind off his health, Elizabeth decided to play catch-up on the whereabouts of a few of their street acquaintances. "Hey Joe, did Buster really hop a freight for California?"

"Naw." Joe sipped his coffee. "Who told you that?"

"Jake was in here the other night and said Buster took off to visit his family out west."

"Is that so?"

The grin in Joe's eyes was unmistakable, but Elizabeth nodded anyway.

"Didn't anyone ever tell you that Jake is a pathological liar?"

Elizabeth nearly choked. "Obviously not."

"Last I heard, Buster's living behind an old warehouse four or five blocks from here." He wrinkled his nose. "Him and that damn little dog he taught to pee on command."

"Whizzer, isn't that his name?" Elizabeth laughed, knowing she'd been partly responsible for the pooch's antics. Fried chicken gizzards had been one heck of an incentive.

"Yep. A nasty little bastard, but smart as a whip."

"How about those three guys that used to come around asking for donations for the rich," she asked, remembering how comical the trio's routine had been.

"The stooges?" Joe chuckled.

"Yeah. Talk about bizarre characters. You see them around anymore?"

"No, but don't knock it. They're working the lower south side and doing pretty well from what I hear."

"Where has Thelma been? I haven't seen her lately."

Joe sat quietly and stared into his cup.

Reaching across the table, she placed her hand on his forearm. "Joe?"

"Huh?"

"I wondered if you'd seen Thelma?"

"Of course I have. I check on her every day." Joe shook his head and frowned. "But she's not a bit good."

Elizabeth leaned forward and suggested, "Maybe I should take her to the clinic."

"No." Joe pulled his arm away. "No doctors."

"But, Joe—"

"I'll look out for her, don't worry."

Elizabeth hesitated. She knew Joe wasn't comfortable with doctors. But she also knew how much he cared about the street people. "Okay, for now," she conceded reluctantly. "But let me know if she gets worse."

Joe drained his cup, then nodded.

She freshened his coffee. "How come you're out so early? You know, you shouldn't roam the neighborhood while it's still dark."

"That's who I am."

The sincerity in Joe's voice immediately caught Elizabeth's attention. He looked her straight in the eye.

"What do you mean it's who you are?"

"It's what I do," he announced with the utmost integrity.

The honesty in his expression and the simplicity of his statement silenced Elizabeth. Every once in a while, she'd catch a glimpse of the type of man Joe was. Strong. Intelligent. Loyal.

Sometimes, like today, her impression came from words spoken with such conviction that she wondered what on earth could have broken him. And, as always, like a thief in the night, the momentary image disappeared. Quickly. Quietly. Without a clue.

"I don't understand, sweetie. What is it that you do?"

"Make my morning rounds, of course."

"Morning rounds?" she repeated as much to herself as to him. He probably means check on everyone, she reasoned. So why was that image so unsettling to her? Something nagged at the back of her mind, itching and burning, desperate to come forward. Dammit, she hated when that happened.

She knew this niggling had something to do with her past, but it stayed just far enough out of reach to thumb its nose at her and taunt her. She let out a frustrated sigh. Or, maybe all making rounds meant to her was that she'd spent far too much time in the hospital. Satisfied for now, she shook off the specter and concentrated on Joe.

"They found another body this morning," she told him, sitting back down at the table.

"So that's what's got you all upset." He patted her hand sympathetically. "Don't worry."

"Joe, there's a murderer out there." She pointed to the back door and searched his weathered face for understanding. "Someone is killing people who live on the street."

He nodded. "I know. They're better off, though." His eyes brightened with reassurance. "They're at peace now."

Elizabeth's stomach lurched. When she'd first met Joe he might have been destitute, but he was always lucid. Lately she'd noticed him losing touch and that was breaking her heart.

"You'd better drink your coffee before it gets cold," Elizabeth said, trying to coax the blank expression from his eyes.

Like a child, he obediently took a sip.

She searched the cabinet for a skillet, hoping breakfast might help get him back on track. "How would you like some scrambled eggs and toast?"

"Sounds real good, Peggy."

Her heart thudded dully against her chest. He really *was* confused this morning. "Look at me, Joe." When he faced her, she continued, "I'm Elizabeth." She watched his muddled expression melt away like April snow.

"Of course you're Elizabeth. Who else would you be?" he retorted.

On the outside, she gave him her most tender smile, and prayed she was wrong....

She waved her wooden spoon regally. "I'd say the

Queen of England, but I don't own one of those ugly hats she wears.''

Joe laughed.

On the inside, she curled into a fetal position and wept, certain she was right.

Nick leaned against the doorjamb and grinned. Dr. Franklin's smooth style on the phone sounded suspiciously like his. And, no one appreciated a fancy verbal tap dance more than he.

Catching sight of him, she smiled, then waved him into her office. She rolled her eyes and made one final promise to "check on that" before cradling the receiver and tossing her pen down in protest.

"I got your message. What's up?" Nick relaxed against the smooth leather chair, knowing full well Mary Franklin wouldn't hesitate telling him exactly what was on her mind.

"I saw Elizabeth this afternoon," she began. "She said you asked her to shut down the kitchen."

"Guilty as charged."

"And, now that you've gotten to *know* her better, were you surprised she turned you down flat?"

Nick ignored her innuendo and shook his head. "Not at all. She's one stubborn *lady*."

"Tell it to me straight." Dr. Franklin leaned forward as she spoke. "How much danger is Elizabeth in?"

His jaw clenched. "Any is too much."

"For you, or for her?" she asked in a soft, coaxing voice.

"Cut to the chase, Doc," Nick insisted, knowing she was about to do just that anyway.

Dr. Franklin clasped her hands together and placed them

in the middle of her desk. "How involved are you and Elizabeth?"

Nick grinned. He'd worked with the good doctor too many times to try to play head games. The woman was a pro and he respected her for that. "Up to my eyeballs—and then some."

She sighed. "That's what I thought."

"Did Elizabeth say anything about me?"

"Not in so many words," she admitted. "But I know her pretty well and I've never seen her so...radiant." She pointed a well-manicured finger at him. "You know exactly what I'm talking about, Davis."

Nick merely shrugged. He'd done a lot of things in his life he wasn't particularly proud of, but betraying a lady's confidence had never been one of them.

Understanding his silence, Mary raised one delicately arched brow and inclined her head. "Touché, Detective."

"Anything else?"

She eased back in her chair. "How are you handling all of this?"

"If you mean the case, technically I'm still undercover, just waiting for a break." Nick shifted his weight. "If you're referring to Elizabeth, there hasn't been anything to handle."

Mary leaned back. "And that surprises you?"

He stood and walked to the window before asking, "Shouldn't it?"

"Not necessarily, Nick." When he remained silent, Mary continued. "Did you think it would be that difficult to begin a new relationship?"

Nick shrugged his shoulders. "I expected guilt," he admitted. "And lots of it."

"But there isn't any."

"No." He turned to face her. "Why not, Doc? I loved

Dani more than life itself. When she died, I thought I would, too.''

"The point is—you didn't.''

"But I wanted to.'' Nick raked a hand through his hair. "God, how I wanted to.''

"That's called grief.'' Out of habit, Mary had picked up her pen and jotted down a few notes. "And, if you've been able to work through it, that would explain why the transition was easier.''

Nick shook his head. "I don't think so, Doc.''

"Why not?''

He thought a moment. "I didn't work through anything. After Dani's death, I was a walking time bomb. If Elizabeth hadn't come along and given me something to focus on, I'd probably be dead by now.''

Mary laid down her pen and looked at him. "You never talked to anyone about your wife's death?''

"No.'' Nick challenged the surprise in her eyes. "What was there to say?'' The edge to his voice was unmistakable.

She waited a moment for his anger to subside. "You could have discussed your feelings. Maybe vented some of your resentment and worked through your denial.''

Nick snorted, but said nothing.

"Can you tell me a little about how your wife died?'' At his hesitation, she gently persuaded, "You'll never truly be able to move forward until you resolve this, Nick.''

He paced as he spoke. "A little more than two and a half years ago, we found out Dani was pregnant. We were so excited….'' His voice trailed off. "About a month later she lost the baby, but we were told she'd be able to have another child, so we tried to accept what had happened and plan for the future.''

Mary sat quietly and listened.

"We were invited to Dani's sister's in Springfield over the Fourth of July weekend, but I had to work. She had her heart set on seeing Amy, so she went alone." Nick pinched the bridge of his nose between his thumb and forefinger. "That Monday, on her way home, her car hit a gas truck…and burst into flames. They said she died instantly." He stopped in front of Dr. Franklin's desk and simply looked at her.

"Who do you blame for Dani's death?" Dr. Franklin asked.

He turned his back on her. "No one. It was an accident."

"How about her sister? After all, she invited Dani."

"Why in the hell would I blame Amy?" He slammed both fists into his pockets. "She was trying her best to help Dani through the miscarriage."

Mary switched tactics. "Was it Dani's fault for going?"

He spun around and faced her. "Dani had just lost our baby," he growled. "She needed some time."

"Who then?"

"Me…me," he raged. "I should have been there. I should have been driving that damned car." He pounded his chest with his fist. "I should have been there."

"And, since you weren't able to save Dani, you've made it your job to save Elizabeth."

Nick took a ragged breath. "Hell, no. You think I don't know the difference between Dani and Elizabeth?" He opened his mouth to speak again, then slightly cocked his head and paused. "You think I'm confusing them?"

"Are you?"

"I don't think so." He sank down in the chair opposite her desk. "They are similar, Doc. At first, I thought it was my imagination, and I was furious at myself for seeing any part of Dani in Elizabeth."

"And now?" Mary tapped her pen on the pad she'd been scribbling on.

"In my mind, the differences are clear, but the similarities are real, too. In fact, I even called her Dani once."

Mary's pen stopped. "How did she react?"

"She didn't."

"Not at all?"

"Nope." He could still feel the way Elizabeth's warm legs had wrapped around him after he'd intimately whispered, "Dani," in her ear. The erotic image alone posed a serious threat to any poker face he'd hoped to put on for the good doctor. "I assumed she didn't hear me."

"Does Elizabeth know about Dani?"

Nick shook his head. "We've never discussed my past."

"Don't you think it's about time you did?"

"It's been on my mind." Unable to sit another minute under Dr. Franklin's scrutiny, he stood again. "Aren't you glad you asked about all of this?"

"Actually, Detective, I'm extremely glad." She offered a reassuring smile. "One more thing."

"What's that?"

"Do you have a picture of Dani with you?"

Without saying a word, he pulled his wallet from his back pocket and flipped it open.

Mary studied the photo, then handed it back. "She certainly was lovely."

Nick nodded.

"By the way," she began. "How did you identify Dani at the time of the accident—dental records?"

"There really wasn't any need." Nick reached beneath his shirt and separated the two chains he wore, pulling out the gold one that held a ring. "They found Dani's wedding band in what was left of her car." He looked out the window. "It's pretty much all that was left."

Mary waited a beat. "And you're sure it's hers?"

Nick's gaze narrowed as he faced her. "It's engraved."

She nodded. "I'd like to think about what we discussed here today, and I'll be in touch."

"Sure, Doc." He stopped before reaching the doorway. "I'm not trying to pound a round peg into a square hole, am I?"

"No, Nick. You're not forcing it." Mary smiled. "I don't believe you're seeing something that isn't there."

The drive back from Dr. Franklin's office seemed endless. Until today, Nick had refused to discuss losing the baby or Dani's death with anyone. Instead, he'd hidden his pain like some unforgivable sin.

Hell, maybe Mary was right. This talking business had to be an improvement, because nothing else he'd tried had given him any peace of mind. He'd grieved for over two years, fighting every emotion that surfaced, pushing away every person who tried to reach out to him.

Cussing hadn't helped and drinking only made matters worse. Brawling had nearly cost him his job. And, in the end, he was still alone. But, now that he'd actually spoken the words, he felt as though a weight had been lifted off his shoulders.

Now there was just one more person he needed to talk to.

Nick swung by a florist, then headed out of town. Rather than pulling up too close, he parked at the bottom of the hill, but made no attempt to get out. Even after driving the long stretch of highway, he still needed a few minutes to compose his thoughts.

Autumn leaves swirled around his ankles as he walked through the lengthening afternoon shadows. Looking ahead, Nick caught a glimpse of a man who appeared to be standing in front of Dani's grave. The scattering of trees between them made it difficult to be certain, so he picked up his pace, hoping to get a better look.

As Nick closed the distance between them, the cop in him was already making mental notes. Over six feet tall. A smoker. Blond hair. Tan jacket. Blue jeans. Before Nick was close enough to get a positive ID, the man walked, with a slight limp, to a nearby car—late model, black over blue sedan—and pulled away.

Nick chalked up his scrutiny of the stranger as one of the hazards of the job. No matter where he was, or what he was doing, he'd never been able to turn off his cop mentality. God help him, not even in the sanctity of a cemetery.

As always, he made it a point to approach the back side of Dani's grave. He'd never been able to face the grim reality of her name carved into the cold, gray stone.

But today, after talking with Dr. Franklin, Nick had decided to confront Dani's death head-on. It was time to accept what had happened and to forgive himself. He had to let go. So, for the first time since the funeral, he stepped to the front of the grave.

Flowers. A fresh bouquet of pumpkin-colored mums rested peacefully against the stone. That man *had* been standing here. Nick ran a frantic mental search, trying to match relatives, friends, or co-workers to the man's description.

Nothing.

An image from Dani's funeral stirred at the outskirts of his mind's eye, but refused to come into focus. Could that be where he'd seen this guy before? Unsure, he backed off—for now.

"Looks like I'm still chasing shadows, doesn't it Dani? Always seeing bad guys, isn't that what you said?" His voice was no more than a whisper. "But, you were different. You never really believed they were out there, did you?"

Dammit, he might not have shared her view of the world, but they'd been connected, body and soul. He remembered being on a stakeout one night and he'd gotten such an odd feeling that he had dispatch call to see if she was all right. They radioed back, saying she was okay now, but she'd been stuck in an elevator at the hospital for several hours.

So, where in God's name had his internal radar been the day of her accident? Why hadn't he sensed it the precise instant she died in that crash? He remembered feeling anxious and edgy that Monday, but nothing clear-cut, nothing he could put his finger on. Hell, that didn't prove a thing because he'd felt that way every single day of his life since she died. How could he still experience such a solid, heartfelt bond…but never at her grave?

Nick cursed the single tear that trickled down his cheek. He snuffed out the smoldering cigarette butt—Marlboro, he noted—with the toe of his shoe. More ashes, he thought bitterly, remembering the smooth black urn he'd buried. Is that all that's ever left?

"If only I could have seen you one last time. Maybe then I could have said goodbye." Heartbreak slashed through Nick with the vicious speed of a switchblade. He took a ragged breath.

"Dani, I want to tell you that I've met someone. You'd really like her. She's stubborn and opinionated. And, talk about a woman with a glorified view of humanity…just like yours."

He wiped his cheek with the back of his hand, erasing the last visible trace of sorrow.

"You have to know that no one will ever take your place in my heart." He stopped to clear his throat.

Determined to make her understand, he continued, "But somewhere deep inside, I believe Elizabeth has a place in my life, too. And, I know you understand that I can feel this way about her and still love you."

Nick laid the red roses next to the other bouquet, hesitated for a moment, then turned and walked away.

Still unsettled by the scene at the cemetery, the last person in the world Nick needed to see when he opened the door to the shelter was—

"What the hell are you doing here?" His eyes narrowed in on Chico as he immediately closed the distance between them.

"Chill out, officer, your lady friend—" he inclined his head across the table "—and I were just—"

Nick lunged forward and raised Chico out of his seat by the front of his shirt. "What are you? Stupid?"

Elizabeth had never seen such unmistakable rage. "Nick, stop. He—"

With Chico still suspended from both his fists, Nick faced her for a split second. His eyes fired two warning shots as he spoke. "Get in the kitchen."

The unexplainable control in his voice made Elizabeth's flesh prickle. She stood, but refused to move. "He came to talk to you about the killer."

Electricity crackled between them.

Taking advantage of the momentary distraction, Chico jerked free and took a step back. "The lady's right, but, if you're not interested…" He made a move to leave.

Nick grabbed the collar of the boy's jacket and slammed him back down into the chair. "Don't play games with me, you little punk. If you've got information, spill your guts."

Chico rolled his shoulders and snorted. "Thought you might want to know we've seen some fresh guy hangin' around the neighborhood lately."

Nick stared Chico down.

"He was in the neighborhood the night of the murder."

"Can you ID him?"

"Nah, he keeps his distance."

"Short? White? In a wheelchair? Come on, man, you gotta have more than that."

"Hey, it was dark except for the streetlight. But he's a tall dude. Light hair, maybe red."

"Well that really narrows it down now, doesn't it?" Nick's voice was heavy with sarcasm. "Hell, that could be my lieutenant."

Chico shrugged, then stood. "Take it or leave it, Davis, it ain't nothin' to me." When Nick didn't make a move to stop him, he headed for the door. "Have a nice day, officer," he drawled before stepping out onto the street.

Nick leveled Elizabeth with one look. "Don't let him in here again."

Elizabeth slammed both hands on her hips. "What am I suppose to do, lock the front door?"

"If you have to."

"Look, I realize we don't exactly agree on most social issues, but this is my kitchen and I'll be damned if I turn my back on the very people I came here to help."

"Let it go, Elizabeth, Chico's a lost cause."

"He came here to try to help you." Elizabeth started to pace. "What in God's name did you do to elicit such civic-minded cooperation from him all of the sudden?"

"We just had a little talk."

She arched one brow. "And that's all it took?"

"Sure. Now that Chico understands me, he's so busy watching his back, he doesn't have time to make trouble."

Elizabeth wondered at his logic. "You're full of it, Davis."

"You think so?" When Elizabeth didn't immediately speak up, he continued. "Then why are he and his gang keeping their eyes peeled? Why was he in here this afternoon squealing like a pig?"

"Threats have been known to do that to people."

Nick shrugged. "I rest my case."

Elizabeth frowned at his nonchalance. "I guess bullying teenagers into being your snitches makes you a real genius, doesn't it?"

"Those *poor misguided boys* you're so concerned about have been in and out of juvy hall since they were big enough to slash their first tire. Call me deranged, but I think it's time they gave a little something back—whether they want to or not."

Elizabeth faltered. "You know I want you to do everything in your power to catch this killer. I just hope you have a handle on your methods, that's all."

"I know how to do my job." His tone softened slightly. "I may push the limits, Elizabeth, but I'm a damn good cop."

"Not to mention humble." She reached behind him and tugged his ponytail. He could look damn cute when he was irate.

He relaxed and grinned. "That, too."

"Truce?"

"Trust me?"

She rolled her eyes. "Didn't anyone ever tell you it was rude to answer a question with a question?"

"Is it?"

Elizabeth breezed past him. "I'll be in the kitchen." Nick's throaty laughter followed her every step of the way.

As Elizabeth stirred the simmering pots of stew, she

shifted her weight, hoping her good leg would lighten the strain—which, in turn, might lighten her mood. Her bad leg got immediate relief. Her bad mood, however, remained intact, leaving her with the same sick feeling she'd had since her earlier conversation with Joe.

She'd spent the better part of a week concerned about his health, especially since he'd agreed to sleep one night at the shelter and hadn't. But what she'd detected in him this morning really had her worried. The blank look in his eyes had reflected his short attention span and he'd confused her with his daughter, Peggy. Coincidences or symptoms? At this point she couldn't be sure. But, what really upset her was his bizarre attitude toward the murder victims.

Had he simply been trying to calm her fears? Or, had the harsh reality of life on the streets finally taken its toll? Did he really believe those people were better off dead? She planned to keep a closer eye on him from now on, regardless of how busy she got.

Forcing herself to shelve Joe's problems for the moment and focus on preparing dinner, she opened the oven door and checked on the loaves of bread she'd popped in earlier. Judging from the mouthwatering aroma that escaped, they were nearly done.

When Nick came in and saw Elizabeth busy at the stove, something restless that lived deep inside him settled. The empty feeling that usually lingered for days after visiting Dani's grave had already dwindled. The guilt from his inability to connect with her at the cemetery had faded sooner, too. He sighed. Maybe time really could heal all wounds.

His eyes were drawn to Elizabeth, watching as she stirred the huge pots on each burner. Was he losing his mind or, when Elizabeth was around, did he actually feel *more* connected to Dani? As nuts as that sounded, his life had finally started working again. And that felt right.

He just had one more hurdle to clear before he was home free. This afternoon he'd told Dani about Elizabeth. Tonight he would tell Elizabeth about Dani. But first...

As naturally as a cat stretching in a spot of early morning sunshine, he eased up behind Elizabeth and wrapped his arms around her. Palms flat against her middle, the sides of his hands supported the fullness of each breast. A wave of emotion pounded through him like surf against the sand, making subtle changes, washing his slate clean.

Elizabeth could feel the heat of Nick's strong, supple fingers through her thin, cotton blouse. When his thumbs began tracing breathtaking circles, then slid slowly over the tips of her breasts, she nearly dropped the wooden spoon that, by now, barely dangled from her fingertips. Grateful for the much needed comfort of his touch, she relaxed and leaned into him. Now *this* was something that could definitely lighten her mood.

His well-muscled thighs pressed against the backs of her legs and buttocks. Her head rested comfortably against the solid expanse of his chest. As she closed her eyes, a sigh escaped her lips.

He pulled her closer and ran the edges of his teeth along her earlobe. "Mmm, what smells so good in here?" Her hair curled softly against his cheek as he nuzzled her neck, inhaling the soft, sweet fragrance lingering there. "It's you," he whispered.

She swayed ever so slightly from side to side as she molded herself to him, fitting each feminine curve into every masculine hollow. "It might be the bread," she teased.

Nick's lips trailed a path of warm kisses down the side

of her neck, well past the collar of her blouse. He took a deep breath. "No," he groaned, "it's definitely you."

Elizabeth felt his hands ease over her breasts, then gently explore the outline of her bra through her blouse.

Her knees buckled slightly.

"Lace." The word was little more than a whisper. His fingertips slid along the seams in an incredibly erotic pattern.

Mesmerized, she raised her arms overhead and tried to clasp her hands behind Nick's neck.

Thump!

The large spoon Elizabeth forgot she'd been holding hit the linoleum. When Nick jumped at the sudden noise and released his hold on her, she nearly landed on the floor beside it.

For the first time since he'd entered the room, she turned to face him. And, as always, he took her breath away. Long, dark hair pulled back in a ponytail, exposing his gold stud earring. His square jaw somewhat flushed. Only the laughter in his heart-stopping, blue eyes betrayed him.

"Are you trying to kill me, woman?"

Totally embarrassed, she pointed to the floor. "With a wooden spoon?" Her cheeks felt as if they were on fire.

Without a word, Nick reached out and straightened the front of her blouse. As he fixed her collar, he could still feel the warmth of her skin through the material. And that made him smile.

She was beautiful. Full lips, parted slightly. Sooty lashes, lowered just enough to be provocative. He reached out and traced her cheek with his fingertip. "I meant," he began softly, "with your body."

His warm breath caressed her cheek as he spoke. Now she *was* on fire. Hell, she was going to burst into flames if he didn't douse her with cold water...or, better yet, take her right there on the kitchen floor.

"Need any help with the stew?"

Joe's voice preceding him through the door was the next best thing to ice water she could have imagined. Elizabeth cleared her throat so the words would actually come out. "Thanks, sweetie, I think it's ready to go."

Stepping aside, she let Joe take the first pot and tossed a couple of oven mitts at Nick. "Stick your busy little hands in these, Davis. Make yourself useful."

"Believe me, lady," he promised with a grin, "I intend to."

After everyone at the soup kitchen had been served, about midway through the meal, Nick positioned himself in the middle of the dining room, stepped up on an empty chair and whistled loudly enough to catch everyone's attention.

"Listen up people. I've got an announcement to make. The killer they're calling The Stalker hit again last night." The room buzzed. He looked past the threadbare clothing and tattered spirits to the faces stark with concern. Beneath the grime and soot, he saw their fear.

When the low whispers and murmurs died down, he continued. "This is serious business. Deadly serious. Since this is the only place we get together, I thought maybe we could talk about it tonight." A few barely discernable nods were all he needed to continue.

"The word on the street has it that this psycho is after street people." He patted his chest with both palms, including himself. Giving him the right to speak.

"So far, he's killed seven women." He waited for the impact of his words to take affect. "Every woman in here is in danger."

"Who wants to be his next victim?" Pointing a finger at a frail woman seated in front of him, Nick asked, "Do you?" Her eyes widened as she sucked in her breath.

He turned quickly in the opposite direction. "How about you?" The woman vehemently shook her head.

He searched one grim expression after another, determined to try that much harder to reach them. "Society doesn't give a damn about us, and the cops can't be everywhere. So we're gonna have to watch out for ourselves."

"Be afraid. That's okay. Maybe, just maybe it will save your life." He pointed his finger. "Don't go out alone—especially after dark. Stay together. If anything suspicious happens or anyone strange starts hanging around or asking questions, put the word out when you come in here to eat."

"Keep your eyes and ears open. Talk to one another. Men, watch out for the women. Ladies, help each other. Until The Stalker is caught, let's pool our information every night."

"Yeah," echoed softly through the group.

"Okay. See you tomorrow night. *All* of you, I hope."

He jumped off the stool. As he passed Elizabeth's astonished expression on the way to the kitchen, he whispered, "Close your mouth. I told you I was going to make myself useful."

Chapter 7

Nick had planned to catch Elizabeth after dinner and tell her about Dani, but she'd disappeared before he had a chance.

After locking the front door, he did a quick check of the downstairs. A glance down the hall told him the living room light was already off—he took a step—or was it?

He found Elizabeth snuggled in an overstuffed chair surrounded by shimmering candles and the soft sounds of Kenny G. Knees tucked beneath her chin, she looked so peaceful, disturbing her seemed almost criminal.

After all, he could tell her about Dani any time. Not that he was really looking forward to it, because he wasn't. He didn't know how she'd react, given his shaky history when it came to honesty in their relationship. The bottom line— undercover work is the art of deception and lies don't breed trust. He started to back out of the doorway, to leave her alone.

Elizabeth lowered her feet to the floor and craned her neck. "Nick?"

He stepped from the dark hallway and leaned against the door frame.

"Come in." Her voice was soft and inviting. "I never got a chance to tell you how touched I was by what you said during dinner tonight."

"*Everybody* deserves to know the truth, Elizabeth." *Including you.* That same surge of emotion he'd felt this afternoon in the kitchen rushed through him like a gust of wind through a tunnel. "We need to talk."

As he took the seat opposite hers, the candles flickered, casting shadows across the planes and angles of his handsome face, glinting off his earring. Elizabeth's heart beat just a little faster. "What about?"

"Me. The fact that you don't know anything about me."

Since their relationship had ignited practically overnight, she'd never stopped to consider that Nick might already be involved with someone. Her breathing became shallow as she scrutinized him. His voice had remained steady when he spoke and his gaze hadn't faltered. Good signs? She wasn't sure. If she'd ever been through anything like this before, she couldn't remember it. Maybe she should stop guessing and just let him say whatever was on his mind. "Like what?"

"The past," he hedged.

Relief washed over her. "I'd love to hear all about you." She settled back in her chair to listen.

"Well, not just me. There's another woman in my life you need to know about."

Elizabeth looked away. *Oh, God, I don't want to hear this.* Desperate to regain her composure, she forced herself to face him and ask, "Who is she?"

Nick hesitated. Even after talking with Dr. Franklin, this

was still difficult to discuss. But when he saw how patiently Elizabeth waited, her eyes darkened with concern, his indecision vanished. He knew exactly what he had to do. After all this woman had been through, the truth was the least of what he owed her.

He braced both elbows on his knees and steepled his hands together. "My wife. I was married three years ago." From the vulnerable expression on Elizabeth's face, Nick hoped he wasn't botching this whole explanation by starting at the beginning. All he wanted to do was tell her the entire story.

Elizabeth felt the blood drain from her cheeks as the *M* word ricocheted through her mind. *Married.* Her memory had been erased, which might account for her gross naiveté, but how in God's name could she have been *this* blind. Shouldn't she have at least sensed that there was someone else? Where in the hell was her woman's intuition?

"I see." The words barely escaped her lips.

"The following June she became pregnant—"

"You have a child?" Elizabeth heard her voice raise several octaves, but couldn't seem to control it.

Nick shook his head. "She had a miscarriage."

Elizabeth's heart pounded.

Anxious to say the final words as fast as he could, Nick continued, "Shortly after losing the baby, my wife died in an automobile accident."

A faraway conversation echoed like a whisper in Elizabeth's ear. She remembered overhearing the nurses at the hospital talking about Nick's devastation after his wife died, how he'd nearly gone over the edge.

One look at the heart-wrenching agony in his eyes dissolved Elizabeth's insecurities like a puff of smoke. She reached for his hand.

Nick squeezed hers. "I went to the cemetery this afternoon." He took a breath. "I wanted to tell Dani about you."

Elizabeth froze. "Dani?" She repeated the name, listening closely to the sound of it.

"Yeah. Her real name was Danielle, but I always called her Dani."

"Did you?" Elizabeth felt a jolt of electricity course through her veins at the mention of the other woman's name again. "I mean...did you tell her about me?"

Nick cleared his throat, wondering if she thought he was nuts for talking to someone who was dead. "Yeah, I told her."

Dani—she said the name to herself. What kind of woman could've had such a strong hold on a man like Nick Davis? A man who, from everything Elizabeth had seen, answered to no one. He made his own rules and didn't mind bending the hell out of the rest. Yet, more than two years after her death, he was still confiding in this Dani woman.

There went that pang again.

Elizabeth squirmed in her chair. "We both had a life before we met. I might not remember mine, but I still had one, and I'm sure it's not easy for you to talk about yours."

He shook his head, then pinned her with his stare. "You're a lot like her, you know."

She shivered at the comparison. Why did it make her feel so...strange? "I'll take that as a compliment."

But do I? she wondered. Or, does it just make me feel like a substitute? *Maybe he doesn't care for me at all. Maybe it's still Dani that he loves.* She willed the voice in her head to shut up.

"Nick, I'm really tired. Can we talk tomorrow?"

"Sure." He'd done enough interrogations to know the

moment someone's guard came up, you backed off. "You go on to bed. I'll be up in a minute."

Elizabeth took a deep breath. As much as she dreaded asking him to leave, she needed time to sort out her feelings. "Maybe you should go home tonight. I think I'd like to be alone."

"No," he argued. "It's not safe for you to stay here by yourself."

"I'll be fine." She'd already made up her mind. "Just lock up before you go."

Like hell! He held his tongue as she turned and walked away.

Elizabeth stopped at the doorway and looked back at him. Nick Davis... For so long the handsome face without a name who'd played hide-and-seek with her imagination. An elusive, mysterious man who had teased her psyche and captivated her heart—even before she'd met him. He *had* been the man in her dreams. *The only man.*

But, one question remained unanswered. Whose face did Nick see at night when he closed his eyes to sleep?

The phone was ringing off the hook. Elizabeth frantically groped through the darkness until her hand located the nightstand next to her bed. "Hello." Silence.

She opened her eyes and cursed the illuminated face of the alarm clock she held to her ear. Tossing it aside, she finally found the receiver. "Hello," she repeated.

"I've got it, Elizabeth."

"Nick?" She sat up. "Where are you?"

"Downstairs."

She raked her disheveled hair out of her eyes with her free hand in order to check the time. "It's 4:00 a.m. I thought I told you to go home."

"Hang up. We'll talk later."

His sharp tone made the hairs prickle on the back of her neck. "What's wrong?"

Dammit, why wouldn't she ever just do what she was told? "There's been another murder—"

Click.

"Davis?" O'Malley snorted. "What the hell's going on? Are you still there?"

"Yeah. Speak to me, boss."

Elizabeth hopped across her bedroom floor sock-footed, struggling to shove one leg in her jeans and yank a sweatshirt out of her closet at the same time. Shoes under one arm, she grabbed her purse and jacket and raced downstairs.

Nick was busy checking his gun when Elizabeth skipped the last three steps and landed at the far end of the dining room with a thud. His head snapped up. "What are you doing?"

She tossed both shoes on the floor and angled her feet into them. "Going with you."

He slapped the cylinder of his gun shut before meeting the impertinent tilt of her chin. "Like hell."

"No, Nick." She secured her purse strap over one shoulder and looked him right in the eye. "Like it or not."

"Forget it." He jammed the gun into his shoulder holster and slipped into his jacket. "It's against policy."

"Since when do *you* go by the rule book?" she challenged.

He refused to be baited. "For God's sake, it's the middle of the night. Go back to bed and get some rest."

"How can I sleep when people around me are dropping like flies, and you've set up police headquarters in my living room?" She glared at him, refusing to budge.

"You have no idea what you're in for."

"Well, don't stand there and act like I've never seen a dead body before—" She stopped midsentence and looked at Nick. He looked back at her.

"These people aren't prettied up like in a funeral home," he warned.

"Don't insult me," she argued. "For some reason, I really feel like I might be able to help."

"How? By getting in the way?" His voice was harsh, but he meant it. How in the hell was he supposed to keep her safe if she insisted on doing as she damn well pleased?

"I'm not sure." She folded her arms tightly across her chest.

"Did you know some of these crazies like to hang around the murder scene and see what goes on after the body's found?" His lips curled back into a snarl. "You can't imagine some of the things they do while they watch. Think about it, Elizabeth. Use your imagination."

Elizabeth fell silent.

"That's right. They get their kicks by watching the rest of us clean up the carnage. For some of these psychos it's a real bonus if the cops lose their lunch or turn away. In their sick, demented minds, pulling people's strings gives them power." Nick was on a roll. If this didn't glue her feet to the spot nothing would.

He stepped closer and forced her to meet his gaze. "Do you really want The Stalker to see you, Elizabeth? Can you go along, wondering if he's lurking just out of sight. Sneaking through the shadows. Looking at you. Or better yet, standing right next to you, camouflaged by a group of gawking bystanders. Close enough to hear you speak, smell your perfume or maybe even brush against you. Do you want this lunatic to be able to recognize you in the daylight?"

Elizabeth prayed Nick had only pulled out the stops to

try to scare her—because it had worked. Unable to say why and despite his warnings, she raised her chin and told him, "I'm either going with you, or I'll follow you there."

He growled as he grabbed her by the hand. "You're coming with me, all right. Maybe after an up-close-and-personal look at what this bastard does, you'll close this place down and come home with me where you belong."

Home with him where I belong? Elizabeth would've asked exactly what he meant by that, but she was too busy being dragged to the car. "Where are we going?"

"Not far. Less than three blocks."

She shuddered at the proximity of the murder. "Then why are we driving?"

He didn't bother to look at her. "The car will be a good place for you to sit after you puke your guts out."

Nick yanked his Kojak light from the back seat, shoved it out the window, and slammed it onto the roof of his car. *Damn her.* He glared at Elizabeth, seated primly on the passenger's side. Her pale face and haunting eyes infuriated him. If she wasn't a case of shock waiting to happen, he'd go to hell for lying.

The squeal of his tires as he peeled away from the curb helped relieve a little of the relentless tension he felt pounding at each temple.

He'd worked hard to insulate her from the horror of these murders. How could he have let her badger him into coming, much less chauffeuring her to the crime scene himself? He must have a screw loose.

Tonight he'd tried to shelter her from the ugly, inhumane side of his job. The side he'd never gotten used to and, hopefully, never would. Because this was the side that gave him the edge. And now that she'd pushed her way into the reality of this mess, protecting her was out of the question.

For Elizabeth, the ride was unnerving. If Nick was driving like a bat out of hell to scare her, he was doing a bang-up job. She just thanked God the streets were deserted.

Pools of light puddled beneath each street lamp, partially illuminating the darkened storefronts as Nick accelerated through each intersection. She watched sporadic gusts of wind carry discarded newspapers and debris down the sidewalk, past the boarded-up doorways. Even the sleazy bars had been closed long enough for the hookers to have called it a night.

Elizabeth knew she'd pushed Nick well beyond his limits when she insisted on coming with him. Not that she expected him to fully understand. How could he, when she wasn't even sure why this seemed so important to her? Who knows? After tonight, maybe they'd both be a step closer to figuring it out.

When Elizabeth saw the flashing blue and red lights of the squad cars, her palms grew damp and her mouth felt as if it were lined with cotton. She took a series of deep, controlled breaths, then let them out slowly, hoping they would calm her.

I can do this, she reminded herself.

Nick brought the car to a screeching halt, leaving her already queasy stomach a good block behind. The alley had been secured with yellow tape.

Elizabeth said a silent prayer.

Several people, with jackets marked Police in iridescent white letters across the back were already at work behind the roped-off area.

Spotting O'Malley, Nick practically jumped out of the car before jamming it into park. "Stay put." It was an order, not a request. He couldn't have gone more than five yards when...

The car door slammed shut behind him.

His step didn't falter at the sound, but he balled both hands into fists and kept on walking.

"What've we got, O'Malley?"

"The lab boys are checking it out right now. Dickey's in there taking pictures and the coroner should be here any minute."

"Same MO?"

"Looks like it. "

Nick felt Elizabeth's presence even before he saw the question reflected in his lieutenant's eyes.

"Evenin', ma'am."

She slipped her ice-cold hand into his much larger one. "Good evening." Sizing up the towering, red-haired lieutenant, she realized he was much larger than she remembered.

"Had any more trouble at the soup kitchen, lass?"

Elizabeth shook her head with conviction. "I'm sure that was the last of it." She pulled herself up a little taller and prayed she was right. "We just had a few kinks to work through, that's all."

"Ahhh," O'Malley crooned, grinning at Nick. "I see."

Nick swore under his breath. He could read this man's mind like a book. Trouble was, from the moment Elizabeth had stepped from the car, O'Malley had been doing the exact same thing to him.

A gangly, slender man with a camera ducked beneath the taped-off area and approached Nick. "She's all yours, Davis. And might I add, she's every bit as lovely as the last one."

He turned to Elizabeth, poking his thumb toward the alley. "You'd better fasten your seat belt, ma'am. Trust me—this ride's not for the faint of heart."

"Beat feet, Dickey," Nick ordered.

Elizabeth swallowed hard as she watched the photographer shrug and walk away. When Nick grabbed her by the arm and headed for the entrance to the alley, the knot in her stomach tightened.

"Stay right by me." The warning in his voice was undeniable because that was exactly what he meant.

They were only a few feet off the street when the unmistakable aura of death greeted them, daring them to venture further.

"Damn," Nick muttered, digging into his pocket. "Her bowels have emptied."

Elizabeth flinched when Nick shoved his glove into her hand. Grateful for any type of filter against the foul stench, she tried to thank him, but her gag reflex nixed that idea in a heartbeat. Hoping a nod would suffice for now, she covered her nose and mouth before taking the last few steps toward the body.

Blood. As they approached, the blood pooled around the body dizzied Elizabeth at first. She'd been so afraid of falling to pieces, but for some strange reason, her nerves steadied somewhat, and her nausea settled instead. An odd sense of calm washed over her.

Even though it was still fairly dark out, except for the partial light from a nearby street lamp, she determined the body was lying in a prone position. The head was lolled to one side exposing a small gash on the left side of the throat.

Fully expecting to scrape Elizabeth off the pavement at any time, Nick watched in amazement when she did more than just hold her own. She actually studied the body. No tears. No hysterics. No projectile vomiting.

Elizabeth stepped forward. The worn cotton material of the victim's dress looked vaguely familiar. She couldn't put her finger on why until she took a closer look and saw the dark green wool....

"Thelma," she whispered, stifling a moan with the back of her hand. "I gave her that sweater." Her voice trembled, but she managed to get the words out.

"You knew her?" Nick pulled a pen and a small notebook from his back pocket.

Elizabeth nodded. "As well as you know anyone who lives on the street."

He shoved his pen behind one ear. "No true ID though."

"No. Everyone just called her Thelma." Overwhelmed by regret, Elizabeth wondered if this woman would still be alive if she'd checked on her yesterday after Joe told her Thelma had been sick. She stepped closer, wishing she could turn back the hands of time...then stopped short. "Her leg?"

"Elizabeth, don't." Nick cupped her elbow in his hand, trying to lead her out of the alley. "You don't want to see that."

She pulled free of his grasp. "I knew the blood over here couldn't have come from that small incision at the carotid—even though that's what killed her." She looked up. "Where's the limb?"

Nick stared at her, certain she wanted the truth. "Under her head."

Unflinching, she faced him. "Were all the other bodies like this?"

"Every one."

"Then I guess you already know you're looking for—"

Incision? Carotid? Hell, if I didn't know better I'd swear Elizabeth sounds like—

"—a doctor," she told him, bending down to take a closer look.

Nick's heart rate accelerated. He remembered watching Dani work ER. She'd been fast and efficient, asking all the right questions, barking out all the right orders.

But, Elizabeth Gleason hadn't been a nurse. She'd been a housewife. He ought to know because he'd done the background check himself.

"Probably a surgeon," she added absently.

He shook his head, wondering how in the hell she'd know. "You don't have to be a doctor to cut off a leg," he answered.

"True. But not everybody can amputate one." She straightened.

This time, he didn't stop until he'd escorted her from the alley. "Look, bringing you along was bad enough. Don't start acting like Sherlock Holmes."

Elizabeth took a gulp of fresh air the moment they reached the street. She wasn't nearly as steady as she'd pretended, but she'd be damned if she'd let Nick know that. Especially not after he'd accused her of playing detective.

"I'm sorry you can't handle my opinion." Not that she had a clue exactly where her opinion had come from. "But, I'm more sorry you'd have preferred I keep my mouth shut and do something more womanly—like work myself up enough to faint."

"I never said—"

"You didn't have to. It's written all over your face. What you wanted, Detective Davis, was to act like the Neanderthal cop you are and carry me out of the alley sobbing hysterically."

Nick had to admit Elizabeth's guts had more than blown him away. He'd seen veteran officers toss their cookies over homicides a lot less graphic than this one. So, how in the hell had she managed to keep her cool, much less make medical deductions about the body?

"Don't give me that woman of the nineties stuff," he bristled. "I appreciate every bit of what it took for you to walk into that alley. What I don't understand is where your—" he hesitated, trying to describe her actions "—clinical detachment came from."

A chilling gust of wind echoed the uncertainty in Nick's voice, and the significance of his words severed Elizabeth's defenses like a knife. As unsure of her answer as he'd been of his question, Elizabeth's anger faded. Suddenly tired and confused, she pulled the flapping lapels of her unbuttoned jacket tighter and looked at him. "If it's any consolation," she began quietly, "I'm a lot more confused than you are."

Nick wondered if Elizabeth had any idea that her haunting eyes and trembling lower lip could have brought him to his knees—right there in front of God and half the police force.

"We can talk about this later." He kept his tone even as he wrapped his arm around her shoulder. "I won't be much longer. Why don't you wait in the car while I finish up."

Elizabeth only made it as far as the front bumper before her knees buckled, and she stopped to lean against the hood. Wherever it had come from, the glue that had held her together in the alley had disappeared. Thelma might not have been her friend, but she certainly wasn't a stranger, either. Suddenly, the cold, early morning air felt good against her skin.

O'Malley sauntered over to Nick. "Don't you think you were a little hard on the lass?"

Nick eyed his lieutenant. "She had no business being here."

"You've got that right," O'Malley agreed. "Does that mean I should be bustin' your chops for bringing her?"

Nick raked a hand through his hair. "It's a long story."

"And, I plan to hear every detail," O'Malley promised.

"But not tonight. Now finish up and take her home—where she belongs."

Elizabeth watched a short bald man with a black medical bag pull up and hurry toward the alley. From what she'd seen of the body, Ed had another long day ahead of him. But then, she knew he'd seen worse—like that plane crash a couple of years ago... *Ed? Why am I on a first-name basis with the coroner? And, what plane crash?*

Elizabeth's head spun with unanswered questions.

"Think this might put a little starch back in your legs?" O'Malley handed her a white plastic cup filled with steaming coffee.

She jumped at the sound of his voice, then regained her composure and offered him a shaky smile. "Thanks, Lieutenant."

He reached into his jacket pocket. "Twinkie?"

Elizabeth touched her belly, praying the coffee would stay down. "I'm not quite ready for that."

O'Malley unwrapped the cake and polished it off in two bites. "If it's any consolation," he began, "you did okay in there."

"I guess so." She eyed him over the rim of her cup. "I just can't imagine how."

He parked his hip against the hood. "The way I figure it, a person's either got it or they don't. Doesn't matter much why."

"I suppose you're right." She faced the burly red-haired man and pointed toward the coroner. "I'm sure glad I don't have Ed's job."

"Amen to that."

She inclined her head toward Nick. "I would imagine Davis leads you a merry chase."

"That he does." The pride in O'Malley's voice was

obvious. "But he's one damned fine cop." He cleared his throat. "Just don't tell him I said so."

"Your secret's safe with me."

Nick waited until they'd loaded the body bag into the back of the coroner's van, then made his way to Elizabeth's side. "You two want to break it up? In case you haven't noticed, the party's over."

O'Malley ignored the snide comment for the moment and turned his attention toward Elizabeth. "I wish the circumstances had been different, ma'am."

His genuine smile was comforting. "So do I, Lieutenant."

"And, as for you." He faced Nick. "Do your explaining in triplicate."

"Yes, sir." Nick mocked a salute as O'Malley walked off.

"On my desk by five o'clock sharp this afternoon," the lieutenant ordered without missing a step.

"Charming, isn't he?" Nick asked as he helped Elizabeth into the car.

She waited for him to slide behind the wheel. "Actually, he was very sweet."

"So is motor oil, but I wouldn't want to put it in my coffee," Nick mumbled as he drove away.

Unwilling to talk and unable to relax, Elizabeth stared out the window at the first signs of daybreak. This, she thought dismally, would not be a beautiful, pastel dawn filled with sunshine and promise. The violence of the night had already stripped away its innocence.

Like the stark, overcast sky, Elizabeth, too, felt she'd been robbed. She mourned the sense of hope that was missing from this bleak morning after. That...and a woman named Thelma.

Nick respected Elizabeth's space on the drive home.

She'd been through a lot tonight, and he figured if she was half as confused as he was, her head must be spinning. The moment he pulled up in front of the soup kitchen and parked the car, he knew he had to talk her out of staying there. Unfortunately, he was also certain that particular discussion would have to wait.

Once they were through the front door, he ordered, "You sit, and I'll make some coffee." He helped her out of her jacket and tossed it around the back of her chair.

Too tired to argue, Elizabeth did as he asked. In a matter of minutes, he sat down opposite her with two steaming mugs in hand.

Nick watched her painstakingly stir the black coffee. With every clink of her spoon, he inched that much closer to snapping. Finally, he grabbed her wrist. "I never got to tell you—back there—that I'm sorry about Thelma."

"So am I." Elizabeth glanced down at her arm, then met his gaze. She felt his hold loosen.

"You know," he began, needing to verbalize the haunting sensation of déjà vu he couldn't shake, "the way you handled seeing that body back there reminded me a lot of Dani."

Elizabeth shuddered again at his mention of the name. "How could it?"

"Dani was a doctor. She had a reputation for being cool and calm in ER—almost detached." He paused before adding, "You were like that today."

Dani this and Dani that. Is Dani all he thinks about? "No big mystery," she lied. "Maybe I'm just one of those people who don't get squeamish."

"Maybe," he speculated. "But that kind of clinical attitude usually comes through training."

"What do you want from me, Nick?" Her words were clipped. She was drop-dead tired and confused out to the max. "I went. I saw. I didn't faint. So just drop it, will you?"

"I wasn't trying to make a big deal out of it. I just thought this aspect of your personality might be a clue to your past."

Elizabeth felt as though her head would split. "*My* past?" she repeated. "Is it really *my* past that concerns you?"

"Of course it is."

She stood and glared at him. "I don't think it's *me* you're interested in at all."

Nick was on his feet now. "What in the hell are you talking about? Who else would I be interested in?"

"Dani." Her voice was low and even.

"That's ridiculous," Nick shouted.

She shook her head. "I don't think it is."

"Elizabeth—"

"Please go. I'd like to be alone."

"Dammit, listen to me." He took a step toward her.

She held up her hand, warning him to stop. "This time, I want you to leave, not just stay downstairs like last night." Without another word, she turned and walked away.

"You're wrong, Elizabeth," he yelled to her retreating form. "I hope," he whispered to the empty kitchen. Turning around, he kicked the closest chair clear across the floor and stormed out.

Elizabeth hurried to her room. "Damn him," she muttered, slamming the door every bit as loudly as the commotion Nick had made downstairs after she'd left. Seeking comfort, she was disappointed that her room lacked its usual warmth. Through her eyes, it looked as bleak as the weather. Too tired to sleep. Too upset to stand still. Elizabeth paced.

After all she'd been through, she had just managed to get her life in some kind of order—and for what? So some gun-toting, egocentric, hot dog of a cop could come along and—

She glanced at the bed.

—kiss her so passionately, so thoroughly, so pleasurably that every bone in her body turned into a lush, warm, liquid.

Stay with me on this one, the little voice inside her warned. *You're angry, remember?*

Elizabeth shook her head to clear it. "Of course, I'm mad," she affirmed out loud. Who wouldn't be? That man had swaggered into her life, threatened to close down her kitchen and ended up—

The bed stared back at her.

"—making love to me," Elizabeth whispered.

The kind of lovemaking that was so intense it's impossible to tell where one lover stops and the other begins. And, I thought it was a once in a lifetime love, Elizabeth admitted silently as hot tears scalded her cheeks. She gave in to exhaustion and turned to the only comfort she could find...a memory.

She lay down on the bed and whispered, "Nick Davis is devoted to one woman, all right—his wife. His dead wife."

Chapter 8

Sleep or no sleep, after storming out of the soup kitchen, Nick spent the remainder of the day at the precinct, trying to play catch-up. Knowing O'Malley hadn't been kidding about submitting his paperwork in triplicate before he left, Nick worked until 8:00 p.m.

Unwilling to face Elizabeth yet, he decided to spend the night at home. He left his name as first on call and ordered back-to-back stakeouts to watch the soup kitchen until morning. He tossed and turned, sleeping fitfully on and off. By dawn, he decided to get up and finish agonizing over a cup of coffee. Damn, he was still trying to get a handle on what had been nagging him ever since he'd thought of Dani working ER. If only he could remember.

"There's something significant I'm forgetting," he muttered, absently filling his mug. "But what? It's more than just her style." He racked his brain, but the elusive memory stayed just out of reach.

He became more frustrated as his thoughts returned to

Elizabeth's accusation that his interest was in Dani, not her. He still believed she was wrong. It may have taken him a long time, but he'd finally accepted his wife's death.

I don't want Elizabeth to be Dani, he mused. *But, God help me, she does remind me of her.*

Nick looked down at his mug and remembered how Elizabeth stirred her black coffee just like Dani had. Some of her mannerisms and patterns of speech—he grinned— especially when she was mad. The eerie similarity of how she approached the body in the alley.

He thought back to the night they'd made love. Two bodies perfectly in sync, moving as one. So totally in tune that, when he'd whispered "Dani," Elizabeth's legs had responded, without question, wrapping around him, pulling him closer—just like Dani used to do.

Nick slammed his fist down hard on the table, spilling hot coffee all over his hand. Oblivious to the pain, he knew if he didn't get some answers—and soon—he would probably *lose it* big time. He grabbed his jacket and snagged his car keys on the way out the door. He had to know once and for all. Was he in love with two women...or one?

Nick shifted restlessly in the chair opposite Mary Franklin's large, highly polished desk. "So that's the long and the short of last night, Doc. She thinks I'm still hung up on Dani."

"Are you?"

"No." His answer was emphatic.

Mary looked at him, but said nothing.

"Well, no," he corrected, "I wouldn't say hung up."

"What would you call it?" she coaxed.

"If anything, I may be confused, but not for the reasons you might suspect." He stood and straightened his shoulders to work out the kinks. "I really believe I have Dani in perspective."

"That's in your head." She tapped her temple with one finger. "How about in your heart?"

He faced his friend. "A part of me will always love Dani, and I don't think that's wrong. After all, she was my wife."

"You're absolutely right, Nick. That kind of love never dies." Mary offered a smile. "So, if it's not that, then what has you confused?"

"Boy, how do I put this?" Frustrated, he walked to the window and searched the clear autumn sky. "At the risk of sounding totally nuts, I'm beginning to wonder if the woman we call Elizabeth really is Elizabeth Gleason."

Mary edged forward in her seat, but said nothing.

He turned around and met her intense gaze, "Can amnesia cause a person's personality to change, Doc?"

"Not drastically, if that's what you're asking."

Nick shook his head in frustration. "I had to stop by the station before I came here, so I pulled Elizabeth's file. Prior to today, I hadn't read it since I compiled the information a year ago." He looked absently out the window again before asking, "Did you know she'd been arrested for shoplifting?"

"Not that I recall." Mary folded her hands. "But, I'm like you, it's been about that long since I reviewed the details of her case."

"That's the kind of change I'm asking about. Can a person have one personality type before amnesia and recover with a different one?"

Mary shook her head. "No. They're still the same person they always were, amnesia just temporarily steals their memory."

"Is the Elizabeth you've come to know this past year a thief?"

"Honestly?" She thought a moment. "No."

"The Elizabeth Gleason listed in the police records mysteriously disappeared after her husband was killed in a fire at their home." Nick shoved both hands in his pockets as he thought. "That could be what snapped her, but I checked with the fire department's arson investigator and found out that fire was no accident."

"You think she could have set it?"

"Not the Elizabeth I know. But, do you see what I'm driving at?" Nick hitched one hip on the sill as he spoke. "It's like I said, there are just too many inconsistencies, Doc." He shook his head. "If Elizabeth has a personality more—say, more like Dani's than the woman described in our reports, then maybe she's not Elizabeth Gleason, after all."

"Have you mentioned this to her?" She scribbled notes without looking up.

"No, and I don't plan to," he assured her. "Not unless something concrete turns up."

She laid her pen down and nodded. "Good."

"Don't worry." He appreciated the concern in her eyes. "I plan to take this one step at a time."

"I know you will."

"Thanks for seeing me on such short notice. I just wanted you to know what's going on with Elizabeth."

She patted his hand. "And you."

"And me." He grinned. "We can't have some whacked-out cop chasing ghosts down the streets of Chicago, now can we?"

"Oh, I don't know. I'm sure it wouldn't be the first time." Mary returned his smile.

"Thanks again, Doc." He started out the door.

"Nick."

He turned.

"Let me know what you come up with."

"Believe me, if any of my suspicions are halfway confirmed, your number will be the first one I dial."

Clunk!

Elizabeth pumped the gas pedal for dear life. "Please don't quit on me now."

Thump!

"Come on, Bessie." She smacked the steering wheel. "Don't you dare leave me stranded in this part of town after dark."

Silence.

"Damn." She checked the gas gauges, then eased her car to the curb—which, from the look of things, was just about as far as she was going to get.

"More to the point, damn Nick Davis. I asked him to fill the tank," Elizabeth muttered. She winced at the sound of his name. Had it only been yesterday that she'd ordered him to leave? Elizabeth pushed back the guilt. After all, he had some serious soul-searching to do. She had realized that a couple of days ago and, by now, so should he. In the meantime, she had a more immediate problem—like figuring out a way to get back to the soup kitchen.

Giving the neighborhood a quick glance, she cringed. No phone booth. No gas station. No help.

"He's always so gung ho, trying to protect me at the kitchen," she griped. "All I needed was a little gas."

Now what? After a moment's consideration, she decided there were two choices. Lock the doors and wait for help. Or walk.

With a sigh of resignation, Elizabeth grabbed her purse and the bag of groceries sitting beside her on the front seat and stepped from the car. Momentarily balancing the sack on the hood, she locked the door, then turned up her collar against the frosty breeze at her back before starting for home on foot.

Summer boredom had apparently taken its toll on the streetlights. Neighborhood kids had shot out or broken most of the bulbs, leaving the sidewalks dark, almost sinister. So Elizabeth hurried along as quickly as she could without drawing attention to herself. She hadn't been walking long—when the sensation of being watched skittered down her spine.

She stopped. Turning around, she scanned the dimly lit street behind her. It *appeared* to be empty. But there were so many abandoned buildings and darkened doorways it was impossible to tell. Someone could be staying back just far enough in the shadows to avoid being seen. Instead of calming her fears, the seemingly vacant street somehow escalated her uneasiness.

Elizabeth forced herself to settle down. She hadn't seen anyone watching her because no one was. It was as simple as that. Walking home through this neighborhood at night had simply spooked her and the rest of her uneasiness was a product of her overactive imagination...or maybe not.

A stranger was coming toward her on the sidewalk. Her already cold hands clutched the bag tighter as though it were a lifeline. She held her breath until the person got close enough to be identified as a woman. Then and only then did Elizabeth allow herself to exhale. Her chauvinistic knee-jerk reaction shamed her—until she remembered that nearly every serial killer to date had been a man.

The woman passed without a word. But the niggling in the back of Elizabeth's mind didn't. She stopped and quickly turned again. Did she just see someone step into the shadows? Or had the motion of her own head played tricks on her?

Nearby a dog barked—Elizabeth jumped—sending several yowling cats racing across her path.

Elizabeth gasped.

She regained her balance, then hitched the grocery bag higher on one hip and shook her head. All she wanted was to get home. Shuddering, she picked up her pace. How could she have ever lived on these streets? Or more to the point, how could she have lived on these streets and not been afraid.

"Got any change?" a rough voice asked, as a man stepped from a darkened doorway, blocking her way.

Elizabeth felt as though she'd just stepped into an empty elevator shaft. Since the light from the street lamp was at his back, she couldn't see his face. She made a split second decision and, without hesitation, chose to ignore his question and move on. Sidestepping him, she prayed he wouldn't try to stop her.

He didn't. Instead, she heard him walk the other way.

As Elizabeth hurried on, she realized that this was the first time she could ever remember turning her back on a fellow human being. Trying to justify her actions, she rationalized that when a serial killer invaded your neighborhood, people were forced to live in fear. And, a very real part of that fear included following your instincts of self-preservation. It was as simple as that. Damn The Stalker, whoever he is, she thought. He's not only robbed us of our freedom, he's stripped away our humanity.

Only two blocks to go, Elizabeth sighed to herself. That's when she heard it. Footsteps. This time when she turned she did catch a glimpse of someone. She was certain because...

Her mind tried desperately to reproduce the image she'd

caught out of the corner of her eye. Like a camera lens clicking into focus, she visualized someone—a man—taking a draw off a cigarette.

He didn't step out immediately. But he was there. In fact, he let her get a good way up the street before he began following her again. The faint click of his heels on the sidewalk behind her caused the hair on her neck to prickle.

Elizabeth was practically running now. Where on earth was everybody? Any other time there were at least a few people around. The sound of his footsteps echoed in her ears. He hadn't closed the distance between them, but stayed just far enough back to let her know he was still there.

She wanted to look. To see exactly how close he was.

Maybe, if he was far enough back, she could outrun him. Maybe what she heard was just the pounding of her heart, not his shoes hitting the pavement. Maybe there was no one there at all.

She turned her head to glance back and thought she saw someone quickly step into the shadows. Stopping to listen, the sound of someone following her *had* stopped—but then so had she. Maybe the echo of her shoes was all she'd heard.

The moment Elizabeth started to walk, she felt someone's presence behind her again. She strained her ears.

One block, that's as far as she had to go. Surely to God she could make it one block. She picked up her pace, fighting the desire to run. Running would make it real. Running would let him know how scared she was. Running...oh, the hell with it! She made a mad dash.

The hand that snagged her arm nearly pulled her off her feet. Her bag flew to the ground and an iron grip steadied her.

"Chico." She was almost too breathless to say his name.

"Hey, kitten, are you all right?" Still holding her arm, Chico inclined his head and two of his *friends* headed down the alley about a half a block behind them.

"Yeah," Elizabeth managed to gasp, trying to catch her breath. Not knowing whether to laugh or cry, she added, "I can't believe it was you."

"What was me?" He gathered the odds and ends that had spilled from her bag onto the sidewalk.

"I—" she began, then stopped. Exactly what had happened? "I thought I heard someone behind me." Elizabeth watched Chico's reaction. He certainly didn't shrug off her concern, but listened intently as she spoke. Maybe she hadn't imagined any of it.

"Anything's possible in this neighborhood." He picked up her sack and refilled it. "Let me walk you the rest of the way."

"Thanks." Her smile was genuine. "That's very nice of you."

He fell in step and returned her grin. "Nice, hell. It's self-defense." At her confused expression, he explained, "Your friend, the good detective, has already warned me about what to expect if anything ever happens to you."

This kid was tough on the outside, but she figured he'd needed to develop that persona to survive on this side of town. So Elizabeth allowed him to save face by implying he'd had no choice but to help her. Not that she doubted Nick's threat. Because she didn't. What she did question was Chico's image. She still believed underneath all that hard-guy facade was someone she could reach.

"Hey, if Davis gives you a hard time, send him to me. If he would've put gas in my car like I asked him to, I wouldn't be walking these streets after dark," she told him, shifting the blame where it belonged.

Chico's laugh rippled through the cold, night air. "I'll bet *you* could hurt him a lot more than I could."

A ghost of a smile was her only answer. She looked up and saw the soup kitchen. They'd finally made it home. "Thanks for walking with me, Chico." When he self-consciously looked down at his feet instead of at her, Elizabeth knew her instincts had been right. Regardless of the front he put up, this kid was not a lost cause.

"No problem."

"How about a cup of coffee?" she offered.

"Can't. I gotta go."

"Okay," she called over one shoulder while unlocking the door. He handed her the sack and she smiled as she watched him leave. "Thanks again." For showing me humanity is alive and well and living in Chicago, she finished silently.

Both legs propped up on his open desk drawer, Nick barely made the stretch to silence the ringing phone. "Davis," he barked, weary from the hours of work he'd been pouring into the latest serial killings.

"And a good evening to you, too, cop man."

"Talk to me Chico. You didn't call me to make nice." He leaned back in his chair. "Cut to the chase."

"Okay. A piece of advice. The next time your lady friend tells you to gas up her car, do it."

Nick's feet hit the floor simultaneously. "What?" His voice could be heard all over the squad room. "I did put gas in her car." He hadn't been back to the soup kitchen in two days, but she couldn't have used the entire tank.

"That's funny. I spotted her walking home after her car quit—"

"What the hell happened to her car?"

"Forget the car. That's not the worst part, badge man."

"Don't jack me around, Chico." The warning in Nick's low, controlled voice was clear.

"She wasn't alone."

"What's that supposed to mean?" Nick was pacing now. "Who was with her?"

"No, not with her, man. Behind her."

The words stopped Nick dead in his tracks. Visions of Elizabeth walking down a dark street flashed through Nick's mind. A stranger stalking her. Moving in and out of the shadows. Watching her every move. An alley. Thelma's dead body. "Someone was following her?"

"Damn, you catch on quick for a cop."

"Cut the bull, Chico," Nick ordered. "Can you ID the guy?"

"Nah. I sent two of my boys after him, but they lost him in an abandoned building."

"Son of a—"

"But don't worry about your pretty lady, Sarge, I walked her the rest of the way home."

Nick fought the desire to track down Chico and lock him up for being anywhere near Elizabeth—until his better judgment caught up with his ego. He uncurled his fist. "Chico?"

"Yeah."

Frustrated, he raked a hand through his hair. "I owe you big."

"You're welcome."

Elizabeth leaned back on the pillows she'd propped against the headboard. Weary, she willed herself to relax even though she knew sleep would be impossible tonight. Her hand absently smoothed the cool, unruffled sheets on the opposite side of the bed. It had been two days since she'd told Nick to leave. God, she missed him. Even surrounded by soft, soothing candlelight in the comfort of her own room, she was edgy—

When the phone rang, Elizabeth's already frazzled nerves nearly snapped. She lunged for the receiver, almost tipping over the cup of tea she had set on the nightstand.

"Hello." She bit her lip, refusing to hope....

"Ms. Gleason?"

Trying to filter the disappointment from her voice, she answered, "Yes."

"This is Officer Evans. Sorry to bother you this evening, but is Sergeant Davis there?"

"No, he's not."

"Will he be stopping by later this evening?"

"No, he won't." Elizabeth closed her eyes and repeated the words as much for herself as for the officer on the phone. "I'm not expecting Sergeant Davis at all tonight."

"Thanks, Ms. Gleason. That's all I needed to know."

"No problem," she assured him.

Elizabeth replaced the receiver. Willing Nick Davis out of her thoughts, she sipped her tea, then absently picked up the book she'd been trying to read. More to the point, the page it had taken her all evening to—

A noise.

She sat up.

Silence.

She strained to listen.

Footsteps.

She cursed her imagination.

The floor at the bottom of the stairs creaked.

She swallowed hard.

A step squeaked.

She held her breath.

Silence.

Without making a sound, Elizabeth exhaled and waited.

The seconds ticked by like hours and still the house was quiet. Not a sound. Daring to release a nervous laugh, she chalked the whole incident up to a bad case of the jitters.

Elizabeth picked up her cup and sighed at the thought, knowing it had simply been a very long day—or two. When the back door slammed, she nearly snapped the delicate china handle between her thumb and finger.

"Elizabeth!" Nick yelled on a dead run.

Instinctively responding to the urgency in his voice, she called, "I'm up here."

He took the steps two at a time, unable to reach her soon enough. Ever since he'd talked to Chico, he'd wanted nothing more than to drive his fist through the nearest wall. His Harley hadn't been fast enough to outrun the endless pictures of Elizabeth racing through his mind.

He'd imagined her fighting for her life in some filthy alley while he sat at the precinct agonizing over the gory details of the last murder. If it hadn't been for Chico, he might have received another dead-body call tonight. Only this time, instead of finding some nameless, faceless woman mutilated and left in the gutter, he would have found Elizabeth.

The instant Nick filled the doorway, Elizabeth set down her cup of tea. The candles she'd lit around the room flickered and cast a warm glow over his windburned cheeks, barely able to soften the frightening intensity of his icy gaze. Alarmed by the whirlwind of emotion surrounding him, she stood.

Nick pulled her into his arms and held her, without saying a word. She tried to lean back, but he pulled her close. Dammit, he was tired of letting go. After what had nearly happened to Elizabeth tonight, he was scared as hell of losing someone again. "Just let me hold you," he whispered.

When he felt her relax against him, something familiar rekindled deep inside. Desire so powerful it sapped his strength. Passion so hot it branded his soul. An awakening so simple it left him speechless.

He needed this woman. To live with and laugh with. To love and protect. Not just today. But every day for the rest of his life.

Tonight, walking home in the dark, fear had wound itself around Elizabeth's heart, shaking her confidence and stealing her innocence. She had hurried inside and sought the solitude of her room to try to sort through her feelings. How could she have faced dying without really knowing who she was or what her life had been?

By the time Nick burst into her room with fire in his eyes and trouble on his mind, she had no defenses left. Nor did she want any.

For this moment, all Elizabeth needed was to feel whole again. If she'd let him, Nick could give her that…that, and so much more. So she surrendered, inhaling the cold night air that clung to his skin. When he pulled her against him, the chill from his black leather jacket seeped through her silky nightshirt, his jeans felt pleasantly rough against her bare legs. Larger than life, he smacked of sex and danger. And, she wanted him.

Never breaking eye contact, she smiled up at his ruggedly handsome face and began tugging off his clothes. She took great pleasure in watching her intentions register on his face—and an even greater pleasure when his fingers nimbly began unbuttoning her nightshirt.

Together they peeled away the layers of material, surrendering to their desperate need for one another.

Nick fought off the demons that demanded he take her immediately, furiously and satisfy himself. The overwhelming hunger he felt for Elizabeth went beyond lust. It was like nothing he'd ever experienced before.

He scooped her into his arms and carried her to the bed to keep from pinning her against the wall and taking her without pretense. Some inborn voice told him her desire was every bit as great as his tonight, that she would respond in kind to his unbridled passion. If that was all he wanted...

Nick shook his head and framed her lovely face with unsteady hands. Fighting to draw an even breath, he outlined her lips with his fingertip. She was real and she was safe. His fear subsided, clearing his mind, allowing him to choose her pleasure over his own.

He traced her jaw and the slender column of her neck, stopping only to sense the tender pulse beating steadily against his fingertips. Rewarded by her soft sighs, he watched her eyes darken with passion as he continued, trailing a path from her shoulders to her wrists and back again.

His light touch glided slowly over each breast, causing her to moan softly. Gently kneading their fullness, he flicked his thumbs over each tip until they hardened in response.

He skimmed down her body, teasing her rib cage, taunting the small of her back. His hands continued past her hips to explore the supple beauty of her long, shapely legs.

Nick smiled as she writhed beneath his touch, making him realize the power had never been in the taking, but in the giving, the seduction.

As Elizabeth grabbed Nick's taut forearms, she realized his patience had taken far more skill than untamed passion ever would have. Raising her lips to meet his, she tasted the lingering sweetness of his soft mouth. She shut her eyes and watched the candlelight dance behind her closed lids.

Desire spread through her veins like liquid fire, igniting in all the right places—secret places—that burned with a need that only Nick could satisfy. Her body hummed beneath him as they rolled across the rumpled bedspread. Through a tangle of arms and legs, she arched to meet him as he slipped inside her.

Nick lowered his mouth to hers, silencing Elizabeth's gasp as they moved, slowly at first, in perfect unison.

When the sweet ache became unbearable, Elizabeth wrapped her legs around him and cried out in ecstasy with one final release.

The instant Nick heard Elizabeth call his name and felt her shudder beneath him, his control dissolved. He buried his face in her hair and, with a need greater than life itself, let himself follow.

As Elizabeth snuggled close, her mind finally able to focus again, she began to wonder what had gotten into Nick. She'd seen him cocky. She'd seen him commanding. Hell, she'd even seen him naked. But tonight, in the privacy of her room, she'd seen him vulnerable for the first time. She brushed her hand along his cheek and locked her eyes with his. "What's going on?"

Nick rolled onto his side and propped himself up on one elbow. "I think they call it making love." Offering her a lopsided grin, he hoped she'd just drop it. He really didn't want to think about what could have happened to her tonight.

"I'm referring to the panic in your eyes when you rushed in here."

His smile faded. "Chico called and told me he'd walked you home."

She eyed him suspiciously. "Surely this wasn't some macho jealous thing, was it?"

"Right analogy, wrong reason."

Elizabeth sat up, tucking the covers under her arms. "Speak English, Davis."

"I should have been there for you tonight."

"You," she corrected, "should have put gas in my car."

"I did."

"But—"

"Exactly." He let the implication soak in.

She sat up and wrapped the sheet around her. "So what *exactly* does that mean?"

"That's what I plan to find out, first thing in the morning." Nick climbed out of bed and pulled on his jeans. "In the meantime, I brought you something." He unearthed his jacket from the pile of clothes next to the bed. Reaching into the pocket he told her, "I'm giving you my flip phone with my pager number already programmed into it. You can leave a voice message—anytime—anywhere." He handed her the telephone. "You'll never be stranded again like you were tonight."

Elizabeth held the small receiver, knowing it was so much more than just a phone. "Thanks." And she meant it. "Was that what you went back after?"

Nick poked his head through the neck of his sweatshirt. "What do you mean?"

"I thought I heard you downstairs—right before you came up." She chewed her lip, feeling a little silly for even mentioning it. "It sounded like you started up the steps, then went back down."

"No." He shoved his arms through the sleeves. "I had the telephone in my jacket pocket all the time."

"Well it wouldn't be the first time tonight I heard people

who weren't there." She shrugged. "Oh, by the way, an Officer Evans called earlier, looking for you."

"Evans?"

"Yeah." She watched Nick's gaze narrow. "He wanted to know if you were here, or if I was expecting you tonight."

His jaw clenched. "Did the call come before you heard the noises downstairs?"

Elizabeth nodded.

"Get dressed," he ordered. "I'll be right back."

Elizabeth didn't much care for his tone, but he ran downstairs too fast for her to argue. She'd hardly slipped into her underwear when he barreled back into the bedroom.

"Pack a bag."

She arched one brow. "What for?"

"You're coming home with me." Even though this didn't quite fit the serial killer's MO, Nick wasn't taking any chances. His gut said to get her out of here, and that's exactly what he was going to do.

Elizabeth shook her head. "No, I'm not."

Take it slow, Davis, she's been through a lot. "After what happened to your car, I don't want you spending another night here."

With one arm in her blouse, she shoved both legs through the waistband of her skirt. "What? Cars don't break down in your neighborhood?"

"Maybe they do, but the people driving them aren't you and those people aren't followed home."

"But it was only Chico—"

On second thought, maybe he was taking it too slow. "No, Elizabeth, it wasn't only Chico." Nick was at the end of his rope. "Chico is probably the only reason you're not lying dead in some alley right now."

Her fingers poised over the last button on her shirt. "Then there *was* someone following me."

Nick met the fear in her eyes. "Yes."

"That's still no reason for me to stay with you," she insisted.

Nick gave up. "I just checked the doors for any evidence that someone had been down there earlier." He watched her eyes widen. "The back door had been jimmied. Whatever noise you heard tonight was not a figment of your imagination, Elizabeth. Someone was in here."

Her knees threatened to give out. "Oh, my God."

He had her by the shoulders. "Dammit, don't you understand how much I care about you? I won't risk losing someone I care about again." Before she had time to say another word, he had ransacked her closet floor and tossed an overnight bag at her feet. "You're coming with me."

Chapter 9

Elizabeth tightened her hold around Nick's waist and buried her head behind his broad shoulders as she leaned into the next turn. If the cold air blasting from every direction didn't do her in, Chicago traffic was bound to. Zipping through these streets at night on a motorcycle held about the same appeal for her as being shoved from a ten-story building. When the motorcycle finally roared to a stop, Elizabeth found the courage to open her eyes.

Nick straddled the bike, holding it upright while he pried her hands from his middle. "You can let go now."

"I know that," she snapped, still aggravated by the chauvinistic tactics he'd used back in her room. Who did he think he was, ordering her to pack like that?

Lucky for him, he'd said he cared for her. Her irritation dissolved at the thought, and a hint of a smile touched her lips. The poor man still didn't realize that after admitting that, he could have just asked her to come home with him—nicely, of course. She admired his rugged silhouette in the darkness and shook her head.

Nick hiked one leg and hopped off the bike. Balancing the frame so Elizabeth could dismount, he extended his hand.

She slapped it away. "After all that," she gestured wildly back toward the city, "and all you're worried about is helping me *off* this monstrosity."

First Dani, now Elizabeth. Did all women hate motorcycles? He ignored the hand that had just smacked his and eased Elizabeth off the bike in spite of herself. Grabbing her bag, he led her up the driveway.

Elizabeth had always wondered what kind of house a man like Nick would live in, but nothing could have prepared her for the shock of walking through his front door. She'd expected chrome and black leather or maybe a massive, Mediterranean decor. Certainly not the same muted earth tones that she'd chosen for her room on Maxwell Street.

Running a hand over the luxuriously overstuffed davenport, she ignored the chill that skittered from her fingertips to her shoulder like the footsteps of a fast-moving spider. "Not exactly how I pictured your place, Davis."

"What can I say?" His eyes snapped with the pleasure of seeing her there. "The caves were all taken."

Normally she appreciated his dry sense of humor, but right now her mind was elsewhere. Ever since they'd driven past the two big bushes at the end of the driveway something just out of reach had been taunting her, daring her to remember. She just couldn't put her finger on what it was.

Surely it couldn't be the stress of the day catching up with me, she thought sarcastically. After all, she'd been stranded, followed, scared half to death, ravaged and relocated. She marveled at the ridiculous irony of it.

"Actually," Nick clarified, "Dani decorated the house."

More to the point, he wondered if Elizabeth could deal with knowing that fact.

She liked the straight-forward way he'd mentioned Dani. No apologies. No excuses. No ghost? "It's lovely—at least what I can make out. That ridiculous toy you've somehow mistaken for transportation played hell with my eyes." She pointed toward the davenport. "Would you hand me my purse?"

Nick tossed her the oversize denim bag and waited while she popped out her contact lenses.

"There." She blinked at him over the lid of her compact. "That's better."

Her eyes! Her eyes weren't green at all. They were hazel. "You wear contacts? I didn't know that. Why in the hell haven't I seen you without them before now?"

Confused by his sharp tone, she answered, "They're the kind you can wear for two weeks without ever taking them out—and you haven't known me that long. Is that a problem?"

"No." He looked again. "No problem," he whispered. They *were* hazel. The exotic golden color of a tiger's eye...the exact shade as Dani's.

His heart banged wildly against his ribs. He slipped her jacket off, then wrapped his arms around her, insuring a closer look. "Make yourself at home while I put your stuff away." Staring into that hauntingly familiar gaze, he had to fight to keep his emotions in check.

She hugged him back. "Thanks, I will."

"How about a glass of wine?" He held her, wanting, no, needing another look.

"Ummm." She ran her tongue provocatively over her lips as she twined both arms around his neck.

He angled his head toward the mantel. "And a fire?"

Desperate, he searched the depths of her eyes. Their true color. Their exact shape and the expressive way she used them.

"Now that sounds romantic." She feathered a sweet kiss onto his lips.

Her mouth curved into a smile beneath his. "Hold that thought. I'll be right back," he promised, disappearing down the hall on legs not nearly as steady as he would have liked.

Compelled to look around the room, Elizabeth found the fireplace stacked and ready to go. She walked directly to the end table and her hand hovered over the top two drawers, then stopped. Without hesitation, she yanked open the third and began rifling through it.

"Nick," she called, "where are the matches?" Her head snapped up when she heard his quick intake of breath from across the room.

His pulse thundered at both temples as he watched in disbelief. "What are you doing?"

"I can't find the matches."

Nick's blood ran cold when she innocently pointed to the drawer. "Why are you looking for matches in there?"

She planted both hands matter-of-factly on her hips. "Because," she stammered in bewilderment, "that's where…"

"I keep them," he finished.

Confused and very shaken, she stood there and merely nodded.

Nick's control snapped. He had to find out once and for all who this woman was because she damned sure wasn't

Elizabeth Gleason. His mind clicked through every detail he'd filed away since he'd met her.

"Let me see your right arm," he demanded, putting the unopened bottle of wine on an end table and closing the distance between them. God, had she always worn long sleeves?

"My what?" Frightened by the urgency in his voice, Elizabeth quickly pushed up her sleeve.

Nick led her across the room and held her arm directly beneath the lamplight. Running his fingertip along her skin, he meticulously searched her forearm. He froze the moment he spotted a small, faded scar midway between her wrist and elbow. "ER." The initials slipped between his clenched teeth, as his mind accelerated into overdrive. "Would you please bring me…a glass of water?"

"Sure." More than a little concerned by his irrational behavior, Elizabeth nodded and hurried to the wet bar.

The moment she turned her back, Nick flipped the switch on his pager, causing it to beep.

"Was that your pager?" Elizabeth asked as she handed him the glass.

"Yeah. I've got to go," Nick told her, slipping into his jacket. "I'll be back as soon as I can."

"But, Nick—"

"I'm really sorry." The confusion on her face was nearly his undoing. "Believe me, I would never go tonight, but this can't wait." He carefully grabbed the glass by its bottom and studied Elizabeth, measuring her inch by inch, recording every detail with his eyes. "Thanks for the water. I'll drink it on the way."

Elizabeth just looked at him. "No problem."

"Lock it" was all he said before slamming the door behind him.

Dumbfounded, she just stood there for a moment, not

knowing whether to laugh or cry. Too tired to do either, Elizabeth realized she was frighteningly close to overload and wouldn't be able to make sense of any of this tonight.

She checked her watch. If Nick wanted to traipse all over Chicago at eleven o'clock at night, so be it. With any luck, she'd be able to fit some of these pieces together tomorrow....

A smile teased the corners of her mouth. It was a long time before morning and Nick *had* insisted she come home with him, then left her all alone with nothing to do. Convinced there couldn't be any harm in snooping around a little, she hurried across the room and locked the front door.

Feeling somewhat entitled, Elizabeth picked up her overnight bag and walked straight into the dining room where she was immediately drawn to the rose-patterned dishes displayed in the hutch. Old, no doubt, she cataloged, even before opening the beveled glass door. She removed one of the delicately balanced cups and traced its exquisite shape with her fingertip. Closing her eyes, she—

Remembered?

—the smell of freshly brewed Earl Grey tea...feeling its heat through the paper-thin china.

Her eyes flew open.

"Janette," she whispered.

Whatever she'd just experienced was a memory of some sort. A definite flashback. She ran her fingertip around the dainty rim. Why would these dishes remind her of someone named Janette? The pounding of her heart made Elizabeth wonder if she'd be better off forgetting the past, leaving it behind where it belonged. Shaken, she quickly replaced the cup and tried to close the door—on more than just the hutch.

Her thoughts returned to the present. Looking around,

Elizabeth decided Nick's kitchen would prove a far better place to explore than the recesses of her mind.

The moment she flipped on the light, every bit of air rushed from her lungs.

A spacious room decorated with copper pots

Her eyes made a frantic search.

woven baskets

Haunted by the flashback she'd experienced one morning back at the soup kitchen, Elizabeth leaned weakly against the doorway.

a crystal vase filled with lilacs on a beautiful window seat

"This kitchen," she murmured.

Hanging on for dear life, she braced herself for another glimpse of her past. This time she recognized herself washing dishes at the sink, then felt a man step up behind her and wrap his strong arms around her waist. Pulling her against him, he whispered provocatively in her ear. She smiled knowingly at his sweet promises, the familiar feel of his hard chest against her back.

Every bone in her body melted as he seductively slipped her skirt down around her ankles—slowly—methodically—inch by inch. He carried her across the floor and she heard a low moan escape his lips as he eased her onto the oak dining table. She could feel the cool, smooth wood beneath her buttocks as he began making deliberate, unbearably erotic love to her. When he'd driven her beyond reason and her body had shuddered its release, her eyes opened and she looked up into his face.

"Nick." The name escaped her lips like a prayer.

Her window to the past shut as quickly as it had opened and she was, once again, slammed back into the present. Reluctantly, she stepped into the kitchen and ran a shaky hand across the wooden tabletop. Could her desire for Nick be distorting her fleeting memories? Overwhelmed by emotions and unanswered questions, she turned off the light and, bag in hand, hurried down the hall straight to Nick's bedroom.

Invited in by the soft glow of a night-light, Elizabeth examined the exquisite quilt that covered the bed, admiring its intricately patterned blocks. So much work, she thought fondly. She could almost see the diligent, nimble fingers laboring patiently over every stitch. *Janette,* she thought again.

Elizabeth shook off the specter and began poking around Nick's dresser, alternately sniffing, then smiling over every bottle. In a small china saucer, she found three paper clips, one stick of Dentyne gum, four bullets and…Nick's wedding ring. She slipped the plain gold band on the third finger of her left hand, wondering what it felt like to belong to someone.

As if pushed through a hole in time, she vividly remembered an altar in a church. Saw herself standing there in her wedding gown. Heard her voice say, "I do." Turned to face her new husband.

These bits and pieces retreated just out of reach before the memory fully developed, leaving her unnerved and alone again. Exhausted and confused, she stripped off her clothing and pulled on a nightshirt. Desperate for some kind of physical closeness, she slipped beneath the smooth, soft covers of the four-poster bed. Not at all conscious of being by herself in this strange house, or more to the point in Nick's bed, Elizabeth surrendered to the unexpected comfort she found and quickly fell asleep.

Nick pulled the file on Elizabeth Gleason, then unceremoniously swiped the top of his desk clean with one arm.

Page by page, he searched for the medical report that had been filled out the night of her accident.

"Bingo," he whispered, separating the doctor's notes from the remainder of the forms. Scanning the details, he found exactly what he was looking for—absolutely nothing. There wasn't one damned word about a laceration on her right forearm.

He read further, then recognized his own primeval groan as he let the sheet of paper drift from his fingertips and flutter to the floor.

"How could *I* have missed this?" Nick jumped to his feet, pacing the floor like a caged animal. "When I think how this whole damn mess might have played out." He punched the old metal filing cabinet in the corner with his fist, then wiped his raw knuckles against the leg of his jeans and reached for the phone.

Elizabeth tossed and turned fitfully as she slept, desperately searching her subconscious for the answers that eluded her waking mind. Complying, her sleep blossomed with images so intense they allowed her to take the final step—the one just beyond the crossroads where her dreams mirrored reality.

Lavender sheets. Cool and smooth against her bare skin. A soft breeze, whispering through an open window, ruffling lacy, champagne-colored curtains. Memories of making love surfaced, so real they scorched a path down her body, settling into private places that made her smile.

What was that wonderful fragrance? She inhaled deeply. Fresh and intoxicating. So familiar...

Elizabeth sat straight up in bed. "Lilacs," she whispered. "The bushes at the end of the driveway are lilacs."

"The photographs?" Nick pinned Mary Franklin with his stare the instant she walked through the door. "Did you find them?''

"Right here.'' Handing him a large manila envelope, she met his gaze. "It's one in the morning, Davis. This had better be good.''

With his free hand, Nick gestured toward the chair opposite his. "Good?'' he echoed with a sneer, still wondering if he'd lost his bloody mind. Hell, he might be totally off the wall with this, but something deep down inside told him otherwise. If he was right…he didn't even have the guts to hope.

Instead, he pulled out the glossy five-by-seven photos of Elizabeth and laid them next to Dani's picture. Nick looked up. "Since you've been Elizabeth's closest contact, I need your opinion. If you disagree, you'll probably want to commit me.''

She waited a beat before asking, "And, if I agree?''

He leveled her with his gaze. "You'll probably have to bury me.''

She raised a concerned brow at his candor. "The stakes are that high?''

"Oh, yeah.'' He turned the photos around so they were facing Dr. Franklin, then took one deep breath before he spoke. "Could these be the same woman?'' God, even the question sounded insane.

Mary looked at Elizabeth's picture first, then the other. The moment she recognized Dani, and after the implication of what he was asking registered, her eyes snapped up, connecting with his. "I assume you have your reasons.''

Unwilling to trust his voice, Nick nodded.

She pulled her glasses from her purse and went over each photo very carefully. "It's possible,'' she offered cautiously, slipping off her glasses. "But, what brought this on tonight?"

"You know all the similarities between Elizabeth and Dani I've mentioned before?"

"The little things," Mary nodded.

"Exactly. Nothing concrete, but just parallel enough to raise the hair on the back of my neck." Nick stood and paced the small area behind his desk. "Until now, I couldn't decide whether I was superimposing Dani's traits on Elizabeth, or simply losing my mind."

"And now?"

"Someone followed Elizabeth home this evening so, rather than let her stay on the south side tonight, I took her back to my house. When I came back into my living room after putting her bag away, she had the end table drawer open, asking where the matches were."

"You keep them there?"

"Yes. And she was really shaken when I asked her why she looked *there*."

"What did she tell you?"

"That she knew that's where I kept them." He stopped pacing and faced her. "And, for some reason, that's when it hit me."

"What?"

"That night in the alley, when her approach to the body was so much like Dani's, I kept thinking there was something else I should remember about watching Dani work ER. Not just the way she moved or her style." He shoved both hands in his pockets. "Tonight I remembered."

"What was it?"

"I was in ER the night some dirtbag on crack went berserk and attacked Dani. I jumped over a gurney after him, but the son of a bitch had punctured her right forearm before I could tackle him. God, all I remember is the blood. I broke his thumb getting that scalpel away from him."

"And when you checked Elizabeth's records?"

"No injuries to her arms arising from the accident. But there was one notation of a faint, preexisting scar on her right forearm."

Mary sat up straighter in her chair. "How about fingerprints?"

This time, Nick's head snapped up. "You're good, Doc. I've already got Dani's on file and I just brought a glass in with Elizabeth's prints on it."

"Why do you already have Dani's?"

"They were elimination prints taken from evidence she inadvertently touched in ER." Nick's mind was racing a mile a minute. He braced both hands on the back of his chair and met Mary's gaze.

"Don't get your hopes up, Nick. You know the odds here are astronomical."

The bottom dropped out of his stomach. "Thanks, Doc. I'll keep that in mind."

By the time he got home, Nick's head was ready to split. He'd dropped off the glass with Elizabeth's prints on it at the lab and put a rush on the results. Now all he had to do was wait. That was a laugh. One phone call and his whole life could be handed back to him—or not.

He followed the light down the hall to his bedroom where he slung his jacket over the chair beside the dresser, then shrugged out of his holster. Surprised to find Elizabeth awake, he told her, "You shouldn't have waited up." He rolled both shoulders, trying to ease the tension that was trapped between them.

"I didn't."

For some reason, Nick's instincts kicked in. He turned to face her. "Couldn't sleep?"

"Sleep?" she echoed softly. "How can I sleep, knowing you've been lying to me?"

It might be three in the morning and he might be ready to lose his mind, but he wasn't too far gone to recognize the pain in Elizabeth's voice. He stopped and took a closer look. She was propped up in bed, her face pale, her expression unreadable. Something was drastically wrong.

"I've never lied to you." He sat down beside her on the edge of the bed.

"How could you have kept all this from me?" Elizabeth's pulse was throbbing, she could feel it pound as she gestured around the room. The onslaught of images and emotions she'd experienced in this house had not simply overwhelmed her, they were definitely significant. She knew that, after tonight, there was no turning back. Her life would never be the same again.

"I haven't kept anything from you."

"Yes, you have," she whispered, flinching as he tried to smooth a lock of hair from her cheek. "You must have."

"Sweetheart, you've been through a lot tonight, and I'm sorry I had to leave you alone. But it was important. You have to know that." He opened his arms. "I'm here now."

Touched by the compassion in his voice and the understanding in his eyes, she moved into his embrace. Maybe they could uncover the truth together. "Oh, Nick, what's going on?" She sobbed against him, grateful for his strength. "So much has happened tonight—so many things I can't explain."

All her thoughts and feelings were so jumbled. How accurate were the flashbacks she'd been having? Were they a true reflection of her past, or a combination of what had happened before and what was happening now? Or what she wanted to happen in the future?

If that was the case, maybe she'd never known Nick before. Out of need, maybe she'd subconsciously used him to fill in her sketchy memories. Maybe he hadn't kept anything from her after all.

Even in the shelter of his embrace, the feeling of fear resurfaced, washing over her like a tidal wave, sapping her strength and threatening to pull her under. With no real memory of her past, her life remained a tangle of dark, frightening streets and, until now, she'd faced every blind alley alone.

"Shhh," he soothed, running a gentle hand down the length of her hair.

"I don't know what's real anymore." She leaned back slightly. "Have I ever been here before?"

The pain in her eyes nearly did him in. He'd never wanted to absorb someone's heartache the way he wanted to ease hers. "I'm not sure, love, but I'm going to help you sort everything out. I'm expecting a call that might explain a lot."

He pulled her close. Needing to comfort her and, at the same time, trying to hide the desperation that was ripping him apart, Nick rocked Elizabeth in his arms. Could this woman really be his Dani?

What kind of selfish bastard would be lucky enough to fall in love with the same woman twice?

Me, he willed silently.

The phone rang.

God, he prayed, let it be me.

Chapter 10

Still holding Elizabeth, Nick snatched the phone from the bedside table. Every frazzled nerve in his body stood at attention, blood pounded in his ears. "Davis." He held his breath.

"We've got another body."

The bottom dropped out of his gut at the sound of O'Malley's voice. Nick swore. Not the call he'd expected. Not the news that would have humbled him before God and the universe.

He closed his eyes as he listened, forced his breathing to steady. For the first time since he'd joined the department, he wanted to hand the dirty work over to someone else. He pinched the bridge of his nose. "Where?"

Elizabeth instinctively sensed the reason for the call. She watched Nick's expression darken as he listened, saw his body switch gears as he reached for his shoulder holster. He distanced himself from her. No longer the attentive lover who'd tenderly cradled her in his arms, instead he slipped into his role as police officer. Regardless of the hours he'd already put in, somehow she knew the adrenaline surging through his veins would replace the fatigue that shadowed his eyes—for now.

Later was another story. She knew exactly how much he'd need her after all the messy details were cleaned up, and the body was carted off to the morgue. She would be there for him then.

Like before?

An eerie sensation prickled at the nape of her neck.

"An alley behind the warehouse on Market Street, but don't come down here," O'Malley instructed. "Meet me at the station."

"The station?" The entire time the lieutenant had been filling him in on the details, Nick was organizing a mental check list of procedures. "What about the investigation?"

"I've already called Ed. Leave the rest of the crime scene to the lab boys."

Davis bristled. "Since when?"

"Since I just nailed some guy leaving the scene."

Nick's head snapped up. "The murderer."

"Looks like it."

Nick's jaw clenched at the thought of getting up close and personal with the psycho who had butchered all those women. Was this guy the same bastard who followed Elizabeth tonight? Bile rose in Nick's throat at the thought, knowing if it hadn't been for Chico...

"On my way." He hung up the receiver and faced Elizabeth. "I guess you heard."

"Uh-huh."

Nick nodded as he grabbed his jacket. "When I get home, we need to talk."

"I'll be here," she assured him.

He cupped her face in his large hands and bent down, burying his head in her hair. "Just like always."

The words were barely a whisper, but she heard his voice crack just the same. Unable to get past the lump in her own throat, she offered a shaky smile before he turned and walked away.

The moment she heard the front door close, Elizabeth echoed softly, "Just like always."

Nick barreled his way through the chaotic squad room. His stomach rolled as he sidestepped a drunk who had just lost the remainder of his Saturday night bar tab in and around a nearby wastebasket.

"Hey, Sarge." Nick shouted to be heard over a heated argument going on between a mother and her teenage son. "You need a mop and a bucket over here."

A gruff voice barked back, "Get in line, Davis."

The end of Nick's rope was getting closer by the minute. By the time he reached the interrogation room, he nearly tore the door off its hinges. Once inside, he stopped dead in his tracks. First gaping at O'Malley, then the suspect, he couldn't believe his eyes.

"This is the guy you busted?" He poked a finger in the direction of the man seated in the center of the room.

O'Malley nodded.

Nick closed the door behind him and approached the suspect. "Joe?" He spoke directly into the blank stare.

"You know him?" O'Malley asked.

"Yeah. He's a regular down at the soup kitchen. Joe, look at me." The man sitting there in tattered clothes turned his smudged face toward Nick, but his eyes didn't seem to focus.

He tried again. "Joe, it's Nick." This time, the older man's brow wrinkled with a spark of recollection.

''Nick?'' He grasped the detective's hand. ''What's going on?''

''Don't worry,'' Nick promised. ''We'll get this straightened out.''

Joe released his grip, then lowered his head into both hands.

Nick kneeled down beside him. ''Just talk to me,'' he coaxed. ''Tell me what you were doing in that alley.''

Joe met his gaze. ''Why, I was doing what I always do.''

''What's that, Joe?'' Fifteen years on the force told him the sinking feeling in the pit of his stomach was right on target.

''What is it that you always do?''

''I spare them,'' he assured Nick matter-of-factly.

''Spare them what?''

Joe's eyes filled with unshed tears. ''The pain. The suffering.'' He nodded, and tears spilled down both ruddy cheeks as he continued, ''The waiting.''

''What causes the pain?''

''They're so sick,'' he stated emphatically, mopping his eyes and shaking his head. ''Dying, really.''

Nick turned when he saw O'Malley head for the door.

''I'll be checkin' it out with Ed,'' the lieutenant told him.

He nodded, then switched his attention back to Joe. ''How do you know they're ill?''

''I'm a doctor,'' Joe stated, as if everyone should know. ''I look in on them every day.''

''Let's try to get some facts, here, Joe.'' Nick straightened and clapped his hand on the other man's shoulder, certain it was going to be a long night. ''I think we're going to need them.''

* * *

Too wound up to sleep, Elizabeth made her way back to the kitchen. Heading straight for the cabinet over the dishwasher, she opened the door on the right side and stood on tiptoe to reach the second shelf. She examined the glass she retrieved, wishing to hell something around this house could speak. After what she'd been through, talking stemware wouldn't seem that crazy. She laughed, hoping to hold on to what was left of her sanity. Too late for that, she thought wearily.

After pouring some milk, she opened a bag of candy corn.

Halloween candy? Who would have thought the good detective would be better prepared than a Boy Scout. She grabbed a handful and grinned. "Trick or treat, Davis. You've got a couple of weeks left to buy some more." She poked through several drawers and nosed around all the nooks and crannies. Everything was in its place.

Exactly as she'd left it?

Ridiculous. The placement of household items was simply a matter of common sense, nothing more. After all, silverware belonged next to the sink, pots and pans by the stove. So, she looked around slyly, where would he keep the crystal vase she'd seen in her flashback?

Simple, she thought, opening the narrow cabinet door next to a built-in lazy Susan. "Damn." There it was.

That was no coincidence.

A spooky October wind howled outside the window. Elizabeth grabbed her milk and hurried out of the kitchen, not stopping until she was halfway down the hall. She flipped on the light in the guest bedroom, only to find it unfurnished. No bed. No dresser. Nothing.

One totally vacant room in an otherwise beautifully decorated home. "That's odd," she muttered, sliding open the closet door. Empty... But there was something on the floor in the back corner. She squatted down and reached in, pulling out a large stuffed toy.

Elizabeth didn't notice that the glass had slipped from her hand and landed with a soft thud on the carpeted floor. The moment she placed her palm on her tummy, right below her belly button, the flashback was immediate.

She was standing at the picture window in the living room, and she saw Nick walking up the driveway, surrounded by blue sky and sunshine. He had a huge spray of lilacs in one hand, a gigantic bear in the other, and the biggest grin she'd ever seen on his face. The front door was open, and she felt the warm spring breeze ruffle her hair. A sense of joy, more intense than anything she'd ever experienced before, overwhelmed her.

He spotted her and waved the bouquet. Her hand raised to greet him...

Just as suddenly as it started, the vision was over. Elizabeth found herself back in the present, facing an empty closet, one hand still gesturing in the air, the other gripping a teddy bear. She looked down and, instead of seeing the spilled milk pooled at her feet, she was overpowered by another image from her past....

Nick was standing in a hospital room. She saw his head—his profile, really—resting heavily against the windowpane. He was trying to hide some great sadness by turning away and looking outside at the rain. But his pain was reflected in the glass. He was suffering because...

For the first time since she had begun having these flashes, Elizabeth was able to snap herself out of one. Shaken to the core by devastating sorrow, she refused to look into the anguish she and Nick had shared. Not yet.

She hurried to Nick's room, stuffed animal in hand. Just like the bear she'd kept from the Dumpster, Elizabeth propped this one on the dresser, then crawled back into bed. The morning would be soon enough for the answers she wanted. And too soon for the ones she didn't.

Nick grabbed the coffee he'd been nursing all night and finished it.

Quit stalling and make the call, Davis. Nobody said this job would be easy.

He tossed the empty cup into his wastebasket, then grabbed the phone. Well, *Nobody* was sure as hell right about that.

When the telephone rang a little after six, Elizabeth rolled over onto her left side and, without groping, answered it.

"Sorry to wake you, sweetheart, but I need you to come down to the station."

"Me?" Her feet had already hit the floor. "What for?"

"I've got Joe down here and he wants to talk to you."

"Joe?" Scrunching the phone between her ear and her shoulder to free both hands, she unzipped her overnight bag she'd left beside the bed and began rifling through it. "What's he doing at the station?"

"I'd rather explain everything in person." Like hell. He'd rather put a gun to his own head. He knew how close Elizabeth was to Joe. How could he ever explain that the same man who saved her life and nursed her back to health had also killed at least seven women in the past year?

She pulled out a pair of jeans and a sweater. "I'll be there as soon as I can."

"Take my car," he offered. "The keys are—"

"—in the wicker basket next to the toaster," she finished.

"Yeah." Nick wiped his suddenly sweaty palms on his jeans.

The question in his voice was unmistakable. "Relax, I saw them there last night." *But, had she?*

"Right." *But, had she?* He shook off his suspicions. Now was not the time. He needed to concentrate on the murder investigation.

Elizabeth hung up and glared at the bear. "Don't start with me," she warned. Today, she would have answers from Nick about the lilacs, Janette, and…the baby? Her heart lurched. She had a right to know. No more games. No more secrets. No matter what. But, for now, first things first.

Nick raked a hand through his hair as he waited for Elizabeth to arrive. Another night spent dealing with one more gruesome, senseless death had shoved him past the point of no return. Hell, he'd been ready to take the murdering bastard apart sight unseen—

Hurry. Hurry. Step right up. See the man-beast serial killer. The son of Satan.

—until he'd come face-to-face with Joe.

Sorry, folks. The show's over. Nobody wins tonight. Everybody goes home a loser.

The hopeless despair Nick had seen in the man's vacant stare had withered his fury, left him drained and empty. Cost him his edge. What was left to hang on to once the rage was gone…?

Elizabeth. He looked up and saw her standing in his doorway. Trusting him.

Sometimes that was enough.

"Where's Joe?" she asked.

Sometimes it wasn't.

The grim lines bracketing Nick's mouth told Elizabeth that whatever he'd rolled her out of bed at the crack of dawn for wasn't good. She stepped into his office and shut the door, gratefully muffling the angry shouts coming from somewhere down the hall.

"I'll take you to him in just a minute." He stood and rounded the front of his desk, parking one hip on its edge. "You'd better sit down."

"What's wrong?" she asked, reluctantly taking the seat in front of him. Nick didn't pull punches and his evasiveness was scaring her. "Is Joe all right?"

"Physically, yes." The best way to handle this was to say it fast. "He's been arrested for murder."

Elizabeth jumped to her feet. "What?"

"O'Malley stopped him running from the alley where the woman was killed."

She shook her head violently. "No. There must be some mistake."

Nick reached out and steadied her hands. They felt cold and small sandwiched between his. "Elizabeth, Joe took O'Malley right to the body."

"He probably just stumbled onto it," she explained, trying to convince herself as much as him. "You don't understand how confused he gets sometimes."

Elizabeth's loyalty, her frantic scramble to explain away the facts and help her friend hit Nick hard. "I'm sure he does." Nick inhaled the crisp autumn breeze that still lingered in her hair as he pulled her close. He let her hold on to him, then broke the truth to her gently. "Joe admitted to everything."

She wrapped her arms around his neck and rested her forehead on his strong, broad chest. "He saved my life," she whimpered. "Took care of me."

"I know, sweetheart. I know he did," Nick assured her. "Did you know Joe was a doctor? He told us all the victims were sick."

Elizabeth leaned back to look at him and shook her

head. "No, but that would explain a lot." She remembered how he'd talked about making rounds and checking on everyone. Her blood ran cold.

"O'Malley verified Joe's diagnosis with the coroner. All the victims were terminally ill."

"How does a man like him end up like this?" she pleaded, desperate for answers.

"Sometimes they just snap. We're doing our best to find out why, but Joe won't tell us any more. He refused to say another word to anyone but you."

"Why me?"

"He said you'd understand." Her fresh tears hastened the rest of his explanation. "I've already called in Dr. Franklin. We'll observe your conversation through a two-way mirror, so you'll be safe."

"That's not necessary," Elizabeth assured him, taking a step back. "Joe won't hurt me."

"I can't take that chance." Nick grabbed her by the arm. "I won't lose you." *Again?*

It seemed like miles to the interrogation room. The long corridors with peeling paint and ammonia-smelling tile floors were dingy and oppressing. Loud voices from adjacent offices bounced off hollow walls like Ping-Pong balls, and phones seemed to ring from every direction.

Elizabeth shuddered, and took a deep breath before stepping through the door. She buried her personal feelings, intent on talking to Joe in a calm professional manner because that was the only way they'd ever get to the bottom of the murders.

"Peggy?"

He sat alone, shoulders slumped and head downcast. The ragged brown sweater she'd come to know so well remained neatly buttoned. "No, sweetie, it's Elizabeth."

She approached him without fear, taking the seat opposite his. "Nick says you want to talk to me."

He squirmed nervously, averting her scrutiny.

She noted how his gaze was riveted on the floor. "Look at me, Joe."

Elizabeth waited until Joe made eye contact, then continued, "What do you want to discuss?"

"The women."

Cold tentacles of fear curled around Elizabeth's heart.

"The ones who were murdered?"

Joe scrubbed his faced with both fists. "I didn't murder them—"

Momentary relief washed over Elizabeth.

"—I just did my job."

Elizabeth steepled her hands to keep from wringing them. She could feel hope slipping away. "What exactly did you do, Joe?"

He grabbed her by the arm.

"I swore I'd never stand by and let anyone else suffer the way she did," Joe insisted.

"Who?" Elizabeth swallowed hard.

He released his hold on her sleeve and looked away. He ignored her question. "You know, they didn't suffer..."

Elizabeth willed herself to listen and, as Joe had hoped, to understand. In order to do that, she crossed an invisible line that had been drawn between them ever since they'd met. "Tell me what happened to Peggy."

"Peggy?" Visibly agitated, his face darkened with emotion. "She never should have died," he cried, smacking his thigh with one palm.

"That quack told her the tumor in her leg was benign," Joe moaned. "Dammit, I'm a doctor. And her father." His hands covered his eyes. "Why didn't she come to me?"

Elizabeth moved to his side and rested her hand on his

shoulder. "I don't know, sweetie." Mulling over the details of their conversation as she stood there quietly, her mind began to click. "What kind of tumor did Peggy have? Was it a malignant melanoma?"

"Yes," he answered mechanically.

She concurred with his diagnosis. His daughter's death had been avoidable. "Amputating Peggy's leg would have saved her life, wouldn't it?"

"Yes, dear God, yes." Joe's head bobbed up and down with certainty.

"So you performed the one procedure on those other women that could have spared your daughter."

"I helped them die first, though," he assured her. "Then, I removed the leg just above the knee." He ran one finger across his pant leg like a scalpel.

"To save Peggy."

Joe nodded. "I knew you'd understand."

She vividly recalled the scene in the alley and mentally separated Thelma from the picture. Her mind sorted through all the technical details she'd observed, and zeroed in on the one that defied explanation.

"Why did you put the part of her leg you cut off under her head?"

"For comfort," he rationalized. "I should have at least been able to offer her that." Shoulders sagging, he blinked away the tears. "If I had it to do over again—ethics be damned. In the end, I *would have* at least spared her the pain."

Elizabeth had coaxed Joe into revealing every detail, regardless of how painful the memory. Cool and clinical, her medical knowledge was irrefutable.

From behind the one-way mirror, Nick's gut wrenched. Mesmerized, he watched her gaze raise slowly to meet his through the mirror. *Dani's eyes!*

That woman…is my wife.

His chest felt as if an elephant had stepped on it. The need to eliminate the barrier separating them was so immediate that Nick turned to Dr. Franklin. "I've heard enough."

She nodded. "We got what we were after, and then some."

He thought of Elizabeth. "That's probably an understatement, Doc."

Nick couldn't get into the interrogation room fast enough, but when he opened the door the heartbreak on Elizabeth's face stopped him. He read her silent plea. Laying a hand Joe's shoulder, he honored her unspoken request. "Come with me, Joe," he said gently.

"Don't worry." Elizabeth patted her friend's hand and gave him a reassuring nod. "Nick will take good care of you now."

Joe tipped his head in Nick's direction. "You've got yourself a good man, little darlin'. Don't forget that."

She swallowed hard at the familiar endearment. "I won't," *forget you, either,* she promised silently.

In her heart, Elizabeth believed that Joe had been a good man most of his life. She could certainly sympathize with the long, winding roads tragedy could take you down. But even they weren't endless. After all, nobody knew better than she did just how far off track a person's life could get—

She felt Nick's eyes burning a hole in her.

—and still be able to find your way back.

As Nick led Joe from the room, Mary Franklin laid a gentle hand on Elizabeth's shoulder. "Rough night, huh?"

She faced her doctor and sighed. "Oh, yeah." All through the night and into the early morning hours she had restrained her emotions, fought to hold them in check. Her role in the investigation might be over, but the strain she'd been under had yet to fade.

"Buy you some breakfast?"

The sound of Dr. Franklin's soothing voice nearly brought tears to her eyes. Grateful for the offer, but not trusting herself to speak, she nodded. Linking arms, they slowly wound their way through the zigzag of corridors leading back to the squad room.

"Jesus loves you, sisters," a man dressed in long white robes professed at the top of his lungs. "Repent, and salvation will be yours."

One of the three uniformed cops struggling to subdue the self-proclaimed prophet, hollered, "Hey, Doc, looks like your next appointment's here."

Razzing Sergeant MacClusky in front of the two rookies, Mary checked her watch. "Who are you trying to kid, Mac? Everybody knows my nine o'clock is reserved for you. Show up late to one more session, though, and I'll have you busted down to a crossing guard."

The mix of easy banter relaxed Elizabeth, allowing the hoots and barbs that followed to uncurl the tension that had coiled in her stomach like a snake.

"O'Malley." Dr. Franklin called to the burly lieutenant, her voice raised slightly to be heard above the commotion, and pointed toward the door. "Tell Davis we went across the street to Maggie's."

He gestured thumbs-up and smiled. "Will do."

The bright sunlight hurt Elizabeth's eyes, causing her to squint as they left the precinct's dreary entryway. Exhausted and downhearted, she stepped out into the real world. The cool breeze that brushed her cheeks revived her just enough to keep her going, reminding her how good it felt to be alive.

Dodging Chicago traffic at this time in the morning, on

the other hand, could result in sudden death. The stream of cars was endless. One obscene gesture and two blaring car horns later found Elizabeth and Mary on the opposite side of the street—surprisingly still in one piece.

As the diner door fanned open, the aroma of freshly brewed coffee and warm doughnuts almost made playing road roulette worth the risk.

During their short jaunt, Elizabeth's mind refused to give her a minute's peace. It was time to pull out the stops and insist on some answers, either from Nick, or Dr. Franklin—or both. And she knew it.

After they were seated and served, Elizabeth took a deep breath and looked Mary Franklin in the eye. "I am not Elizabeth Gleason," she said with certainty.

Mary paused, then settled her cup into its saucer. "What makes you think you're not?"

"So many things," Elizabeth answered truthfully. "You saw me this morning with Joe. How could I possibly know about that tumor, and why did I feel so competent—like I'd been in that situation a hundred times before?"

"You tell me," Mary coaxed. She watched with interest as Elizabeth stirred her black coffee—just as Nick had said.

"Joe not only saved my life, but I thought of him as a father," she reasoned, trying to connect some of the facts. "And, don't forget, I saw a body right after the murder. That should have curled my toes, but it didn't."

"Did your reaction to the crime scene make you feel uncomfortable?"

"No." Elizabeth shook her head. "Just the opposite. The details fascinated me. Even having known Thelma, I was able to leave my personal feelings on the other side of the door when I went in to question Joe. Don't you think maintaining that kind of objectivity goes beyond anything I could have read in some magazine or seen on a talk show?''

"Yes, I do." Mary sat quietly and waited.

"Then there's the small matter of Nick. I feel like I've had some kind of past with him, not to mention...his house."

"What about his house?"

Elizabeth couldn't stop talking because every word that tumbled from her lips brought her a little closer to freedom. "The moment I walked through the front door, I sensed an eerie communication, a connection of some kind. It whispered secrets in my ear, then nudged me from room to room, baiting me with glimpses of my past."

"Were these images good or bad?"

"Most were happy. But I found a teddy bear in the back of a closet and immediately remembered seeing Nick in my hospital room. He'd been devastated, and the feeling of sorrow I experienced was tremendous. But I don't think this was when I was hospitalized after my accident."

"Why not?"

Elizabeth shrugged. "Just a feeling, I guess."

"Think back and try to recall every detail," Dr. Franklin suggested.

She closed her eyes and concentrated. "No, it wasn't just a hunch." Her lashes flew open. "I remember running my fingers through my hair."

"Why is that important?"

Already on edge, Elizabeth had to wait while the waitress freshened their coffee. After offering a stiff, "Thank you," she leaned forward and met Mary's gaze. "My hair was short, Dr. Franklin."

Mary thought a minute. "I've never seen your hair short."

"Exactly."

Mary nodded slowly in agreement. "Let's face it—too many things don't add up. Elizabeth wouldn't have any reason to feel connected to Nick, much less his home. And from everything we know about her, she was a high school graduate with no medical training. Certainly nothing that could explain the clinical exchange you just shared with Joe." She took Elizabeth's hands in hers. "You need to sort this through, but I agree. You're not Elizabeth Gleason."

Elizabeth's breath caught in her chest. "Then who in God's name am I?"

Chapter 11

The well-worn bell above the diner's entrance let out an irritated clank as the door swung open. The moment Nick stepped inside, Elizabeth was relieved to see that the deep furrows between his brows and the harsh lines offsetting his mouth had softened. She smiled and raised her hand to catch his attention, then waved him over.

Mary turned. "Now there's one man who could help trace your identity," she suggested.

Even before he sat down beside Elizabeth, Nick reached out and tucked an errant curl behind her ear. At that very moment, he needed to touch her more than he needed to breathe. "Using my name in vain again, Doc?" His words were directed to Mary, but not his eyes. They were riveted to Elizabeth.

"Not and let you catch me at it," Mary vowed. "As far as I'm concerned, Detective, you really are one of Chicago's finest."

"You know the old saying," he teased. " 'Don't tell me, tell my boss.' "

The conversation screeched to an abrupt halt the second Elizabeth's spoon clinked against the inside of her cup....

Nick's gaze locked with Mary's.

Mary glanced from the black coffee back to Nick.

"In reference to what we discussed in the wee hours this morning—" his words were deliberate "—I finally got a chance to speak to Venucci."

Mary edged forward in her seat. "The guy down in fingerprints?"

"Yeah."

"I hope you found what you were looking for?"

"Thanks, Doc." Nick winked, tossing down several dollar bills. "This one's on me."

The inflection in his voice as he and Dr. Franklin played word games hadn't gone unnoticed. Elizabeth felt as if she'd pressed her nose against someone else's windowpane.

Wanting nothing more than to fold her in his arms, he took Elizabeth by the hand. "Let's go home."

"Thanks for all your help, Dr. Franklin." She slid from the booth. "I'll be in touch."

Mary relaxed against the back of the booth and smiled. "I'm sure you will."

Nick's gut was on fire. The caffeine buzz that had gotten him through the night had settled in the pit of his stomach. He popped an antacid in his mouth as he drove, and glanced sideways toward the woman seated next to him. She'd leaned her head back, her eyes closed. So damn vulnerable, he thought. Too fragile to have her world turned upside down one more time.

He saw her shudder and flipped up the heater a notch, even though he figured her chill was probably more emotional than physical. Just the same, he left the car running while he made one quick stop on the way home. He wasn't sure how to handle what he was about to do, but he felt he had to set the stage to make it right.

Elizabeth's mind was spinning. The endless night she'd spent at Nick's, experiencing one flashback after another, nearly put her over the edge. And now this. Joe wasn't who she'd thought him to be…and neither was she.

She braced herself the moment they pulled into the driveway and drove past the now barren lilac bushes. The house had waited for her return. Elizabeth could feel it. But, instead of the haunting veil of uncertainty she'd expected, a sense of peace settled over her.

Before Nick opened the car door, he grabbed the brown paper bag from the back seat, then battled a blast of bitter wind to usher Elizabeth inside. He set the sack on the coffee table before heading down the hall to hang up their jackets.

When he didn't return, Elizabeth stepped around the corner and found him. Moving beside him, she asked quietly, "Are you all right?"

"Sure." He stood there, staring, wondering how something so ordinary could be so significant. Two coats. Hanging side by side. In reality that's all they were. But, that's not what he saw. He saw his life, his dreams. Everything he ever wanted was in that closet. If he lived forever, he could never ask for more.

"Nick?"

When he turned to face Elizabeth, he noticed she'd hugged both arms to her chest, so he closed the door and led her into the living room. "Are you cold?"

"A little."

"How about a fire?" he suggested.

"I'd like that." Silently repeating his question and her

answer, not once, but twice, a smile tugged the corners of Elizabeth's mouth. There was something so familiar about this, but more than that, right now she was certain that she'd *always* had a "thing" for roaring fires and...

"Champagne?"

That was it. Fascinated, she watched him pull out the long, slender bottle he'd bought on the way home. "You took the word right out of my mouth," she murmured under her breath.

Nick spotted the unmistakable gleam of recognition in her eyes and took advantage of the moment to try to prod her memory further. "I'll start the fire. You get the glasses." He stood very still, waiting to see what she would do.

Elizabeth walked straight to the dry sink in the far corner of the living room. She bent down, opened the leaded glass door that concealed a neat row of delicate stemware, and retrieved two.

Nick didn't move.

She straightened, holding one in each hand, then hesitated, glancing bewilderedly from the glasses to the cabinet.

Nick didn't breathe.

As she turned and lifted her gaze, he felt the blood rush through his veins like a runaway river. Pulse pounding. Chest aching. Nick watched her carefree expression crumble into confusion. He closed the distance between them only to discover her beautiful, *hazel* eyes brimming with tears.

"Help me," she whispered.

Taking the glasses from her, he laid them aside. "I will," he promised, pulling her into his arms. Heart to heart, they stood together. He held her. He loved her. He knew her.

"Wait here." As promised, he started a fire, then retrieved both glasses and the bottle. He unceremoniously popped the cork and filled each glass. Handing Elizabeth hers, he set his on the end table, sat down on the over-stuffed chair that faced the fireplace and settled her on his lap.

"Do you remember," he began in a slow, husky tone, his lips brushing her ear, "the December night we walked along the lake nearly four years ago?"

Elizabeth shook her head, barely able to breathe.

"Close your eyes and think back." His voice stayed low and soothing, willing her to relax. "The sky was clear as a bell. And it was cold. Really cold. We had a snowball fight and you made the most beautiful snow angel I've ever seen. Lying there together, dusted in white, we looked up at the heavens—"

"And the sky glowed." Elizabeth began to relax. "The stars, the light."

Nick offered a silent thank you. "Yes. Do you remember what we saw?"

"The Orion nebula." She opened her eyes and searched his face.

"Yeah. Now think back again," he coaxed. "Do you remember the hot summer afternoon we spent on the beach? Not just an ordinary day. A special one." He watched carefully, hoping for some hint of recognition.

He tried again. "Listen to my description and try to visualize everything I say. It was June. Remember how blue the sky was? Not a cloud in sight. Feel the warm breeze against your skin, the sand between your toes. You were wearing a hot pink bathing suit and insisted we sit under your huge blue-and-white umbrella for shade."

Elizabeth angled her finger in his direction. "You put champagne in our thermos."

"Yes." Nick grinned. "We listened to your favorite tape while watching the sunset."

"Kenny G," she responded, suddenly eager to take over. "For a few minutes, the sun looked like a huge ball of flames, slipping past the horizon to hide beneath the water. You lit a fire. I remember the way it crackled and hissed and the cool breeze off the lake that carried its sweet aroma back to us."

"Do you remember what happened when I poured your last drink?" He watched her face light up.

Elizabeth gasped. "I found a diamond ring in my glass." Eyes wide, her hand came up to her throat. "You slipped it on my finger...."

Never breaking eye contact, he pretended to slide a ring on the third finger of her left hand.

"...and I proposed," he finished, fighting to keep from selfishly blurting out every detail. But, he knew walking her through these memories one step at a time would lessen the shock.

"Now, do you remember a beautiful autumn day, three years ago?" he continued. "Let your mind's eye see the orange and red leaves scattered across the sidewalk in front of the church. Feel the hint of frost in the air."

Her trembling fingers made their way to her lips, but she couldn't speak.

"You wore a beautiful, beaded ivory gown and carried a bouquet of gardenias. Remember their sweet fragrance as we stood together, side by side, vowing—"

"Until death do us part," she whispered.

Nick kissed the warm tears from her cheeks. Resting his forehead against hers, he sighed, "Welcome home, Dani."

"What did you say?" Elizabeth eased back and searched his face. The memory of those haunting, blue eyes had gotten her through life on the street. Given her hope when there was none. Offered strength when all she'd wanted to do was give up.

And now, as she searched them for answers, all she saw was the truth. The only truth there ever could have been. The walls seemed to be closer than they'd been just minutes before. The fire warmer. She forced herself to focus on Nick.

"You don't know how long I've waited, how hard I've prayed," he confided, his voice breaking slightly. "Welcome home, Dani." This time the enunciation was clear and concise.

"My husband?" she murmured.

Nick cupped her face in his hands and planted tender kisses on her cheeks and eyelids, the corners of her mouth and the tip of her chin, but his elation was cut short when he pulled away and saw Dani's hand slip down to her tummy. He looked away quickly, then took a deep breath and faced her.

"Do you remember the stormy summer night you spent in the hospital?"

"The teddy bear in the closet." Dani bit her lip as new tears began falling. "We lost our baby, didn't we?"

Nick nodded.

She wrapped her arms around his neck. "Hold me."

"Always and forever," he promised.

"My God, how long have you known?"

"I wasn't really sure until this morning." He pulled her closer. "Don't worry, love. We'll piece it all together."

For a moment Nick simply held her. In his head, he knew that through some twist of fate the woman he'd come to know as Elizabeth was really Dani. But, in his heart, the reality of actually being able to hold his wife again was almost too much to bear.

His wife. Even the words were sacred. Every prayer he'd

said had been answered. And because of that, every promise he'd made would be kept.

Her face was a little too pale for his liking. He set their glasses aside and rubbed her hands briskly between his. "Let's put the champagne on ice for later. Why don't you go stretch out on the love seat while I revive the fire and make you some hot tea." As he stood and helped her up, Dani grabbed him by the arm.

"Earl Grey?"

Nick nodded, meeting her questioning gaze. "I saved it."

"Why?" she asked, barely able to steady her voice. "You never liked it."

"But you did."

Swallowing the sob that rose in her throat, Elizabeth offered a shaky smile and sat down. She watched him rearrange the logs, sending sparks flying up the chimney, before heading toward the kitchen. She wiped away tears that had spilled down both cheeks and closed her eyes. For what it was worth, release held its own kind of comfort.

By the time Nick returned and handed her the steamy mug, he found she'd pulled herself together. Strength had always been Dani's strong suit. Thank God, some things never changed.

"Ummm," she sighed after taking a sip. "I'd forgotten how good this is."

He sat next to her. "I know this must be difficult for you," he started.

Elizabeth leveled her gaze. "Nick, are you sure that I'm your wife? That you're not just wishing it to be true, and maybe I'm just close enough to make it seem possible?"

"Yes, I'm sure." Because he understood her apprehension, his answer left no room for doubt. "We used fingerprints to confirm your identity."

"Where did you get my fingerprints?"

"Remember that glass of water you got for me last night?"

Elizabeth nodded.

"The boys in the lab put through a rush."

"And, you're sure?" she repeated.

"Positive." He knew her frame of mind was fragile, at best. She would need time to adjust and get reacquainted with her life—and him. To ease that transition period, he'd move heaven and earth to make her feel as safe and secure as possible. "I had them double-check."

"I see." She sipped her tea thoughtfully. "Did I have a career?"

Nick answered her with a question. "Do you remember the night we met? It was late November. Cold and foggy. I'd just brought a doper who was high into ER. Tall and wiry with red hair and an attitude to match. Put up one helluva fight before we got there."

Elizabeth grabbed her sweater sleeve and yanked it up, exposing the faint scar on her forearm. "This wasn't a result of the accident. That man attacked me with a scalpel he grabbed from the tray," she looked into Nick's face, "and you tackled him. When you wrestled it out of his hand...you broke his thumb."

"Right." He waited a beat. "Do you remember why you were there?"

Without a second thought, she answered, "I was working the graveyard shift."

He watched her eyes widen.

"I was a doctor?"

The surprise in her voice made him smile. "You *are* a doctor," he corrected. "The best."

"So that's why my reaction to seeing Thelma's body confused me."

"Exactly."

She sat up a little straighter. "My curiosity bothered me because I'd known her. She was so sweet and kind, and being more interested than repulsed when I looked at her worried me."

"That's because you were always so thorough, had to have all the answers."

"I was really good?" She felt a smile tug her lips.

"You *are* great."

Elizabeth sipped her tea. "Where do we go from here?"

Nick steepled both elbows on his knees. "Tell me what else you remember."

She closed her eyes for a moment and took a slow breath. "A huge bouquet of lilacs in a tall crystal vase."

He slipped a throw pillow behind her back and pulled her feet into his lap before answering. "I brought you lilacs whenever I could get them because they were your favorites. And the vase was a wedding present—" he grinned "—believe it or not, from O'Malley."

"Maureen must have picked it out," she concluded absently.

Nick could see the significance of rattling off O'Malley's wife's name hadn't registered with Dani.

She pointed toward the dining room. "When I looked at the rose-patterned china, it brought to mind the name Janette."

"She was your aunt—"

Elizabeth sucked in her breath. "Who died right after we were married. A beautiful woman with dark hair, blue eyes and the most wonderful sense of humor in the world. She was like a second mother to me, and I loved her with all my heart."

Nick nodded.

"She made that exquisite quilt in the bedroom, didn't she?"

"Uh-huh. It was always your favorite."

Sadness washed over Elizabeth. "So was she."

"I know. That's why I left it on the bed. I'd have done anything to keep you close. Anything."

She reached for his hand. Such tenderness. Such strength. Such a wonderful man.

The peaceful expression on Dani's face pleased Nick. "What else?"

"I had a flashback of the copper pots and the window seat."

He smiled. "So you recognized the kitchen?"

"Yes."

When she blushed like a schoolgirl, Nick asked, "Was there something else about that room?"

"Maybe you can tell me." Her cheeks felt as if they were on fire. "Should I remember something *special* about the table?"

Nick nearly choked. "Well, I'll be damned."

"You may very well be," she retorted, trying to hide her embarrassment.

He just shook his head.

"What?" she asked, questioning whether or not she really wanted to know.

"This is all too weird," he admitted. "Wonderful, but weird."

She smiled in agreement. "So, what are we going to do about it?"

"Part of me wants to howl at the moon." At her giggle, he continued, "And, the rest of me wants to tie you up and never let you out of my sight again."

Needing the comic relief, she teased, "Didn't we do that once?"

Now, it was Nick's turn to laugh. "Actually it was twice, but who's counting."

Dani gasped so hard, he had to pat her on the back.

"Relax, I was just kidding," he assured her.

"You'd better be."

Her smile enchanted him. "But, can you be sure?"

"About some things I can." She knew what he was really asking.

"And others?" He studied the sudden faraway look in her eyes.

She sighed and shrugged.

"They'll come, sweetheart. They really will."

"I suppose Dr. Franklin could help us," she began, "but right now, I'd just like to be with you, if that's all right?"

"Are you kidding?" He settled back, his tone serious. "I could spend every hour of every day right here with you."

His sweet declaration touched her. "I know we've got a lot to sort through, but I need some time to catch my breath."

"Talk about an understatement." He took her hand. "I look at you now, and you're not Elizabeth anymore. All I see is Dani."

She angled her head. "Excuse me?"

"You know, the peculiar little things you do," he began, pointing toward the door. "Like, always taking your shoes off when you come in."

Dani shrugged. "I'm sure lots of people do that."

"Kick out of them, maybe, but not line the damn things up—toes flush against the wall—like you do."

Checking, Dani glanced over her shoulder and shrugged. "So, I'm neat."

"How about the way you tuck your legs in the seat of the chair when you sit."

"It's comfy, Nick." She hated it when he beat around the bush like this. "What's your point?"

"A few similarities between the woman I called Elizabeth and you sneaked past my defenses, but I suppressed so many. It took all my strength not to compare the two of you, and by doing that I refused to recognize what was right in front of my face.

"Namely, my own wife."

The blame in his voice broke Dani's heart. "Not seeing me in Elizabeth wasn't your fault," she assured him. "As it was, your psyche probably had to work overtime to stay one step ahead," she gave his hand a squeeze. "To protect you."

He shook his head and gazed into the fire. "Maybe, but I'm a police officer. A trained observer."

She pulled free and placed her palm over his heart and felt the strong, steady beat beneath her fingers. When he turned to face her, she told him quietly, "But this was your life, not your job. There's a big difference."

Lifting her hand to his lips Nick feathered a kiss in her palm. "You're right."

She smiled at the warmth of his lips on her skin. As much as she wanted to lose herself in him, she needed answers more. "Tell me what happened. Why you thought I was dead."

Nick took a deep breath. "You'd been at your sister's—"

"My sister." Dani brightened. "Honey blond hair…big brown eyes…Amy."

Nick nodded. "I called her from the office before I met you at Maggie's and broke the good news to her as gently as possible under the circumstances. I explained as much as I could and told her you'd call her later."

"All right," Dani agreed, still desperate for information.

She'd reacquaint herself with Amy soon enough. Right now, she and Nick needed to sort through all their confusion.

"It was the Monday after the July Fourth weekend. You were supposed to be driving back from Springfield when I received a phone call." Nick momentarily blocked the horror but, for the first time, he was finally able to face it.

"They said your car had collided with a gas truck and had burst into flames upon impact."

Suddenly aware of his shallow breathing, Elizabeth, no! *Dani,* steadied his shaking hands in hers. Even with her seated right by his side, she could see how quickly his anguish resurfaced. She moved into his arms and returned some of the comfort he'd shown her.

He held her close and inhaled her familiar scent, making sure she was real, before he continued, "What was left of—" he cleared his throat "—the body they found in your car was burned beyond recognition. But, this—" he pulled the chain over his head and handed her the gold band "—survived the fire."

Her hands were shaking so badly she could barely unhook the clasp and slip the ring off the chain. When she checked the inscription, her eyes met Nick's.

Feeling as though his chest would burst, Nick slipped the ring back onto her finger—where it belonged—and continued quietly, "Since you were expected back around the time of the accident, and we found your wedding ring in the car, there wasn't any reason to believe that woman wasn't you."

Dani shook her head. "So, who in God's name was in my car?"

"I don't know." Finding Dani alive posed a new mystery and Nick's mind was already sifting through the facts. "But, I'm sure as hell going to find out."

"I guess that brings us back full circle. That woman wasn't me and I wasn't Elizabeth. Why did you think that was my name in the first place?"

Nick stood, needing to pace off some of his anxiety. "When I hit you, the purse you were carrying contained Elizabeth Gleason's ID. You two were approximately the same age and weight and, at the time of the accident, an eyewitness identified you as Elizabeth Gleason."

"In other words, you did the best you could," she assured him. "After all, from what I've read, Elizabeth's story pretty much fit the profile of a homeless person. She'd been missing since Stewart died in the fire that destroyed their home. That's definitely the type of trauma that could drive a woman to live on the street."

"Maybe, but then, the nature of that fire was questionable."

She loved to watch him work. Wheels were already turning in that cop mind of his. Rolling over facts on mental three-by-five inch cards. Weighing every angle. His mind stashed details, regardless of their immediate significance. One at a time, they were methodically filed away.

"I'm sure you'll figure it out, Nick." She offered him a confident smile. "You always do."

His grin was genuine. "I love to hear you say that word."

Dani stood and wrapped her arms around his neck. The memories were working their way to the surface faster than she thought possible. "What word is that?"

"Always," he repeated, gently placing a kiss on the tip of her nose. "That tells me you remember."

Dani tugged his ponytail. "Well, I don't recall this."

"And?"

"And," she hedged, ignoring his male ego, "is that my earring?"

Nick's eyebrow shot up, as he touched the small, gold stud. "Do you remember when I gave you these?"

She thought a moment, then rattled off excitedly. "The New Year's Eve after we met. The Penthouse Grill. A candlelight dinner for two."

Her joy was contagious. "You've really had quite a breakthrough, lady."

Her stomach growled, causing Nick to realize it was late afternoon, and they hadn't eaten since breakfast. "You must be starving." He sat her down on the love seat, propping up her feet and plumping the toss pillow behind her head. "Enjoy the fire and leave the rest to me."

He disappeared into the kitchen only to stick his head back around the corner. "So..." He held up his ponytail.

She shrugged.

"And..." He touched his earlobe.

She laughed. "I love them."

Twenty minutes later, Nick found her dozing comfortably in the now-darkened living room. The gentle glow of the fire played off the angles and planes of her face. Concerned about the stress she'd been under, Nick frowned, wondering if he should let her sleep. Content to simply lean against the doorway and watch her, he waited a few more minutes before whispering, "Hey, pretty lady."

It took a moment for Dani's eyes to focus on her dimly lit surroundings...and Nick. Home, she thought with a smile, then closed her eyes again.

Nick kneeled down and feathered kisses at both corners of her mouth. She wiggled her nose in response and turned onto her side, facing him. "Are you hungry?" he asked.

Stretching, she yawned as her eyes fluttered open.

"Starved. What's for dinner?"

"Two of your favorites." He helped her to her feet, then led her to the blanket he'd spread in front of the fireplace.

He pointed to the chilled bucket of champagne. "Sit and pour. I'll be right back."

On his way to the kitchen, she watched him light the assortment of candles scattered around the room.

He turned back and called over one shoulder. "Ambience, remember? I nearly blew my cover trying to impress you."

"Lucky for you, it worked." She filled the glasses and was still grinning when he came back and placed a wooden serving tray on the floor between them.

She picked up one of the bowls, then looked at Nick. "Macaroni and cheese?" she squealed.

He handed her a spoon. "Runny—just the way you like it."

"This is sooo wonderful," she managed to say between bites. She examined her plate and, without peeking, guessed, "Not peanut butter and banana."

Nick grinned. "White bread. No crust."

She sampled one. "Oh God, I can't believe how good these are."

This was the "Dani" Nick remembered. Watching her now, he knew why he'd have given his life for hers, no questions asked. Why he'd never been able to walk to the front of the grave with her name on it. Why, on that hot July afternoon, he hadn't felt their bond being severed the moment the coroner projected she took her last breath. He looked at her again and felt his heart shift. This was exactly why.

After Dani's death, he'd heard the talk at work. At the hospital. Words like *denial* and *grief* spoken behind his back. Whispers that he was out of control—out of his mind.

But, none of those people knew. He was the only one who did. And, for the first time in his life, he hadn't followed his gut instinct. Never again, he vowed silently. Never again.

She pointed to his plate and grinned sheepishly. "They really are a lot smaller with the edges cut off."

He handed her the uneaten half of his sandwich and watched with great pleasure as she wolfed it down. "That's because they're girlie sandwiches," he teased, enjoying the familiar arch of her brow.

"As opposed to what? Raw meat?" she returned.

Nick's smile was easy. "Something like that." He stacked the dishes to one side and helped her to her feet. The contentment in her eyes tugged at his heart. "It's late. Let's go to bed." He wrapped his arm around her waist and smiled when she did the same. Arm in arm, they walked down the hallway.

Moving in sync, they talked and laughed, sidestepping one another as they got ready for bed. He tossed her clothes in the hamper while she brushed her teeth. She turned down the bed while he pulled on boxer shorts. Lights out and snuggled beneath the covers, Dani asked, "I must look different now, don't I?"

Nick grinned in the dark, wondering if this was one of those damned-if-you-do, damned-if-you-don't questions. "Yes."

"Better?" she asked quickly, while she still had the nerve.

"You were beautiful then, and you're beautiful now," he answered truthfully. "I was attracted to you twice, remember?"

Dani propped herself up on one elbow. "Did I have short hair before?"

His whole body ached for rest, but he couldn't deny her. If she wanted, he'd talk until dawn. "Why? Do you remember that?"

"No, but in one of my flashbacks I swore it was just about to here." She ran her finger along the base of his ponytail.

"Yes, it was always short." He skimmed the length of her silky hair with his hand. "But this is really nice."

Satisfied by the husky sincerity in his voice, she lay back down. When his strong arms wrapped around her, she sighed, losing her battle with exhaustion. "Thank you so much for finding me," she murmured.

Nick closed his eyes. Gratitude? Was that all she felt for him? Had he been a fool to assume she'd still love him? He listened to the sound of her even breathing and relived every agonizing night he'd spent alone in his bed.

Tonight, his wife was really back, but nothing had changed. For the first time in over two years, Nick Davis was able to whisper, "I love you, Dani," but this time was just like all the rest. No one answered.

The cigarette fell from his lips and scorched the scarred linoleum before he stopped reading long enough to grind it out.

LOCAL DOCTOR FOUND ALIVE AND VICTIM OF AMNESIA

CHICAGO (AP)—Dr. Danielle Davis, age 33, thought dead in a fiery collision that occurred over two years ago, was discovered alive and running a soup kitchen on Chicago's lower south side. Ironically, the discovery was made by Nick Davis, a detective for the Chicago Police Department, and the husband of Dr. Davis. A police department source stated that the identification was a result of a fingerprint comparison request made by Detective Davis early yesterday morning. When contacted, Davis refused to divulge details, but stated that his wife had been suffering from amnesia and living under the identity of Elizabeth Gleason.

Lieutenant O'Malley stated that Dr. Davis was unable to shed any light on the new mystery of who died in her vehicle, but is expected to regain the balance of her memory in the near future. The Chicago Police Department is reopening the investigation of the traffic accident that claimed the life of the now unknown woman driving Davis's car and John Stevens, the driver of the Sonoil tanker.

He wadded up the newspaper and crammed it into the garbage can. Grabbing his matches, he struck one and watched in fascination as the flame burned down, meeting his fingertips, testing his will. Then and only then, did he toss it on the pyre. "Say goodbye, Dr. Danielle Davis. You should have stayed dead."

Chapter 12

Nick woke early. With too much on his mind to sleep, he quietly slipped out of bed and pulled on his jeans. Lying next to Dani last night had been a disturbing combination of heaven and hell. As he watched her now, still sleeping like an angel, his heart shifted. Surely to God they'd have a second chance. Running a finger down her warm cheek, he wondered how he could live through losing her again.

Backing quietly out of the bedroom, he headed for the kitchen, grabbing the dirty dishes off the living room floor on his way. His mind slowly replayed the events of the past few weeks while he cleaned up. Something still nagged at him, but what? Maybe just a detail. Possibly a stray fact. One loose end. He shrugged off his impatience, knowing whatever was bothering him would surface eventually.

Elizabeth awoke grinning and patted the bed next to her. Cold. Her smile faded as she rolled over on her side and hugged the pillow to her middle...

What if her memories of yesterday had only been a dream? Some kind of subconscious wish her heart had made. What if *this* was really yesterday morning and Nick had never called her to the station? What if he had never told her she was Dani?

She swallowed hard, trying to control the sick feeling that overwhelmed her. "Think logically," she pleaded. Nick was a man with a past, but his wife was dead. She was a woman whose history was sketchy, at best, but she was alive. Together they could concentrate on filling the void in one another's lives. Maybe that alone would be enough to see them through, regardless of who she was.

"Bull." She sat straight up in bed and heaved her pillow across the room. When panic threatened to take over, she hurried to the living room, searching for the courage to confront her worst nightmare. No blanket. No champagne bucket. No dishes. Her heart hammered against her ribs.

"I thought I heard you."

She spun around at the sound of Nick's voice. Freshly showered and shaved, he smelled of soap and shampoo. Standing there bare chested, wet hair hanging to his shoulders, his presence obliterated any hope of an attention span longer than a sigh.

When she just stood there staring, he asked, "Are you all right?"

She tore her gaze from his pale blue eyes and pointed toward the floor. "The picnic?"

"All taken care of." Giving in to the urge to touch her, he ran his fingertip the length of her arm. He couldn't help but wonder if things would ever be the same between them.

"Then yesterday wasn't a dream—last night really happened—and today really is today, not yesterday," she babbled, crisscrossing her fingers for emphasis.

Nick stood there a beat, digesting what she'd asked. "No it wasn't. Yes it did. And, yes it is." His low laugh softened the lines of concern and confusion on Dani's face. He took her by the hand and led her into the kitchen. "Come with me."

Dani sat down opposite the window seat as Nick filled her cup with coffee and topped off his. Unable to get enough of her, he sat down and patted her hand. "I was afraid the phone woke you."

Dani shook her head. "Who called?"

"Dr. Franklin. The press already got wind of your story." Nick took a sip of coffee. "She wanted to forewarn you before you read it in this morning's paper."

"If nothing else, I guess it will save a lot of repetitious explaining." The thought of cultivating old friendships brought a wistful smile to her lips.

"Dr. Franklin also said she'd like you to run by her office some time today."

Dani grinned. "She must have been reading my mind. I wanted to talk to her about a few things anyway."

Nick leaned back in his chair. Desperate to pin her down and ask exactly how she felt about him but not wanting to push, he asked, "How does it feel to be back?"

"Too good to put into words," she admitted with a sigh. Glancing out the bow window, the brilliant autumn colors in the backyard caught her attention, so she moved to take a closer look. Resting one knee on the cushion of the window seat, she pointed. "Have those beautiful oaks always been there? I don't remember them."

Pleased that she at least seemed genuinely happy to be home, Nick shook his head. "You wouldn't. I planted them two years ago in September."

The hollow ring to his voice caused her to turn and face him.

Nick cleared his throat. "One for you and one for the baby."

She fought to control her swirling emotions as she moved to his side. Without a word, she cradled his head to her breast and stroked his damp hair. "You are magnificent."

Accepting her comfort, Nick wrapped his arms around her waist. Every beat of her heart brought him a little closer to being whole again. Surely that wouldn't be taken from him twice in one lifetime. "You're too kind."

She planted a kiss on top of his head, then sat back down. "We've got a lot to discuss, don't we?"

"That we do, love." He nodded, then smiled at the sweet familiar sound of her impatience.

"Like my work." She began, counting down each subsequent idea on her fingers. "Will I continue with my practice? What about the soup kitchen? The hospital? How am I—"

He leaned across the table and silenced her with a slow deliberate kiss, intended to sidetrack her—

"Dammit, Dani," he murmured, his lips never leaving hers.

—not derail him.

Her lips curled into a smile beneath his. "Trying to shut me up?" She punctuated her point by tracing his mouth with the tip of her tongue.

He was sure he could speak, but nodded anyway—just in case.

"Okay, you win." She pulled away playfully, then teased, "Satisfied?"

"Not exactly," he groaned. Standing, he grabbed the front of her nightshirt and pulled her to her feet. Slowly, very slowly, he eased her closer until their bodies were pressed together. His fingers wandered the expanse of her back, finding her slender waist and traveling beyond. Her eyes widened and her body trembled when he cupped her buttocks and pressed her center to his.

Mesmerized, she couldn't look away. His eyes stayed open as he slid his mouth over hers. Gently gliding and savoring. Licking and tasting. What started out a gentle, coaxing kiss already had her pulse pounding. The buzz in her head grew louder until she barely recognized her own throaty moan as he slipped his tongue between her lips.

He had thought about this for hours. *This* was exactly why he'd been wide awake before daybreak. He wanted his wife back—in every way. But he had to back off. As *grateful* as Dani had been to be home, she'd never said she loved him.

Even now, the pleasure from feeling her shudder or the arch of her back as she molded herself to him wouldn't justify his actions. Dani desperately needed to rest and decide if what she felt for Nick went beyond gratitude. Besides, something in the forefront of his mind kept warning him to keep a clear head.

A lifetime of street smarts and fifteen years of police work had taught him how to teeter dangerously on the edge of control. Balancing there, until his mind was reeling with visions of Dani, he took just a little bit more for himself before pulling back. He supported her by the shoulders until her lashes fluttered open and her eyes focused again.

"Now I'm satisfied," he lied.

Her legs managed one wobbly step backward as she found her chair. "Well, good," she told him, barely able to breathe.

Nick leaned against the refrigerator. He had to lock his jaw and clench both fists to keep from carrying her off to bed. A little distance, he decided, would do them both good. Dani needed some time to readjust and he needed to scratch the itch he'd developed trying to wrap up the murder investigations. "I'm going to run to the station for a little while. I've got to sort through a few things."

She might still be feeling a bit light-headed, but there was no way she could miss that cop look in his eyes. "What's got you bugged, Davis?"

"Nothing." The arch of her brow told Nick he wasn't off the hook, so he leveled with her. "I'm not sure yet."

She felt the color drain from her face, knowing she had to ask the one question that could destroy her future. If he wasn't positive she was Dani, she needed to know, right now. And, if he was certain she was Dani, but wasn't equally as sure that he wanted her back in his life, she had to be told that, too. Watching his expression carefully, she held her breath and prayed. "Are you having second thoughts about my identity?"

"Relax, sweetheart, fingerprints don't lie." Steadier now, he took her hands in his. "You are, and always have been Dani."

Searching his handsome face for doubt, she found none—at least about her identity. Maybe it was just as simple as that.

"Why don't you just relax around the house today."

Dani shook her head. "I want to go down to the kitchen—"

"No." She flinched at his abrupt tone, so Nick tempered his voice before continuing, "At least not today. You've been through way too much. Besides, I called the kitchen first thing this morning and checked—the volunteer schedule is filled through next week."

"But—"

"They said everything is fine. You had already pre-planned the meals and the groceries have been taken care of. So there's no reason whatsoever for you to go. You can just stay here and rest, at least a couple of days. Please?"

She may not remember everything about Nick Davis yet, but she could certainly tell when he was preoccupied with work. Which he was. Not to mention what it cost him to say please. Which he had. "On one condition," she bargained.

He smiled, knowing damned good and well she wouldn't give up without attempting some kind of compromise. "Name it."

"I'll just run down there and pick up my clothes, then come right home." She arched one brow and offered her most innocent smile.

Nick leaned down and whispered in her ear, "Forget it. Those were Elizabeth's clothes, not yours." Before she could start, he reached into his jeans pocket and grabbed his billfold. Rifling through it, he found what he was looking for and tossed her a credit card. "Buy yourself some new ones, Mrs. Davis."

"So, why am I remembering every aspect of my life except what happened to me the day I was driving home?" Dani asked Dr. Franklin. She looked around the beautifully decorated office, grateful that she didn't feel any different sitting here today—as Dani, instead of Elizabeth.

Since the day she woke up in the hospital over a year ago, this haven had been the only constant in her life. She looked across the familiar mahogany desk at the woman who had become her mentor. Dr. Franklin had given her the courage to want to go on and the strength to follow through.

"Whatever happened to you that day was apparently very traumatic," Dr. Franklin began. "Our minds have a way of blocking painful memories to protect us."

"For how long?" Dani asked, desperate to put her life into perspective.

"That's hard to say." Dr. Franklin tapped her pen on the tablet for a moment, then met Dani's unwavering gaze. "I've been considering hypnosis."

Determined to find some answers, Dani nodded. "Let's do it."

Within minutes, Dr. Franklin had talked Dani into a state of total and complete relaxation. With very little prompting, Dani recalled visiting her sister and leaving Springfield late that Monday morning. She remembered her drive home as pleasant but, anxious to see Nick, she'd ignored his warning about taking a short cut through one of the seedier parts of Chicago.

She grabbed the arms of the chair and lunged forward. "My car! They hit my car!"

"Look into your rearview mirror and tell me who's behind you."

"A man is driving, and the passenger is a woman. She's waving me over."

"What do they look like?"

"He's fair. She has dark hair. I'm pulling to the curb and they're right behind me."

"What are they doing now?"

"They're both getting out and walking toward me."

"What are you doing?"

"I'm rolling down my window and..."

"And?"

"And, he tapped me on the shoulder, but the sun's so bright, I have to shade my eyes."

"Take a deep breath. Now, look up at the man."

Dani flinched, then grabbed her cheek. "He hit me."

"Dani, it's all right. You're safe here with me. Just try to tell me everything."

"No! No!" She pulled back. "He won't quit." She wiped her lip as if she were bleeding. "He's opening my door. Stop! What do you want? He's pulling me out." Dani violently shook her head. "Don't, please don't hurt me." She reached out, grasping at air, then stared at her fist.

"What's in your hand?"

"Something from the woman."

"What is it? Look at it, Dani."

Dani wrinkled her brow. "A leather strap. I'm not sure."

"Take your time."

"Wait," Dani nodded. "It's her purse...but it can't be."

"Why not?"

"Because it's mine. It's the brown one I've always had. The one with my ID in it. I've got it away from her—oh, no." Dani pulled back.

"What now?"

"He's got a gun." She covered her face with both arms. "He hit me across the face with it. I'm falling. I hit my head on something hard. God, it hurts."

"Are they gone?"

"No. The woman grabbed my hand. My ring. Please don't take my wedding ring." Her breathing was ragged as she slumped down in the chair. "The darkness feels so good. No more pain. But wait! I don't want to die...I don't want to die..."

"I don't give a damn what it takes, I want the tombstone off that grave today," Nick shouted. "I already told your assistant, there's been a mistake. My wife is alive." He paused, uncurling his fist. "Yes, I'm positive." He slammed his fist down on the desk and ordered, through gritted teeth, "Just do it."

The thought of Dani's name being on the grave marker another day was more than he could bear. With the phone call to the monument company out of the way, Nick mentally checked off his first order of business and prepared to focus all his attention on the investigation.

His office was scattered with files and folders. More so than usual. Something wasn't coming together on this case and he was damn sure going to find out exactly what that something was.

He dug out all the information he had on Elizabeth Gleason and found some interesting handwritten notes scribbled in the margin of the detective's report:

Blanche Kent Interview (nosy next-door neighbor)
Re: Residential fire at 1122 West Virginia Ave.
Occupants: Stewart and Elizabeth Gleason
1.Gleasons don't get along.
2.Positive Mrs. Gleason has a boyfriend.
3.Description of boyfriend:
Around 40 years old
6' to 6'2"
Medium build—but muscular
Light to sandy hair—over the collar
Blue eyes
Slight limp
Always drives fancy cars—but never the same one?
4.Boyfriend ticked Kent woman off by tossing cigarette butts, Marlboro to be exact, in her yard (No, Mrs. Kent, that's not a felony!)

Something was inching its way to the front of Nick's mind—just not fast enough to suit him. Tired of waiting, he decided to kick his thoughts into gear by using his bulletin board.

He tacked up a sheet of paper marked JOE—STALKER in the center. Beneath that he lined up the seven victims, one identified as Thelma and the remainder listed as Jane Does one to six. He made a notation beneath each of these: Terminally Ill.

One sheet was added for Elizabeth Gleason and another for Elizabeth Gleason's Boyfriend. Nick paced back and forth. He must have busted hundreds of dirtbags fitting that description, but something bugged him about this guy.

Dani was added to the puzzle. The only disturbing memory she'd confided to him was the one about the man she'd seen through a window who had hurt her. What kind of window would she be facing? So close someone could reach through and hurt her? And where was the glass?

He posted a sheet labeled Woman Who Died in Dani's Car. Nick felt a twinge knowing that woman had been buried in Dani's grave, and his reluctant visits to the cemetery flashed through his mind. "Son of a—" Elizabeth Gleason's boyfriend matched the description of the man at Dani's grave—right down to the damn cigarette butts and the limp. Nick scribbled another card entitled Man at the Cemetery.

He racked his brain for details of everything significant that had happened over the past few weeks and one thing came to mind that bothered him. Chico insisted Dani was being followed the night he walked her home. By Joe? After all, he was The Stalker.

Nick shook his head. She didn't fit the profile of his victims. Besides, Joe liked Dani. Hell, if he'd have wanted to, he could have killed her the first time he found her. But he didn't. Instead, he saved her life. He wouldn't turn around and murder her after that.

So, if Joe wasn't following Dani that night, who was? And why? Nick scribbled Dani's Stalker on another piece of paper and his jaw clenched when he pinned it to the board. He couldn't help but wonder where the hell this guy was now.

Thank God he'd steered Dani away from the soup kitchen today. He didn't want her anywhere near that place, without him.

"I couldn't wait to tell you about Dani's breakthrough this afternoon," Dr. Franklin told Nick. "She came in here so determined to find out what happened that I hypnotised her."

He began to pace. "And that worked?"

"Like a charm. She remembered what happened when she was driving home—"

The tumblers in Nick's mind clicked into place—an automobile window. "Carjacking."

"How did you know?"

"Something she told me a while back finally fell into place," he admitted.

"Did you know there was a woman accomplice?"

"No, but they work in teams to scam the victim. Most people will pull over for a nice-looking couple."

"Psychologically speaking, that's very clever on their part."

"Anything else?"

"Yes. You know the brown purse with Elizabeth's ID in it that Dani had when you found her?"

"What about it?"

"Dani grabbed it away from the woman in the struggle."

"I'll be damned."

"You and me both."

Nick slammed his hand down on the desk. "Elizabeth Gleason was one of the carjackers." He dropped into his chair. "She's the one who died in Dani's car—the body we buried."

"Exactly. Dani remembered the woman taking her wedding ring."

His blood ran cold. "I hate to cut you short, Doc, but I've got to go." He slammed down the receiver, knowing the pieces were falling into place almost faster than he could process them.

Desperate to get the facts in order, Nick counted them off one by one. "Dani's gas was syphoned so she'd be stranded. The person who did it followed her that night."

Too angry to sit, he stood. "An Officer Evans called Dani asking for me."

He pulled a roster from his desk drawer and scanned it for an Officer Evans. None listed.

"Shortly after Evans called, Dani heard someone downstairs." He began to pace. "I checked the door that night and it had been tampered with." He cursed the confines of his office. "Whoever broke in, called first to make sure I wasn't there." He blamed himself for staying away.

"This wasn't Joe. None of this matches the serial killer's MO." He sidestepped his opened drawer. "But Dani is definitely the target. So, what's the motive?" He kicked the drawer shut.

"For the past two and a half years, the only thing Dani's been involved in is the carjacking." He steepled his hands and concentrated. "That's got to be it. But that still doesn't explain the motive."

His mind turned over the details of the carjacking. "Dani was probably bumped and pulled over. The struggle ensued. Elizabeth took off in Dani's car, panicked and ran the red light. Her partner stayed behind to drive their car.

She hit the tanker—'' His voice trailed off. "That's it!''
He pounded his palm with his fist. "Accident or not, the
commission of a felony directly resulted in the tanker driver's death. The fact that the carjackers were committing a
crime at the time of the wreck changes the trucker's death
from accidental to murder. Whether or not Elizabeth's
partner was in the car is immaterial. He's still an accessory.
And he's after Dani because he's afraid she can identify
him.''

Nick ripped through Elizabeth's file and pulled out the
neighbor's complaint on her boyfriend—tall, early forties,
blond hair, slight limp, smoked Marlboros. "Son of a—''
The guy at the cemetery. The guy who couldn't take his
eyes off her at the shelter. "This bastard's been watching
her all along. Right under my nose.''

He unclenched his fist in order to dial home. With every
ring, he coaxed, "Come on, Dani. Be there.'' After fifteen
rings he hung up. "Dammit.''

He prowled his office, racking his brain. Where would
she go to shop—as if he'd really be able to figure that one
out. He shook his head. Catching her at home would be
his best bet.

Twenty phone calls later, his patience was shot. Not to
mention his telephone. The last time he'd slammed down
the receiver, he busted it.

If she didn't go home, where do you think she went?

Nick jumped up, grabbed his jacket and nearly tore his
office door off the hinges.

Dani had said good night to the last of the volunteers at
the soup kitchen and was upstairs packing when she heard
the noise. She cocked her head to one side and strained to
listen. Nothing specific. Just something unfamiliar. Like a
floor creaking underfoot. If this hadn't happened before,
she would have fluffed it off. Tonight, she wasn't about to

take any chances. Hopefully one of the others had simply forgotten something.

Closing her suitcase, she decided there was nothing she'd rather do than go home to her husband. Grabbing the bag, she turned out the light and headed downstairs.

That's when she saw him. Standing in the dimly lit dining room, a man's silhouette blocked the outside door. Dani gasped.

"I didn't mean to scare you," he said softly.

Dani's heart was pounding so hard it took her a moment to realize the volunteers probably just forgot to lock up when they left. She regained her composure and spoke in a calm, even tone. "I'm sorry. That door should have been locked." She kept her distance, but gestured around. "As you can see, the kitchen's closed, and I was just about to leave. We serve dinner between five and seven every evening."

The man didn't move. "I don't think I can wait another day."

The man's low, almost desperate tone caused Dani to hesitate. "Tell you what," she began, "I'll pack you some leftovers to go. How does that sound?"

"Very kind of you, Dr. Davis."

Halfway to the kitchen, Dani stopped, but the chill that slithered down her spine didn't. She spun around and asked, "How do you know my name?"

The man stepped toward her. "You're front page news."

Dani didn't like the turn this conversation had taken. "I'll just be a minute," she assured him. Suddenly frightened, Dani tried to convince herself he was harmless and hungry and probably had gotten her name from the newspaper.

But her instincts screamed for her to slip out the back door and verify the details later. If he was truly looking for food, the refrigerator was full. No harm done. If he was dangerous, at least she wouldn't be around to find out.

Flipping on the light, Dani entered the kitchen and saw a large, perfectly cut hole in the window over the sink. The bottom fell out of her stomach. She raced toward the back door, until a strong hand snaked out and grabbed her by the arm.

"Did I mention that I didn't come in through the front door, Danielle?"

The shrill ring of the phone diverted the man's attention long enough for her to snag the receiver...

Nick was running lights and sirens. He'd vowed to go with his instincts, and that was exactly what he was doing. A burning need to reach Dani had pushed him beyond reason. He'd dialed the soup kitchen's number, only able to unclench his jaw after someone picked up the phone.

Thank God, he'd found her. Within a split second, his muscles relaxed, the death grip he had on the steering wheel loosened.

"Dani—"

The bloodcurdling scream that followed drained every ounce of sanity from Nick's body. He punched the gas pedal to the floor. "Daaannniii!" he shouted, careering his car through the streets like a madman.

Nick grabbed his mike and radioed in. "Dispatch, L-57."

"L-57, go ahead."

"I have an assault in progress with a female complainant at the Maxwell Street soup kitchen. Do you show any vehicles available in sector thirty-four?"

"That's a negative, L-57, I show all vehicles 10-6 at an armed robbery with shots fired. I have a vehicle available in sector thirty-five. Do you want me to dispatch?"

"Dispatch them as backup. I'm closer. ETA five minutes." *Hold on, Dani. Just hold on.*

Dani's arm stung where the man had slapped the receiver from her hand. Right before he'd yanked the phone out of the wall, she'd heard Nick yelling her name. He had to be on his way. But how long would it take him? She had to stall until he got there.

As she rubbed her forearm, she examined the man carefully. Light hair. Blue eyes. Large frame. He seemed vaguely familiar, but she couldn't place him. "Look, I don't know who you are, but—"

"But you will eventually." He sneered. "You see, that's the problem."

Dani moved behind the chair. "What problem?"

"I read all about how your memory is coming back. To quote the paper, you'll 'regain the balance of your memory in the near future.'"

"Why does that concern you?" She racked her brain for possible weapons—a wooden spoon, a meat fork, a knife—if she was lucky enough to get the drawer open.

"Let's just say we met once before." He took a step in her direction.

"Well, I'm sure whatever happened between us can be left in the past. I'm ready to go on with my life." She gripped the back of the chair.

"Tsk. Tsk. Tsk." He shook his head. "I'm afraid it's not that simple."

As he lunged at her, Dani shoved the chair into his path and ran as fast as she could. She almost made it to the back door before he tackled her, sending both of them sprawling onto the hallway floor. Dani tried to struggle from underneath him, but he held her around the waist and roughly hauled her to her feet.

"Get up," he snarled.

Dani's mind flashed back to a man's voice. *"Get out,"* *he'd snarled.*

He dragged her back to the kitchen and slammed her down in a chair. Slipping a hand into his back pocket, he pulled out a set of handcuffs and dangled them in front of Dani's face.

"I'll bet you and that cop husband of yours have used these on more than one Saturday night," he said smirking.

Watching the perverted glint in his eyes as he twirled the metal cuffs on one finger, she cringed.

He yanked her arms behind her and anchored both wrists to the rungs on the chair. "Don't get your hopes up, sweetheart, this pair isn't fur lined."

His sadistic laugh filled the room, making Dani's flesh crawl. She prayed for Nick to hurry.

He flicked his finger across the top few buttons on her shirt. "Thanks to that damned phone call, I don't even have time to make this worth my while."

Dani called on every ounce of strength she had not to flinch under his repulsive touch. "Why are you doing this?" As she sat there and looked up at him, the ceiling light made her squint. The carjacking flashed through her mind like a bolt of lightning. "You," she whispered. *My God, he'd been through the line at the soup kitchen.*

"Now you remember, don't you, Dr. Davis?"

"Look, I don't give a damn about the car. I won't press charges. I'll drop the whole thing," she rattled off in a desperate attempt to convince him.

"You think you're going to die over a petty car theft?" He laughed. "Not hardly. You, my dear, are my only link back to Elizabeth and that accident. *That* is why you have to be dealt with."

"Elizabeth Gleason was the woman you were working with, wasn't she? The one who died in my car."

"Right on both counts. Now they can charge me with the death of that truck driver." He started for the dining room, but turned back. "If only she could have stayed dead."

Dani shook her head. "I don't understand. Elizabeth is dead."

"But you're not. You see, *you* didn't let her die. You resurrected her. Imagine my surprise when I picked up the paper and found out that my dearly departed girlfriend was opening a soup kitchen. I even came through the dinner line one night to see if you recognized me and you didn't."

Dani bit her lip.

"You were safe for a while. But not now. We just can't have you blabbing to the police, can we? Don't go away, sweetheart. I'll be right back."

Dani jerked both hands until she felt the metal cut into her wrists. Ignoring the pain, she yanked them even harder. Sweat trickled down her back and between her breasts as she pushed with her feet and tried to scoot across the floor, but was only able to move a few feet.

When the man returned, Dani saw the gas can and remembered the blackened shell of a house on Wisconsin Avenue. "Stewart." The name slipped past her lips. "You murdered Elizabeth's husband, too."

"Damned if we didn't. I see you've done your homework—but it wasn't like that at all." After noticing Dani had been able to move her chair, he unlocked her restraints and dragged her across the room where he recuffed her to the door of the walk-in freezer. "Lizzie and I just invited old Stewart to a barbecue. Only thing was, we didn't tell hubby dearest that he was the main course." His macabre laughter echoed through the huge commercial-size kitchen as he began trickling a fine line of gasoline around its perimeter.

Dani could see he'd been pushed too far. Perspiration beaded his forehead and upper lip. And his voice had taken on the high-pitched sound of a violin string that had been stretched too tight. She had to throw him off course. Even though she remembered it, Dani stalled for time by asking, "What's your name?"

He stopped momentarily. "Huh?"

"I asked you your name."

He set the can down and looked at her.

Thank God, she'd caught his attention enough to make him pause. "Is that too much to ask?" Her tone was quiet as she tried her best to calm him.

"What the hell," he said offhandedly. "Reaper. The Grim Reaper." He burst out laughing as he struck a match and held it over the trail of gas on the far side of the kitchen.

"I mean, your real name," she coaxed, playing for time.

"It's LeRoy Stratton. I told you that night I came through the line at the soup kitchen." He leered. "I was standing right in front of you."

"Don't do this, LeRoy," Dani pleaded. "For your sake, just let me go."

"And spend the rest of my life in prison? Forget it." He pulled out a gun. I haven't decided whether to blow your brains out, or..."

She watched a hideous grin spread across his face as he dropped the match and watched in fascination as the flames danced along the floor.

Nick silenced the sirens a couple of blocks away from the soup kitchen and cut the lights and engine, before coasting into the driveway. The kitchen was well lit, so he

raced to the window and looked in. Dani was secured to
the freezer and the son of a bitch had started a small fire
on the floor near the far wall. No time to sneak in the front
door. Nick had to get in and he had to do it now.

Backing up to get a running start, Nick tucked his head
and crashed through the large kitchen window right behind
the man. He rolled through the flames and shattered glass.
Just before he came up into a shooting position, one shot
was fired.

Dani saw the impact of the bullet knock Nick backward.
"Nooo!" she screamed, writhing against her constraints.
As Nick sprawled on the floor at her feet, a bright red stain
spread across the front of his shirt. She struggled against
the metal shackles that kept her from him. Pulling and
tugging, she jerked wildly, trying desperately to reach him.

"Looks like the good sergeant has interfered once too
often."

Tears streaming down her cheeks, Dani pleaded, "What
are you talking about?"

"Who do you think shot out the front window? Who
do you think broke in and would have finished you off, if
it hadn't been for Davis?"

"You," she gasped, realizing it hadn't been Chico and
it hadn't been her imagination. It had been LeRoy Stratton
all along.

"Looks like the third time really is the charm." The
man sneered at Nick as he stuffed the gun into the back
pocket of his pants. "After I charbroil the two of you, I
can finally rest in peace." He taunted Dani with a grin.
"No pun intended."

"Stop this," Dani begged, shaking her head in disbelief.
God couldn't have brought her and Nick together again
just to end it like this. Her eyes darted around the huge

room as the small path of gasoline began to burn. "Please, don't. He's hurt. Just let us go."

Ignoring her pleas, LeRoy began filling a bucket with gasoline. "Elizabeth died this way. It's only fitting that you do, too."

Nick fought through the soothing darkness, clawing his way back to the pounding ache in his shoulder…and Dani. He clamped his teeth together to keep from moaning. Through a pain-filled haze, he saw the man fill the bucket. He watched the gasoline splash over the side and trickle toward Dani.

Dani saw that faint flutter of Nick's lashes. *Thank God, he's alive. We can't give up now, Nick,* she told him silently. *We've come too far.* That's when she saw his fingers twitch….

"No, it's not right that I die the same way Elizabeth did," she yelled, trying to divert the man's attention from Nick. "It's not fitting at all. Elizabeth screwed up everything and got you into this mess. But I can get you out." Playing for time, she continued, trying hard not to focus on the faint smell of gas surrounding her. "If you let us go, I can get my hands on money—lots of it," she promised.

"Like hell," he growled. "The only thing I'll get out of you is hard time in the joint."

Nick silently inched his fingers around the cool metal of his 9mm automatic. When the man pulled back and started to toss the gas, Nick called on every ounce of strength he had to raise his gun and fire.

He heard Dani scream as the man's body pitched forward and landed on the now blood-splattered floor. The gas from the bucket fanned across the tile like deadly tentacles, every one reaching straight for Dani.

Nick made it to his feet and staggered through the kitchen.

"It's no use. I can't get out of these." Dani choked, straining against the cuffs. "Save yourself."

"Cover your mouth and hold still," he ordered. Smoke burning his eyes, he leaned against the freezer and dug through his pocket to find his key ring. He slipped the cuff key into the lock and jiggled it to the right. No luck. Blinking, he squinted. They had to get out, the flames were spreading fast. The fire had already cut off any hope of getting out the back door.

"Damn, they're double locked." This time, he flipped the key left, then right and the cuffs clicked open. He peeled them from Dani's bleeding wrists. "Get down, closer to the floor." Nick grabbed her arm and tugged her halfway to the floor, but before he could take a step, he slid down the front of the freezer. His head was spinning. He couldn't get his bearings. "Go on—out through the dining room," he told her. "I'll be right behind you."

"No, Nick, get up," Dani pleaded, frightened by the amount of blood he'd already lost. She pressed her hand down hard on the wound to try to control some of the bleeding. "We're getting out of here together." She tried to haul him to his feet, but couldn't. "Stay with me, Nick. You've got to help me."

He forced his way past the pain that ripped through his shoulder. "You go, dammit. I already called for backup. They can come back for me."

The crackling sound of the flames and the hiss of the fire urged Dani to hurry as she propped her shoulder under his good arm. Time was running out. "Forget it, Davis. Either we both walk out of here, or we'll die together." She wiped his sweat-streaked face with her palm. "I love you and I can't live without you again."

"Damn stubborn woman loves me," he moaned, pushing himself to his knees. He'd do this for Dani, if it killed him.

"Hang on, Nick," Dani pleaded, balancing his weight against her own and helping him to his feet. "You can do it."

Once they struggled to maintain their equilibrium, Dani wrapped her arm around his waist to steady him as they started for the door. They wove their way through the curling smoke, sidestepping the pools of gasoline that seemed to be igniting faster than they could maneuver.

They were nearly to the dining room when Dani felt Nick's knees buckle. Thank God, she heard the first siren. When his dead weight became impossible to handle, she had to lower him to the floor. Coughing, she screamed, "Help. Somebody help us. We're in here."

O'Malley was first on the scene.

"Hurry, Lieutenant." Dani waved her arm.

"Are you all right?"

"Not me," Dani sobbed. "Nick's been shot."

Kevin knelt, then scooped Nick's body into his arms. "Hold on to my sleeve, lass, and let's get him out of here."

Even Nick's eyelids ached...until he forced them open and saw Dani standing there, so still, so thoughtful. Looking pale and tired, she rested her head against the window and looked expectantly into the darkness beyond the glass. Such a beautiful soul to have suffered so much, he thought sadly.

"Dani."

A cry of relief escaped her lips, "Nick." She rushed to his bedside and smoothed a gentle hand over his brow.

"How long have I been out?" he rasped.

"Shhh, they just brought you in a little while ago." Dani kissed the tip of her finger and touched it to his lips. "Close your eyes and rest, love. You're going to be fine." Taking his hand, she assured him, "I'll be right here. I'm not going anywhere without you."

He squeezed her fingers and managed a lopsided grin before his eyes fluttered shut. "...not gonna leave me again," he muttered.

One night of sleeping in the chair beside Nick's bed had Dani pacing the room to stretch out the kinks. She rolled her shoulders as she monitored his progress for the umpteenth time.

Checking his vitals again, she noted his blood pressure had finally stabilized and his temperature had returned to normal and stayed there. She stopped long enough to smile at his sleeping form.

It's no wonder nothing short of death could have erased such a gorgeous image from her memory, Dani thought with a sigh. Dark hair tousled around his shoulders. Thick lashes resting on cheeks that had finally regained their color. Angles and planes of his square jaw, now rough with stubble.

Pouring herself a cup of what the hospital jokingly called coffee, she propped her feet up and settled in for a long evening.

"Hey, pretty lady."

Dani's shoes hit the floor the moment Nick spoke. She traveled the well-worn path to his side and released the metal bed rail, sliding it down to straighten the sheet. "You realize we have to stop meeting like this."

He laughed, then winced. "You've got that right." He struggled past the stiffness he felt in every joint to try to push himself into a sitting position. Running his finger down the sensitive flesh on the inside of Dani's arm, he suggested, "Home would be nice." He took her hand and pressed it to his lips.

"How does tomorrow sound?" She didn't miss the suggestive gleam in his eye.

"Not as good as today would." He ignored the slow burn in his shoulder as he flipped the covers back and patted the empty space next to him. "But, I might be persuaded to take it."

Unable to resist, Dani returned his wicked grin. "I'll have to admit your offer is tempting, but you're not in *that* good of shape...yet."

"Maybe not," he shrugged sheepishly, trying desperately to ignore the pain.

"The bullet hole was clean. It passed straight through, but you lost a lot of blood."

Suddenly serious, he met and held her gaze. "Just lie here, Dani," he whispered. "That's all I want. I need to feel you next to me."

Dani responded to Nick's request like the delicate petals of a flower opening to the sun. Unsure which one of them needed comforting more, she slipped beneath the sheets and settled her body close to his. Resting one hand carefully across his chest, she felt the strong, steady beat of his heart and said a silent prayer of thanks. For sparing the man of her dreams. For returning her past. But more than that, for the promise of her future.

"I love you, Dani."

"I love you, too." She sighed, knowing tonight there were no shadows across her heart.

Epilogue

Dani slipped out of the cramped hospital bed and went home to shower and change. On the way, she stopped at the store to pick up a few groceries. That way, she wouldn't have to leave again after Nick came home.

Home.

Just the sound of the word brightened her spirits. Not that she could feel much better than she did at this very moment. That, she thought, would be virtually impossible.

Parking at the entrance designated for the pickup of patients being released, she made a quick stop at the nurses' station. "How's he doing this morning, Katherine?"

"He's ready to go home." The RN smiled and affectionately patted Dani's arm. "It's so good to have you back, I still can't believe it's you, Dr. Davis."

"You think *you* were shocked." Dani shook her head. "Well, I'd better get going. I'm surprised Nick hasn't already taken a cab home."

Katherine giggled.

Dani's eyes widened. "He hasn't, has he?"

"No," the snickering nurse assured her. "He's definitely been waiting for you."

"Then I'd better get going." Had Katherine always acted this...*giddy?* Strange, Dani thought, she hadn't noticed it before today. Shaking it off, she headed down the hall and into Nick's room. She was pleased to see he was not only wide awake but had obviously showered and shaved. Even though he was somewhat pale, and not entirely himself yet, Nick Davis still took her breath away.

"My God, Nick, who died?" she teased, pointing to the exquisite roses that lined both window sills and perched on every available table in the room.

"No one." He jerked his thumb in the direction of the curtain that had been drawn around the bed next to his.

Dani raised her head from the fragrant, white roses long enough to mouth the word *Wow*.

Unpretentious, he thought. How like Dani. A grin tugged at his lips when he realized she truly was coming into her own again. He watched her walk from one bouquet to the next, sniffing and smiling over the dozen or so pots that had been delivered earlier.

"Finally got a roommate, huh?" she whispered, bending to check out both pairs of black pumps and the spit-shined wing tips visible beneath the cotton drape. Straightening, she quipped, "I thought maybe the staff bribed you with roses to get you out of here."

"Very funny."

"Well, Detective Davis," she began, stroking a satiny pedal, "you haven't been the most cooperative patient."

"I swear, those ugly rumors you heard are all lies." He crossed his heart with one finger. "The nurses around here love me."

"Sure they do."

God, she was glad to see him. The feeling washed over her like a warm ocean breeze. "You sure look a whole lot better this morning." She stopped at the foot of the bed to glance over his chart. Nodding at all the handwritten notations, she asked, "How would you like to go home before lunch?"

"That's my woman," he sighed. "But first, come here."

Dani stepped closer. Unable to resist the need to touch him, she combed her fingers through his hair. Satisfied he was still warm and very much alive, a feeling of contentment snuggled deep inside her.

He patted the sheet, inviting her to sit beside him, then took her hand in his. Gazing up into the beautiful golden eyes he had feared he would never see again, Nick asked, "Did you realize we missed our anniversary a couple of weeks ago?"

She paused a beat to think. "I guess we did, didn't we?" Her sigh wasn't for the time they'd lost, but in anticipation of all the special occasions to come. "Once you're one hundred percent, we'll celebrate. How does that sound?"

He grinned. "I've got a better idea."

Had Dani not been so relieved by Nick's recovery—so anxious to put their life back on track—she'd have recognized the familiar twitch bracketing his mouth. That subtle sign she'd seen a hundred times before should have warned her that he was up to something. "What do you propose we do?"

Nick's seductive laugh echoed halfway down the hall. "You're priceless, you know that?" *And she was.*

Suddenly anxious, Dani took a closer look at him. She picked up on the electrifying buzz of excitement pulsing just below the surface. "You know how I hate these little games of yours."

He loved to watch her curiosity muscle its way past her

logic. But even Dani could only take so much. He crooked his finger to draw her closer. Eyes locked, lips less than a breath apart, he whispered, "Will you marry me, Dani?"

Stroking his smooth, strong jaw with the back of her hand, she rested her forehead against his. "I thought we were married."

"We are." He steadied her wrist and slightly angled his mouth to brush a row of warm kisses over her knuckles. "Wouldn't you like to renew our vows before we start our life together again?"

Dani remembered Nick as a romantic, but somehow his proposal struck a special chord. Unshed tears stung her eyes at the thought of coming full circle to find this man again. "Of course I would."

He looked at her. Despite the physical changes, Dani was now and always would be the only woman he ever loved. Her hair might be longer. Her nose a bit more perfect. But, those beautiful, hazel eyes would always be the windows to Dani's soul—no one else's. "Then how about right now?" he whispered.

"Well, we can hardly get married here." She swallowed the sentimentality that had made her voice crack, eager to save it for her actual wedding day.

He pushed himself up in bed. "Why not?"

Dani blew out a frustrated breath that ruffled her bangs, ruing the day she remembered how stubborn Nick Davis could be. "Well, for one thing—" she racked her brain "—we don't have your wedding ring."

He reached in the pocket of his robe and produced his gold band.

"How did you get that?" Enjoying the lively twinkle in his eyes even more than she wanted to admit, she told him, "The last time I saw that ring, it was on your dresser."

Nick shrugged. "You must be mistaken."

"I don't—"

"What else would it take to pull off our wedding today?"

Looking down at her jeans and oversize sweater, she grinned. "I can hardly get married dressed like this."

Nick pointed to the closet.

Dani hesitated, then shook her head. "No way."

"See for yourself."

She opened the door. "Oh, my God," she whispered. Her breath caught at the sight of her beautifully beaded wedding gown and his tux. She spun around only to meet his unreadable, pale blue gaze. "How—? When—? Who—?"

He tried unsuccessfully to summon his most authoritative voice. "You're babbling." Damned if she wasn't even more beautiful standing there, looking totally confused.

"I know." Two syllables were about all she was worth at the moment.

"Take a deep breath, and tell me what else we'd need."

Her gaze narrowed. He couldn't be serious. She lifted her chin and rattled off, "Music, a cake, witnesses and a minister."

When her brow raised, challenging him, Nick reached over and hit the Play button on the tape recorder next to his bed.

Instead of Neil Diamond's pulsating rendition of "Brother Love's Traveling Salvation Show" that had rattled the windows the day before, Dani recognized the "Wedding March."

"While you're at it, you might want to check the bathroom," Nick offered.

She eased the door open as though it were booby-trapped, but the only thing that exploded was her heart. A beautiful, two-tier wedding cake, complete with a bride-

and-groom topper, waited for her on the other side. "Oh, Nick." Her voice reverberated off the tile walls as she recognized the delicate white flowers they'd had on their first cake—white roses!

"Hey, Davis, those aren't your roommate's flowers," she accused. She backed out of the rest room just in time to see the curtain around the other bed being shoved opened.

For a split second, time stood still. Dani felt as if her feet had been riveted to the linoleum. Speechless, her mouth dropped open and both hands frantically found their way to her cheeks. "Amy!"

"Dani?" The honey blonde stared, registering the new look and sound of her sister.

Through laughter and tears, they ran into one another's arms.

Kevin and Maureen O'Malley, who had followed Amy from behind the drape, joined Nick at his bedside.

"Ya done good, Davis," O'Malley swore, finding his wife's hand and giving it a tender squeeze.

"I did, didn't I?" Nick swallowed hard, finally appreciating Dani's belief in goodness and mercy. Looking at her today, he realized he'd certainly found his share of both.

"I was never much for miracles," O'Malley admitted, "but you can bet your sweet a— Let's just say I'll be sitting in church come Sunday morning."

"You and me both, Lieutenant." And that was just one of the promises Nick planned to keep.

With that, the minister, along with half the hospital staff, filed into the room.

In the midst of congratulatory hoots and hollers, Nick's gaze zeroed in on Dani. His wife. His reason for living. A sense of peace settled over him. Life as they had known it was about to begin again. Two souls, bound together for eternity.

With one arm around her sister, Dani made her way through the crowded room. Along the way, she hugged her brother-in-law, Phil, and gave Lieutenant O'Malley and Maureen both an affectionate peck on the cheek. Without hesitation, as her friends and family looked on, she planted a kiss on Nick that would last…at least until the honeymoon.

Finally, she'd come full circle. Her world was complete again. Looking around, Dani knew, without a doubt, she had more than regained her life. In her search for yesterday, she had found her tomorrow.

* * * * *

TRACI ON THE SPOT   BY TRACI

1

Morgan Brigham slowly set down his coffee cup on the kitchen table and stared at the comic strip in the center of his paper. It was nestled in among approximately twenty others that were spread out across two pages. But this was the only one he made a point of reading faithfully each morning at breakfast.

This was the only one that mirrored *her* life.

He read each panel twice, as if he couldn't trust his own eyes. But he could. It was there, in black and white.

Morgan folded the paper slowly, thoughtfully, his mind not on his task. So Traci was getting engaged.

The realization gnawed at the lining of his stomach. He hadn't a clue as to why.

He had even less of a clue why he did what he did next.

Abandoning his coffee, now cool, and the newspaper, and ignoring the fact that this was going to make him late for the office, Morgan went to get a sheet of stationery from the den.

He didn't have much time.

Traci Richardson stared at the last frame she had just drawn. Debating, she glanced at the creature sprawled out on the kitchen floor.

"What do you think, Jeremiah? Too blunt?"

The dog, part bloodhound, part mutt, idly looked up from his rawhide bone at the sound of his name. Jeremiah gave her a look she felt free to interpret as ambivalent.

"Fine help you are. What if Daniel actually reads this and puts two and two together?"

Not that there was all that much chance that the man who had proposed to her, the very prosperous and busy Dr. Daniel Thane, would actually see the comic strip she drew for a living. Not unless the strip was taped to a bicuspid he was examining. Lately Daniel had gotten so busy he'd stopped reading anything but the morning headlines of the *Times*.

Still, you never knew. "I don't want to hurt his feelings," Traci continued, using Jeremiah as a sounding board. "It's just that Traci is overwhelmed by Donald's proposal and, see, she thinks the ring is going to swallow her up." To prove her point, Traci held up the drawing for the dog to view.

This time, he didn't even bother to lift his head.

Traci stared moodily at the small velvet box on the kitchen counter. It had sat there since Daniel had asked her to marry him last Sunday. Even if Daniel never read her comic strip, he was going to suspect something eventually. The very fact that she hadn't grabbed the ring from his hand and slid it onto her finger should have told him that she had doubts about their union.

Traci sighed. Daniel was a catch by any definition. So what was her problem? She kept waiting to be struck by that sunny ray of happiness. Daniel said he wanted to take care of her, to fulfill her every wish.

And he was even willing to let her think about it before she gave him her answer.

Guilt nibbled at her. She should be dancing up and down, not wavering like a weather vane in a gale.

Pronouncing the strip completed, she scribbled her signature in the corner of the last frame and then sighed. Another week's work put to bed. She glanced at the pile of mail on the counter. She'd been bringing it in steadily from the mailbox since Monday, but the stack had gotten no farther than her kitchen. Sorting letters seemed the least heinous of all the annoying chores that faced her.

Traci paused as she noted a long envelope. Morgan Brigham. Why would Morgan be writing to her?

Curious, she tore open the envelope and quickly scanned the short note inside.

Dear Traci,
I'm putting the summerhouse up for sale. Thought you might want to come up and see it one more time before it goes up on the block. Or make a bid for it yourself. If memory serves, you once said you wanted to buy it. Either way, let me know. My number's on the card.

Take care,
Morgan

P.S. Got a kick out of *Traci on the Spot* this week.

Traci folded the letter. He read her strip. She hadn't known that. A feeling of pride silently coaxed a smile to her lips. After a beat, though, the rest of his note seeped into her consciousness. He was selling the house.

The summerhouse. A faded white building with brick trim. Suddenly, memories flooded her mind. Long, lazy afternoons that felt as if they would never end.

Morgan.

She looked at the far wall in the family room. There was a large framed photograph of her and Morgan standing before the summerhouse. Traci and Morgan. Morgan and Traci. Back then, it seemed their lives had been permanently intertwined. A bittersweet feeling of loss passed over her.

Traci quickly pulled the telephone over to her on the counter and tapped out the number on the keypad.

* * * * *

Look for TRACI ON THE SPOT
by Marie Ferrarella, coming to
Silhouette YOURS TRULY
in March 1997.

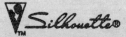

MILLION DOLLAR SWEEPSTAKES
OFFICIAL RULES
NO PURCHASE NECESSARY TO ENTER

1. To enter, follow the directions published. Method of entry may vary. For eligibility, entries must be received no later than March 31, 1998. No liability is assumed for printing errors, lost, late, non-delivered or misdirected entries.

   To determine winners, the sweepstakes numbers assigned to submitted entries will be compared against a list of randomly, preselected prize winning numbers. In the event all prizes are not claimed via the return of prize winning numbers, random drawings will be held from among all other entries received to award unclaimed prizes.

2. Prize winners will be determined no later than June 30, 1998. Selection of winning numbers and random drawings are under the supervision of D. L. Blair, Inc., an independent judging organization whose decisions are final. Limit: one prize to a family or organization. No substitution will be made for any prize, except as offered. Taxes and duties on all prizes are the sole responsibility of winners. Winners will be notified by mail. Odds of winning are determined by the number of eligible entries distributed and received.

3. Sweepstakes open to residents of the U.S. (except Puerto Rico), Canada and Europe who are 18 years of age or older, except employees and immediate family members of Torstar Corp., D. L. Blair, Inc., their affiliates, subsidiaries, and all other agencies, entities, and persons connected with the use, marketing or conduct of this sweepstakes. All applicable laws and regulations apply. Sweepstakes offer void wherever prohibited by law. Any litigation within the province of Quebec respecting the conduct and awarding of a prize in this sweepstakes must be submitted to the Régie des alcools, des courses et des jeux. In order to win a prize, residents of Canada will be required to correctly answer a time-limited arithmetical skill-testing question to be administered by mail.

4. Winners of major prizes (Grand through Fourth) will be obligated to sign and return an Affidavit of Eligibility and Release of Liability within 30 days of notification. In the event of non-compliance within this time period or if a prize is returned as undeliverable, D. L. Blair, Inc. may at its sole discretion, award that prize to an alternate winner. By acceptance of their prize, winners consent to use of their names, photographs or other likeness for purposes of advertising, trade and promotion on behalf of Torstar Corp., its affiliates and subsidiaries, without further compensation unless prohibited by law. Torstar Corp. and D. L. Blair, Inc., their affiliates and subsidiaries are not responsible for errors in printing of sweepstakes and prize winning numbers. In the event a duplication of a prize winning number occurs, a random drawing will be held from among all entries received with that prize winning number to award that prize.

5. This sweepstakes is presented by Torstar Corp., its subsidiaries and affiliates in conjunction with book, merchandise and/or product offerings. The number of prizes to be awarded and their value are as follows: Grand Prize — $1,000,000 (payable at $33,333.33 a year for 30 years); First Prize — $50,000; Second Prize — $10,000; Third Prize — $5,000; 3 Fourth Prizes — $1,000 each; 10 Fifth Prizes — $250 each; 1,000 Sixth Prizes — $10 each. Values of all prizes are in U.S. currency. Prizes in each level will be presented in different creative executions, including various currencies, vehicles, merchandise and travel. Any presentation of a prize level in a currency other than U.S. currency represents an approximate equivalent to the U.S. currency prize for that level, at that time. Prize winners will have the opportunity of selecting any prize offered for that level; however, the actual non U.S. currency equivalent prize if offered and selected, shall be awarded at the exchange rate existing at 3:00 P.M. New York time on March 31, 1998. A travel prize option, if offered and selected by winner, must be completed within 12 months of selection and is subject to: traveling companion(s) completing and returning of a Release of Liability prior to travel; and hotel and flight accommodations availability. For a current list of all prize options offered within prize levels, send a self-addressed, stamped envelope (WA residents need not affix postage) to: MILLION DOLLAR SWEEPSTAKES Prize Options, P.O. Box 4456, Blair, NE 68009-4456, USA.

6. For a list of prize winners (available after July 31, 1998) send a separate, stamped, self-addressed envelope to: MILLION DOLLAR SWEEPSTAKES Winners, P.O. Box 4459, Blair, NE 68009-4459, USA.

COMING NEXT MONTH

From the bestselling author of *Scandalous*

CANDACE CAMP

Cam Monroe vowed revenge when
Angela Stanhope's family accused him
of a crime he didn't commit.

Fifteen years later he returns from exile, wealthy
and powerful, to demand Angela's hand in marriage.
It is then that the strange "accidents" begin. Are the
Stanhopes trying to remove him from their lives
one last time, or is there a more insidious,
mysterious explanation?

Impulse

Available this March at your favorite retail outlet.

As seen on TV!

Free Gift Offer

With a Free Gift proof-of-purchase from any Silhouette® book,
you can receive a beautiful cubic zirconia pendant.

This gorgeous marquise-shaped stone is a genuine cubic
zirconia—accented by an 18" gold tone necklace.

(Approximate retail value $19.95)

Send for yours today...

compliments of ▼ *Silhouette*®

To receive your free gift, a cubic zirconia pendant, send us one original proof-of-
purchase, photocopies not accepted, from the back of any Silhouette Romance™,
Silhouette Desire®, Silhouette Special Edition®, Silhouette Intimate Moments®
or Silhouette Yours Truly™ title available in February, March and April at your favorite
retail outlet, together with the Free Gift Certificate, plus a check or money order for
$1.65 U.S./$2.15 CAN. (do not send cash) to cover postage and handling, payable
to Silhouette Free Gift Offer. We will send you the specified gift. Allow 6 to 8 weeks for
delivery. Offer good until April 30, 1997 or while quantities last. Offer valid in the
U.S. and Canada only.

Free Gift Certificate

Name: _____

Address: _____

City: _____ State/Province: _____ Zip/Postal Code: _____

Mail this certificate, one proof-of-purchase and a check or money order for postage
and handling to: SILHOUETTE FREE GIFT OFFER 1997. In the U.S.: 3010 Walden
Avenue, P.O. Box 9077, Buffalo NY 14269-9077. In Canada: P.O. Box 613, Fort Erie,
Ontario L2Z 5X3.

FREE GIFT OFFER   084-KFD
ONE PROOF-OF-PURCHASE
To collect your fabulous FREE GIFT, a cubic zirconia pendant, you must include this
original proof-of-purchase for each gift with the properly completed Free Gift Certificate.

084-KFD

You're About to Become a

Privileged Woman

Reap the rewards of fabulous free gifts and benefits with proofs-of-purchase from Silhouette and Harlequin books

Pages & Privileges™

It's our way of thanking you for buying our books at your favorite retail stores.

PROOF OF PURCHASE

SIM-PP22

Offer expires March 31, 1997

Pages & Privileges ™

Harlequin and Silhouette— the most privileged readers in the world!

For more information about Harlequin and Silhouette's PAGES & PRIVILEGES program call the Pages & Privileges Benefits Desk: 1-503-794-2499

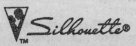

Silhouette®

SIM-PP22